THE FATAL CREATION

AN ABSOLUTELY GRIPPING PSYCHOLOGICAL THRILLER

A SERGEANT EVELYN "MAC" MCGREGOR
THRILLER

BOOK 1

JULIE BERGMAN

Copyright Page

This book is dedicated to my supportive husband, who has supported me, been my sounding board, lent me his creative mind, and believed in me throughout —and to my beautiful children, who have shown me unwavering support and always encouraged me to follow my dreams. I appreciate all my family and friends who stepped in to help with the editing process and have shown me tremendous support. A special thanks to my friend who listened to all my crazy ideas on our afternoon walks, made suggestions and supported me along the way.

"There is only one thing that makes a dream impossible to achieve: the fear of failure." – Paulo Coelho

JOIN THE NEWSLETTER

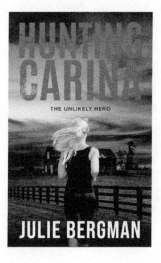

PROLOGUE

KILLING WAS the only thing he thought about anymore. It put his mind and soul at peace while everything around him seemed chaotic. It was cold out, and he thought about going home to his nice warm cabin. He didn't want to be here, but he knew he had to be. If he didn't take care of her, she would just hurt others, and he would never find closure—and after all, she deserved it. He just wanted his world to be quiet again. The anger was eating him from the inside. Control, deep breaths, counting, and there she was.

He had been watching her for weeks now. She was so beautiful. It was frigid out during October in Spokane, Washington, and the cold wind played with her hair as she stood on the sidewalk. She didn't look like the other girls on Sprague Avenue. She seemed almost innocent and somehow serene. Her large, dark almond eyes looked over at his truck for a moment, begging him to save her from this life. He knew she would welcome death when it came. His heart began to race, thinking she could see him, but that wasn't possible. He was tucked back in the shadows, inside the darkened cab of his truck. It was safe to watch for now.

Abigail had been working on Sprague for a couple of years. She had followed her boyfriend here a few years ago, and then he took off, leaving her to fend for herself. The business was good, and she had several regulars, which made it easier in this line of work. However, she knew her profession was a high-risk career. Lately, she had felt a little uneasy because the same dark pickup truck had been coming around for the past few weeks. The driver never approached the girls; he just sat back and watched them. It gave her the creeps. She had learned early on that you had to trust your instincts and always watch your back. This was the most dangerous job she could have chosen, but she no longer knew how to change her circumstances. She had tried to take on some odd jobs and even went back to school once, but she couldn't make enough money. She was saving up all her money to move away from this frigid place and go somewhere warm.

Most people told Abigail she was beautiful, but she felt average, though she couldn't argue that she was one of the best earners on the streets. She had beautiful, long raven hair that fell down her back. She had full lips that made her look pouty and a little sad, which seemed to turn on her clients. She was about to turn twenty-eight but looked like she couldn't be any older than twenty. She was petite with a tiny waist and small breasts. She dressed more like an innocent schoolgirl with cardigan sweaters and leggings. Her clients wanted to "save her" and give her a better life. She had a couple of older men that would give her extra money, clothes, and gifts, to help keep her off the streets. She would just put it all in her nest egg, waiting for the opportunity to get away from this place and live a fully clothed, normal life during the daytime instead of this awful existence. Maybe, just maybe, she could fall in love and start a family one day.

This night-shift business was wearing on her. She felt tired most of the time, and her body ached from standing in the cold. She hated what she did for a living, letting men paw at her body for money. Some men weren't bad and treated her nicely, but others were rough and smelled terrible. One man was so heavy he'd almost crushed her the night before. He had to have been over 300 pounds and was sweating profusely the entire time. She thought he would have a heart attack, but he didn't. He got off quickly, and her business was done. She was happy that he'd paid well, and she could take a shower.

She was lost in thought when she finally noticed the blue pickup truck that had been sitting there, watching them for weeks, slowly creeping toward her. She raised her guard, ready to flee if there was something wrong with the person inside. The nice thing about dressing like a schoolgirl was that she didn't wear those ridiculously high heels like the other girls, which let her run faster. She was looking for her best exit plan when the truck stopped in front of her. For some reason, her internal alarms were freaking out. Her heart felt like it was about to jump out of her chest. She told herself to calm down and to stop being so paranoid.

When he finally stopped in front of her and rolled down his window, she was surprised to see a clean-cut man sitting behind the wheel. This explained a lot. It was illegal for anyone to solicit a prostitute in Washington State, but that didn't stop most people. It wasn't something that was heavily enforced, anyway. As long as the girls got their regular checkups at the clinic and didn't give the local police a hard time, they were usually left alone. On occasion, she would provide sexual favors to some of the men on the force, keeping them at bay for a while. The other girls did the same. It was part of the price of doing business.

The man in front of her was quite handsome. He was a bit older, probably mid- to late-forties. It was hard to tell these days. This one seemed to be in great shape, but she sensed he was older than he looked.

"Hi handsome, would you like to have some fun tonight?" Abigail asked.

"Yes," he said, looking down at his hands. He appeared ashamed of what he was about to ask for. That was common in Abigail's line of work, but she had no idea what he had in mind for her.

"How much for the entire night with you?" he asked in a husky voice.

Abigail smiled; this was going to be easy money. "I won't take less than five hundred." It was higher than her standard rate, but she figured he was good for it.

The man smiled back at her. "That's more than reasonable to spend time with a beautiful lady."

She mentally kicked herself; she should have asked for more.

Most guys said they wanted her for the entire night, but they usually fell asleep once she got them off, and she was out of there. She would just have one of her friends pick her up. She and her roommate had a system: Abigail would text her when she got to the place, and then text her when she was done, safe, and headed home. So far it had been a pretty good system and seemed to work well. Even if her friend was working, she had backups. There was an Uber driver she knew who had a crush on her and would pick her up anytime, anywhere without asking questions. He always said she reminded him of his sister, and he wanted to help her.

She climbed into the man's truck.

———

He smelled good and was nicely dressed in dark jeans and a button-down shirt. This might be a pleasant job. She settled herself into the comfortable worn seats.

"Would you mind going back to my place?" he asked in a low voice. She looked a little surprised. "I have a small hunting cabin about forty-five minutes out of town. It's private, and we can enjoy our evening without interruption."

She hesitated; the hairs on the back of her neck stood up again. What was her problem? This was a good-looking, well-dressed man, not the typical scum that would try and pick her up. He wasn't going to hurt her. He just wanted to have a good time in private where he wouldn't get into trouble, and no one would interrupt. He was probably married and worried his wife might see him.

He sensed her hesitation. "I can pay you extra," he said, raising his left eyebrow and giving her his most disarming smile.

She guessed this guy was a little higher up on the food chain, and it would be bad for him to be caught with her, especially since he probably thought she was half his age. Not quite, but he was definitely a bit older than her.

"We can do that if you want, sugar, but it'll cost you an additional two hundred," she said, smiling sweetly.

"That won't be a problem," he said without hesitation.

She settled into the seat, starting small talk. He didn't want to talk about himself; he wanted to know where she was from, how she'd ended up on the streets, and all the usual things. She seemed to bring that out in men. They always wanted to find out how they could save her. She pulled in more money than most women she worked with and was just waiting for the right time to get out. She owed her handler time at this point and could not get out of his grip until she paid him off. If she slipped away without finishing the agreed-upon time, he wouldn't come after her; he would take it out on her roommate or someone else she cared about. That was not an option.

She rattled off the usual story about how she had only been on the streets for a few months, and she was just trying to earn enough money to get home to her parents in Indiana.

He seemed to buy the story and told her to continue.

"My parents live on a farm out there," she said. "I spent my whole life trying to get away from that small town, and now I'm spending all my time trying to get back."

"How did you end up on the streets?"

"I followed the love of my life. He told me we were going to start a family together. He left me for someone else." That last part was true. That was precisely how she had ended up in Washington State, but she hadn't been fresh off the farm. She was from California and had been trying to make her start as an actress there. One wrong choice after another led her to this cold place, making money on her back. But the guys always liked the sob story of the innocent farm girl. The truth was, she didn't mind it very much. It was easy money and much better than working full-time at a minimum-wage job, barely making enough to pay the rent.

She's lying, he thought to himself. He knew where she was from, and that she was here trying to finish what she had started. *Even though she's beautiful and charming, she's pure evil deep down in her soul.* He hadn't seen it the first time he'd met her, but now he could tell that the devil lived in this woman. He had tried to kill her before, but she simply refused to die. It was hard to kill this demon, but just maybe, this time, he would be successful. Last time she had outsmarted him, but this time would be different.

She kept talking but trailed off when she realized they were driving outside of town—*way* outside of town. He took a turn onto a dirt road and kept going. True to his word, about forty-five minutes into the drive they stopped at a small cabin in the middle of nowhere. There wasn't anything in sight. She knew they were out by a lake, but that was about it. She checked her phone but had no signal. That concerned her because she wasn't exactly sure how she would get out of there. Once he shut off the truck, she could only hear the sounds of the forest. It was peaceful, but also frightening; no one would hear her if she cried for help. The thought made her visibly shiver.

If he had seen it, he didn't say anything. He stopped and looked at her, and her breath caught because of the cold look in his gray eyes. But then his face softened, and he looked at her kindly. "Let's get you inside. You look cold." Then he came around the truck to open her door like a true gentleman.

She smiled to herself, thinking that you just didn't see that much anymore. He offered his hand and helped her out of the truck. He stood there staring at her for a moment, just drinking her in. He extended his arm, indicating she should go up to the cabin.

Inside, things were much nicer than what the outside had suggested. Everything had a warm, rustic feel: the overstuffed, comfortable-looking furniture, an old wood-burning stove that he started a fire in while she looked around the cabin. She eventually sat down in one of the old leather recliners, trying to look sexy, but the chair was so big that she felt like she was being swallowed by it.

He sat across from her and just stared for a while.

"So, honey, what's your guilty pleasure?" she said, giving him her best smolder. Abigail was good at negotiating with men. Most wanted to help or protect her due to her young, innocent look.

He let her rattle on about what she was willing to do with him, which was quite a lot, to his surprise. He was bewildered because she didn't know who he was. This had to be Sahar. They had spent so much time together in the past that he knew she should know him, but she seemed to have no clue. This made him angry. After all she had done to him, the least she could do was acknowledge him and apologize. Deep down, that was all he wanted from her.

Finally, he stood up, and she smiled. "Okay, let's get started," she said. She looked up at him with her most innocent look, only to see the darkness creep back into his eyes. He seemed lost in thought and didn't really look at her but through her. She moved toward him and touched his chest. He froze and then slowly looked down at her with that same dark look in his eyes. His face contorted into something evil and black. Then he reached down and grabbed her by the neck in one swift move. She clawed at his arms with her fingers, trying to get him to let go. She gasped for air, her eyes bulging out of her head.

No, not like this. Don't let me die. I'm not ready, she screamed, but nothing came out. She couldn't scream or make any noise at all. She felt a darkness around her eyes start to creep in. Her body began to welcome the looming unconsciousness because the reality of what was happening to her was too terrible to process. She passed out, dangling from the man's grasp like a rag doll.

He stood there staring at her face as it turned strange shades of purple, and then he dropped her. She fell to the floor. Sweet air came rushing back into her lungs as she sputtered and coughed, trying to catch her breath. She finally began to regain her bearings when something hard hit her across the back of the head. White light exploded behind her eyes, and her head swam. Nausea gripped her body as her eyes rolled back into her head. It felt like her head was going to explode. She lay very still, trying not to throw up and play dead. She tried to think of how to escape but came up with nothing; the pain in her head was blinding.

She felt him pick her up off the ground and move her to the couch. He caressed her hair and put a blanket over her still body. "Sahar, how could you do this to me?" he whispered.

Who the hell is Sahar? She thought and realized she didn't care as long as he let her go. She could play the part of Sahar. Maybe he wouldn't hurt her if he believed she was this woman. She slowly opened her eyes and submissively smiled at him. "You know I missed you," she said, trying her best to be convincing.

He looked at her and remembered the love he had felt for her. He ran his hands through her hair and caressed her cheek softly. Then her betrayal cut through his memory like a sharp knife. It caused him pain right behind his eyes. It physically hurt and blurred his vision. He felt his balance sway. He sat down beside her and took a few deep breaths. He had to get rid of the pain in his head. There was only one way. She had to die to make it quiet again.

He leaned down and kissed her on the forehead. "Don't worry, my love, I'll take care of everything," he said in a low voice.

She thought she might have a chance; she just had to play along until there was an opening to escape. But then he gently wrapped his hands around her pretty neck and began to squeeze once more. She squirmed under his weight, spitting and kicking until she passed out. He looked down at her beautiful face with regret. He reached into his bag and grabbed his combat knife. He looked at it for a few moments, enjoying how it felt in his large hand. It was a beautiful seven-inch steel blade, curved at the top like the small of a woman's back. His finger played with the blade's handle, fantasizing about gliding it to the hilt. He found himself getting an erection just thinking about it.

She had already taken off her sweater and was lying there unconscious in a dark-blue silk blouse and leggings. Her skin was soft to the touch. The contrast of the bruises beginning to form around her neck enticed him. He pressed the knife under her dark-blue shirt and cut it from the bottom to the neckline with a practiced motion. It was excruciating to wait, but the timing had to be just right. He stripped her black leggings off her, taking her tiny black thong panties with them. It was easier to slice the little piece of fabric that held the front of her lacy bra in place. He could tell she was beginning to regain consciousness. It would be time soon.

He stood over her, slowly taking off his clothes. The excitement was almost more than he could handle. She would be his forever. He lowered himself on top of her, stuffing himself inside. To his enjoyment, she was wet. Her eyes shot open as he plunged the knife deep into her chest and abdomen. Her sticky, sweet blood smeared all over his chest. It was warm and metallic. Her eyes rolled back into her head, and he could feel the life leave her body as he shuddered in ecstasy.

He woke up the next morning feeling the chill of the dark cabin crawling across his skin. He had slept for a long time and felt groggy and out of sorts. It took him a moment to figure out where he was. He lay there for a while trying to remember the night before, but nothing came to him, and then he rolled over and saw her lying there. She was already cold and getting stiff. Rigor mortis was setting in. He had wrapped her body in a plastic sheet to keep the mess under control. Even though the cabin was cold, she would begin to smell soon. *At least we can be together, for now,* he thought. *She looks so peaceful lying there.* Her bare skin was turning slightly blue but still gorgeous. He ran his hand down her bare stomach feeling slightly aroused. It had been such a long time since he had been with her. After Sahar had left him, he had felt so alone. It was comforting to have her back. He brushed his hands through her hair, breathing in the faint scent of shampoo.

He looked at the clock and realized how late it had gotten. He had to get his day started; otherwise, he would run out of time. It was Saturday, which would typically leave him with the entire weekend to do as he wished, but he had to attend an awards ceremony this weekend. If he didn't show up at the event, they would notice.

He slowly got out of bed and went to the kitchen to start the coffee and get some breakfast. He knew he had a lot to do today, but first, he needed to make sure she was safely in his garden. He went back to her looking closely at her cold skin. In the light of day, he realized that this girl wasn't Sahar after all. She had looked just like Sahar at the moment but now that he looked at the dead woman lying on his bed, he could see the differences. It had happened before when he thought he had the right woman. They were sleeping in his garden now.

It would be hard to dig in the frozen ground by his cabin. He had prepared and cleared the area, but a soft covering of snow had fallen while he slept. If he started a fire over her gravesite, it would soften the earth. No one would notice some disturbed earth at the back of his cabin, he hoped. After he ate, he went out to get his supplies to start the fire. He always enjoyed sitting out by the fire and enjoying a cold morning. It was an excellent start to the day.

He tried to clear his mind, but the thought of losing her again became overwhelming. It saddened him that this hadn't worked out the way he had hoped. Every time, it turned out the exact same way. He tried to be charming and did everything he could, but she kept slipping through his fingers, and he didn't know why. All he wanted was to be held in Sahar's warm embrace again. He would figure it out. It was just a matter of time before she returned to him for good. He thought this one had been her, but it was clear she was not the right one. He would just have to keep looking. He knew she was out there waiting for him. She told him so all the time.

He ran his hand slowly across the scar on the back of his head. He had received the scar the last time he had seen her. He knew she didn't mean to hurt him. She couldn't have. He knew she loved him and that they would be together again. He would find her. He had to. It was the only way to calm the anger growing inside him. He struggled to keep things under wraps most of the time, but his anger would show every once in a while, and he would have to step away. In his position, few people questioned him, but they would find him out if he ever truly lost it in front of anyone. They would see the demon he kept at bay. Sahar would make it all better. He just had to find her, and she would fix everything.

The doctors said he had a traumatic brain injury, among other things, but he knew that she could fix him. He just needed to find her again. He took a deep breath and walked into the bedroom to look at the one that wasn't right. She was lying there so peacefully. How had he been so blind to think that she could have been right? It was now obvious to him that there was no way she could have been Sahar. His quest for her had blinded him again. He had thought all the others were right as well, but they were not. He began preparing her. He took several pictures of her still-naked body for his book. He liked his collection of beautiful things. It made him feel calm when he looked at it.

They were all so beautiful even though they weren't her. He gently cut off a large piece of her hair and tucked it inside a small clear bag. The preparation had to be done just right. He ran his hand across her face and down her beautiful body then went to retrieve a washcloth with hot water and bleach. He meticulously cleaned each section of her body, especially under her nails and between her legs. He did not want to leave any of himself behind. "Goodbye for now," he whispered. He rolled her in the sheet she was lying on and then carried her out to her new home, gently placing her on the soft earth. She would be a beautiful addition to his growing masterpiece.

CHAPTER
ONE

TECHNICAL SERGEANT EVELYN MCGREGOR— THOUGH everyone called her "Mac"—rolled over, confused by the incessant noise invading her sleep. It simply had to be too early to get out of bed. She slowly opened one eye to see her room still engulfed in darkness. Yup, it couldn't possibly be time to get up yet—and then she remembered: she had set her alarm for this awful hour because her PT test was coming up in only two short months. She hit snooze on the alarm and lay there cursing herself for not staying up on her running throughout the year. Running was the bane of her existence. She hated it. The pounding and abuse it caused her body. It was the last thing she wanted to do. Overall, she was in good shape, but she preferred to exercise by hiking or playing outdoors. The last thing she wanted to do was get on a treadmill and feel like a hamster running in place for an hour or running around in circles on the indoor track.

She finally rolled out of bed and grumpily padded to the bathroom to get in her PT gear. The base gym wasn't far, and if she got there soon, she could finish in time to have breakfast at the office before meeting with her first client. *Mmm, breakfast... Ooh, and coffee, lots of coffee... but not until the workout is done.* She got ready, thinking to herself that there was something she needed to remember to pick up today. Right, she was almost out of coffee! *Coffee. Put coffee on the list, put coffee on the list, put coffee on the list,* she kept repeating to herself as she got ready. She put her hair up in a ponytail and grabbed her running shoes. *Coffee, what was it about coffee? Oh yeah, coffee sounds good. Hmm. What was I supposed to do again?*

She left the house without putting coffee on her grocery list. She hated working out in the morning but knew if she didn't get it done first thing, it would never happen. She would get busy with her clients and never get a workout in, and then she would fail her PT test and receive disciplinary paperwork. If that happened, she could lose her career in the military. That was not acceptable. She was going to make it. She wasn't going to fail, even though her father said she wasn't cut out for military service. She wanted to prove him wrong. She missed him every day.

Mac was stationed at Fairchild Air Force Base in Washington, where it was cold most mornings. Often, the base remained cold throughout the day, not just in the mornings. This morning it was freezing. There was a fine layer of frost on the ground, and the trees had a majestic, crystallized look that reminded her of a pixie fairy movie she used to watch as a kid. She could see her frozen breath as she stepped outside and climbed into her little SUV. Everyone here had a four-wheel drive; it came with the territory. Few people were crazy enough to drive two-wheel in wintry conditions.

She was only a short twenty-minute drive to the base. She normally took the back roads, but not in the winter when they were covered in black ice. She had learned that the hard way when she had tipped her last truck on its side after spinning around on slick, unforgiving black ice. One moment she was singing along to the radio while sipping on her coffee, the next she was in a ditch. She had been fine, but her old truck was totaled. That had angered her at first because it was paid off, but such is life. Her new SUV was nice because it had remote start and heated seats. She felt like she was moving up in the world with her sweet little new ride.

As she pulled in line to wait her turn to get on base, she thought about how quiet it had been at the office recently. She moved up in line, waiting her turn. When she arrived at the small guard shack, a security force member checked her ID and allowed her on base. The base itself was quite beautiful in the wintertime. It was covered in large trees that towered above her as she drove. They all had that beautiful, crystallized look she had only ever seen in Washington. The ice here was treacherous but very pretty. The buildings all looked similar. Some of them were older with a yellowing color, while others were newer brick buildings. She passed the Wing Headquarters building. It was a relatively new two-story brick building with lots of windows.

She followed Bong Street around and made a few turns until she pulled into the gym parking lot, found a spot, and quickly walked inside so she wouldn't freeze to death. She always felt like a mess going to the gym in the morning. She had been told over the years that she was attractive, but she felt like a mix between Medusa and Droopy the Dog. She could feel the bags under her eyes, and even though she had pinned her hair back, it always had a bunch of flyaways and looked crazy. Mornings were not her thing. If she had her way, everyone would start their days after 0900 hours. *Oh well, I'm here, might as well get this over with.* She distractedly acknowledged some of the other early morning gym-goers and started her run. She always felt awkward when she ran. One of the other ladies ran by looking majestic, like she was almost gliding.

Mac became lost in thought as she ran. She wondered why it looked so easy for others. She was in good shape with a lean, athletic body, but had also been cursed with curvy Latino hips and a bigger butt, which made it difficult to bound along the ground. Overall, she liked how she was built and enjoyed working out, but she just didn't enjoy running. No one should have to bounce that much. She was breathing hard with sweat running down her face, barely able to keep going, when a lady she knew from the JAG came running up to her.

Jody was a tall, slender black woman with large round eyes. Mac always thought she looked a little surprised. "We had a murder on base last night," Jody said, her eyes widening even bigger than before. "Some guy killed his wife. Can you believe it?"

Mac just stared at her, thinking she had heard wrong.

Jody continued in a high-pitched voice, "They found a dead woman in base housing, and the main suspect is, of course, her husband. He was found with his wife's body all covered in blood. They said the house looked like a massacre!"

Mac thanked Jody for the heads-up and quickly walked toward the stairs. *Well, that just ended my workout.* She couldn't recall a murder case happening on base before, though admittedly she hadn't researched it. There certainly hadn't been one during her career. Murders rarely happened in the military, and certainly not on base. Before she even made it to the shower, her phone beeped with a text from her boss. *COME IN ASAP!*

She rushed into the shower. *Dammit, I forgot my shower shoes again.* She quickly went about her business, trying not to slip on the nasty floor. She dried her shoulder-length hair and quickly put it up in a bun. She liked that she didn't have to worry about what she was wearing every day. As long as she wore the correct uniform for that day's activities—which was usually the same as everyone else—she was wearing the right thing. Outside of work she was normally a jeans-and-t-shirt girl. She did like to dress up on occasion, but just as often found it uncomfortable; people would stare at her, and she could never be sure why. She usually figured she looked ridiculous or had a booger in her nose.

She climbed back into her vehicle; thankful it was still warm inside since her hair was starting to freeze right to her head. When she arrived at her office, she found her boss talking on the phone. She dropped her stuff in one of the chairs and started booting up her computer. Government computers were slow, so while she waited, she headed to the little kitchen attached to their office for some coffee and breakfast. She never could remember to pack her food, and there was usually no time for lunch, so she just bought separate groceries for both the office and home.

Mac worked at the Area Defense Counsel's office as a paralegal and occasionally as a defense investigator, though she really enjoyed the rare occasions when her boss sent her out into the field to do investigative work. In the Air Force, everyone had to wear many hats. Her Air Force Service Code—"51J071"—designated her as a paralegal, but she often held many different roles: defense investigator, court witness, and witness examiner, not to mention all the things she did for office administration like budgeting, scheduling her bosses' travel, and making sure the office ran well.

Her boss poked his head into the kitchen. "Aww, coffee! We're going to need that today." His face already showed signs of stress and it wasn't even 0900 yet.

CHAPTER
TWO

THE ADC OFFICE was always busy. They jokingly referred to it as "the pressure cooker." Captain Stanton was of average height with short-cropped blond hair. He looked older than his years due to the pressure and stress of his job. The lines at the side of his eyes were starting to spread, and he constantly looked tired. His superiors were always having him travel from base to base defending airmen in court. His wife and two kids seemed okay with it, but Mac figured it had to be hard being a mother when your husband was always on the road. The nice thing about a murder case was that it would be a high priority, and he wouldn't be going anywhere for a while—not that he would be home much, but at least he would be in the same state as his family. Sometimes his wife, Emma, and kids Adam and Franklin would stop by with dinner when he was working a late case, or the night before a court date, which always ran late. Emma was a kind woman with a huge heart who always brought enough food for Mac. She was a wonderful lady. Stanton knew he was a lucky man.

Stanton walked up beside Mac and grabbed a cup of coffee and a muffin.

"So, what do we have so far?" Mac asked.

"Not much, I'm afraid. Last night, Senior Airman Terrell Johnson from the Security Forces Squadron was found next to his wife's body.

He was covered in her blood and screaming. One of the neighbors called the cops when they heard his screams. They arrested him on the spot. They cleaned him up and put him in a holding cell on suicide watch. He's still there now but won't talk to anyone, which is a good thing. We need to get over there as soon as possible."

They took their coffee and breakfast with them to the SFS squadron. Mac thought about the first time she had met Johnson. They had worked together on a drug case once and done some sparring at the gym a few times. Mac had been trained at a young age to defend herself, and she liked to keep her skills sharp. When she first met Johnson, he had supplied her office with evidence and made sure she and her counsel had discovery on the drug case. He had come across as a kind and gentle guy, which was not often the case with the cops on base. They were usually a bit gruffer and sometimes a little edgy, but Johnson was friendly and accommodating. He had never given her any indication that he would do something like this. She had always felt she was good at reading people, but now she was questioning that ability.

They walked in and found Johnson sitting in the holding cell in his boxers. When you're on suicide watch in the military, you're left with nothing you can use to hurt yourself. At least this cell was clean and didn't smell like the ones downtown. Sometimes their clients were held in the Spokane County Jail when they were in pretrial confinement. Mac figured there were worse places, but it was still nasty. Their guys were kept away from the general population, but county always smelled of urine, and grime seemed to be stuck to the gray walls and brown floor.

Technical Sergeant Branson came over to greet them. Branson was the confinement non-commissioned officer. His job was to monitor and manage the confinement facility and ensure the right manning was assigned when they had an accused in custody. He was a tall, good-looking man with a bald head. He reminded Mac of Mr. Clean from those old commercials. Branson looked exhausted and worried, with a strained look on his face.

"Hey Captain Stanton, Mac—it's good to see both of you. I'm glad you're here. Johnson used to be one of my troops. I can't imagine he did what he's accused of. He worshipped his wife. She was everything to him. He's in shock and won't talk to anyone. I have the interview room ready for you guys. If you want to take a seat, I'll get some clothes on him and bring him to you shortly."

They thanked him and went into the interview room.

The room was small with uncomfortable chairs. The chill in the room crept into Mac's uniform. She wondered why they always had to keep military confinement facilities so cold. But, of course, most on-base facilities were either too cold or too warm. It seemed they could never quite get it right, always turning on the air conditioning in the winter or the heater in the summer.

"So, what do you think?" Stanton asked.

Mac liked her boss. He always treated her kindly, like he was her partner rather than her boss. He always wanted to discuss cases with her and valued her insight and opinions. There had been a couple of cases that they had worked together where she had seen things in the evidence that he had not. Plus, their clients liked talking to her because she was easygoing, which sometimes allowed her to get more information than her boss could. Most enlisted were leery of talking to officers openly because officers and enlisted weren't allowed to be friends or have relationships in the military world. Fraternization could get you in a lot of trouble; there was a rank structure for a reason.

She was lost in thought when Stanton asked his question again.

"I don't know for sure," she said. "My instincts tell me that Johnson is a good guy, but we've been doing this for a while and have seen people do all kinds of things that we never thought they would do. Plus, he was caught with his wife. I'm not saying that means he did it, but that looks very incriminating. I think we'll have to get more evidence on this one to come to any conclusions."

"I agree," Stanton said. "We'll have to see what the evidence shows, but I also think we should do some digging of our own. It isn't every day we get the opportunity to defend an airman accused of murder. The closest I think we ever came to a case like this was that NCO who came back from Korea last year and lured his wife's lover into a motel room and stabbed him thirty-two times. Now *that* was an interesting case, and the guy confessed, but the civilians kept jurisdiction so we didn't get as involved as I would have liked."

She smiled, thinking about how much Stanton enjoyed what he did. He was an excellent attorney, and he had one trait that most attorneys couldn't fake: people liked him the instant they met him. It came across in the courtroom when he interviewed witnesses and the accused. People simply wanted to like him. His charisma alone had gone far to help them win some complicated cases.

Johnson was brought into the small room. His head was down, his curly hair matted. His eyes looked distant and tired, like he hadn't slept in days. Mac thought back to the times she had been around him in the past. He had been young and full of life with kind brown eyes. She had even thought him good-looking, though a little young for her, and of course, he was married, which in Mac's mind made him completely off-limits. She had girlfriends who liked chasing married men, but that wasn't her thing. The only thing she wanted was a solid relationship with a man she could be friends with and trust. Except she rarely trusted anyone. Most men just wanted to get into her pants, which had resulted in her current status: single.

Johnson lifted his eyes and looked directly at her. She saw sorrow in his deep brown eyes. No hatred or deception, just loss and fear. He reminded her of the puppy she'd had when she was a young girl. She had an urge to hug him and tell him everything would be okay, but she couldn't. It would have been highly unprofessional—in general, the military frowned upon hugging fellow military members, and certainly not clients. Public displays of affection were discouraged and could get you in trouble if witnessed by the wrong person.

Johnson slid into a chair; his large shoulders slumped. The chair creaked beneath his weight. He was a large black man; she guessed at least 220, with a young babyface looking much older than a twenty-six-year-old should. Mac suspected that one of Johnson's parents wasn't black because he had beautiful, light mocha skin that made him look like he had spent time on the beach.

Captain Stanton greeted Johnson and asked, "How are you holding up?" Mac thought that was a silly question, but it was just Stanton's way of starting a conversation.

"As good as can be expected, I guess," Johnson said.

"I know this is difficult, but could you tell us what happened from the beginning?" Stanton said. Mac's job during these interviews was to take notes and ask questions at the end. It was the basic routine for interviewing people. Her boss would always start the questioning, and then she would complete the interview with her own follow-up questions. As the defense, they weren't trying to get anyone to confess; they were just trying to get the accused's side of the story so they could start crafting a viable defense.

This was one of her favorite parts. She enjoyed her job thoroughly, especially investigations, and wished she could simply do this for the rest of her career. Unfortunately, if she made rank, they would move her into a leadership position. That was not her thing. She loved the opportunity to take care of the underdog and help defend them against the big bad government. Stanton always told her she should go to law school and be a defense attorney, but she wasn't sure she could do what he did in the courtroom. She enjoyed the investigative part more. Finding the evidence necessary for her client to be set free—or, in some cases, supporting the client while facing court and prison time—was what gave her fulfillment. These cases were demanding yet rewarding; everyone turned their backs on the accused, but she got to stand by their side.

"You have complete confidentiality," Stanton said to Johnson, "and nothing you say will go outside this office without your consent."

Johnson nodded and signed the forms to accept Stanton as his defense counsel.

"Have you been read your Article 32 rights?" Stanton asked. Article 32 rights were similar to Miranda rights in the civilian world.

"I, um, yes…they read me my rights when they took me from the scene. You have to believe me…I did not kill my wife. I loved Zonira with everything I had. We were talking about having a baby. She was going to get off birth control so we could start trying. She was my entire world. I would never hurt her."

"We believe you," Stanton said, "but we have to be able to prove what happened. Please describe your day starting when you woke up yesterday."

Johnson sighed. "My day was normal, like any other day. I got up at oh-seven hundred hours to work out. It was my day off, but I have a PT test soon and wanted to get in shape since I had recently taken a month off. So, I got in a great workout and then went to the coffee shop on base to pick up some coffee and breakfast for Zonira and me. Zonira had just gotten up when I got home. She was so beautiful standing there in one of my old t-shirts. Her hair was all a mess, and she looked so sexy." He stared past them, remembering his last moments with his wife. "I tossed aside the food, and we made love right there on the kitchen table. I can't believe she's gone. It doesn't matter what happens to me. I can't imagine my life without her."

He took a few more deep breaths before continuing. "Zonira was going to go see her sister in Coeur d'Alene. We've appreciated being stationed at Fairchild Air Force Base because that's allowed her to be closer to her sister. After we finished breakfast, she went to get ready. I kissed her goodbye, and she left the house. That's the last time I saw her. I decided I would go out and do some fishing and hiking. It'd been a while since I got out to enjoy nature. I thought it would be a good way to clear my head and get ready to get back to work since my R&R was about over."

"Zonira and I had agreed to meet up later that evening for dinner. I texted her to let her know I'd be running a little late, but she didn't respond. When I came back to base, I thought maybe I'd find her angry with me for losing track of time." He leaned back in the chair and stared absently at the ceiling. "In my head, I was coming up with all kinds of apologies. When I walked into the house, I took off my muddy boots because I knew she would be mad if I tracked mud into the house. I walked into the kitchen, and there she was." A tear rolled down his cheek.

"At first, all I saw was her feet, and then I came around the island, and—" He gasped, the words catching in his throat. "She was just lying there. I'm not sure what happened after that. The next thing I knew, I was being pulled off her and taken away, and then I was in a cell. There was so much blood. It was all over the place, all over the kitchen, all over the cabinets; it was everywhere. I've never seen so much blood. It was almost like someone had painted using my wife's insides." He dropped his head to the table, his big shoulders rising and falling. Finally, he looked up again at them, his dark skin ashen.

Stanton looked at Mac and nodded. Turning back, he said in a soft voice, "Johnson, tell me about your deployment."

"Nothing really to tell. It was out of the blue. I wasn't supposed to deploy, but I magically got orders and prepared for deployment shortly after we got here. It went fine overall. It was my first time, and I didn't know what to expect, but I got there and did my job then came home."

"During your time abroad did your wife say anything to you that stood out? Anything strange in letters?" Mac asked.

"Not really. She was so brave. She always told me not to worry and that she would be fine. She said some of the people from my shop sometimes stopped by to check on her. After that, she returned to school and kept busy, but nothing more."

"I need to ask...do you think there's any way she was having an affair while you were gone?"

"No way. She wouldn't do that," Johnson said and looked away. Mac thought there might be more to that but figured now wasn't the time.

Stanton reassured Johnson that they would do everything they could for him. Mac knew they never promised certain outcomes to clients because there was no way to know how things would turn out. All they could guarantee was that they would do everything in their power to help their client, which was never a lie. They would turn over every stone to find the truth, whatever it was. Their job wasn't to free their client but to make sure the justice system worked properly and ensure their client didn't get railroaded.

CHAPTER
THREE

STANTON AND MAC got up and let Technical Sergeant Branson know they were done. He came in to retrieve Johnson from his chair and said, "Do you guys' mind hanging out for a few? I'll be right back." They agreed. He took Johnson back to the holding cell and got him settled in.

Mac and Stanton sat silently waiting for him. They knew better than to discuss their case in an open environment. Branson came back in and said, "Our new shirt would really like to meet with you. Would you mind waiting for a little bit? He's almost done with his meeting."

They agreed and were led to the shirt's office. While they waited, they looked around his office. Mac recognized the diamond on one of his plaques signifying the first sergeant symbol. He had won the award for being the top-enlisted advisor on base. He had an impressive wall decorated with going-away gifts, awards, and decorations. Apparently, he was a well-liked leader.

Mac had heard about this guy. Someone had told her he was a huge beast of a man, somewhere around six foot seven, maybe six foot eight. If nothing else, she was curious about meeting him. A first sergeant could be a huge asset when defending a military member in her line of work. The shirt typically knew everything going on in his squadron and had a good idea of who they should interview, who were friends with who, and each member's reputation within the squadron. Though rumors weren't facts, there was typically some truth to them.

Still, Mac wasn't hoping for much, because this guy was brand new to the squadron. Many first sergeants moved from squadron to squadron around a base. They were usually reassigned to a different squadron every two years or so. She had never met this shirt because he had previously worked over on the "Survival Evasion Resistance and Escape" side of the base. She knew they got into trouble over there, but they usually took care of their own. She had heard that many people feared this guy because of his size, but she knew that size didn't always mean everything.

She was off in her own little world when Stanton let out a soft whistle. "Damn, that guy is huge."

Mac looked down the hall following Stanton's gaze and there stood the biggest man she had ever seen. "Holy shit!" she muttered; her eyes wide. She was trying not to stare at him, but couldn't help but think, *Wow!* The mammoth man finished his conversation and started walking toward his office. Mac's heart was racing, and she felt pissed at herself for not maintaining control, but this man was *gorgeous.* There was no better word for him. She guessed he was Italian or Greek or descended from some other place that gods come from. He looked like someone who could grace the cover of a popular bodybuilding magazine with his lean, massive body.

As he walked into the office, he had to duck slightly to clear the doorway. He stood there for just a moment, filling up the entire doorframe with his wide shoulders and strong chest.

Stanton stood up and looked like he had somehow shrunk next to this man. He stretched out his hand. "Hi, I'm Captain Stanton, and this is Mac—I mean, Sergeant McGregor. We're the defense counsel in the Johnson case."

The big man shook Stanton's hand, then turned to Mac and shook her hand as well. His hands were so big that hers disappeared in his. She liked how big and intimidating he was. It made her somehow feel safer. He smiled down at them, making Mac feel like a little kid. His smile was warm and reached his eyes.

"Yes," he said in a deep, baritone voice. "Branson said you would be waiting for me. Thank you for your patience. I'm Master Sergeant Gavin Hudson. I just got to the squadron and am having a hell of a time so far." He smiled again, this time directly at Mac, and she felt a little weak in the knees.

Dammit, where does this guy get off making me feel this way? Her fight or flight instincts started kicking in—*get away, get away, danger, danger, this one could really be trouble!* She smiled back at him and saw a twinkle of mischief in his hazel eyes.

Hudson came the rest of the way into the office. "I wanted to meet with you because I feel there's more to this case than meets the eye. I have a buddy of mine downtown that gave a tip about a case they're looking into. Joe and I have known each other for a long time. He and I were talking preliminaries over a cold beer, and it turns out our victim on base looks almost identical to a missing person's case from downtown. Our on-base murder investigation is, of course, being led by OSI because the accused is one of ours, and that's directly in their wheelhouse. I told them about the downtown case, but they dismissed it. They said that just because the two women look alike doesn't mean the cases are connected."

"Makes sense," Stanton said.

"I just have a feeling about this," Hudson said and took his phone out of his pocket to show them two pictures. One was of Johnson's wife, and the other was of the missing woman downtown. The similarity was uncanny. "Since OSI is investigating, I really can't stick my nose where it doesn't belong. My buddy's name is Joe Romero at the Spokane Police Department." Hudson said. He pulled one of his business cards out of his pocket and wrote Joe's information on it. "Call me if you need anything." He handed the card to Mac and walked away.

Mac watched him walk down the hall before realizing she was staring at his ass. Staring at other military members' asses, especially while in uniform, was frowned upon. But it was such a nice ass, attached to such an amazing body.

Stanton came up next to her with a big, goofy grin on his face. He winked at her and said, "I see you like the view."

She nudged him back with a sheepish grin.

CHAPTER
FOUR

Afghanistan - four and a half years ago

THE SERGEANT STOOD strong and confident in front of his airmen. They had been in the hot desert of Afghanistan for months. Exhaustion showed on everyone's faces and his most of all. The entire team was sitting on old crates in the dusty hangar, waiting to hear about the day's activities. The hot air felt made it feel like his uniform was melting on his body. The heat seared their lungs in the hangar, creating an oven-like atmosphere rather than providing shelter. The temperature outside had already climbed to over ninety degrees. It was nearly unbearable in July, especially when they were out in the field under the hot, unrelenting sun. They always packed tons of water and sunscreen, but it was never enough.

Bagram Air Base had been their home for nearly half a year. They were all ready to go home. The eleven men and women that were part of his team had shown amazing strength and endurance during their deployment. He was as proud of them as a father would be of his own children. "Listen up, we only have another couple of weeks in this shit-hole and then we get to go home." They all cheered. "That's the good news. The bad news is, we're going outside the wire today. We are scheduled to meet with Afghan Air Force officials at ten hundred hours. They'll link us up with the same team we've been working with during our relaxing vacation here." They all laughed. "Even though we know these people and we've been working with them, that doesn't mean we don't need to keep our guard up. Heads on a swivel, folks. We all know what can happen when people become complacent. Right?"

They all nodded in acknowledgment.

One of his airmen raised his hand like he was in class. He still had a baby face and looked up to his leadership the same way he imagined the young man regarded his parents. With wide eyes, the young airman smiled at his team leader. "So, boss, will she be there today?" A big grin spread across his young face, and the others started chuckling quietly.

They knew their team leader had a crush on the woman who worked as a liaison for the Afghan Air Force, but they didn't know the half of it. They had been working to build up the Afghan Air Force and help the people of this country protect themselves. It had been a long and frustrating process.

The female liaison they had been working with during their deployment was something else. Women in Afghanistan were not treated well, and it had taken a long time to gain her trust. In this country, it was even frowned upon to use a woman's name in public; Afghan law stated that only men's names were to be used in public. The sergeant had been shocked to learn that after an Afghan woman gave birth, her name was left off the birth certificate. They only showed the name of the father. The same went for when a woman married or died; her name did not appear on the wedding invitation or the death certificate. Women in Afghanistan had been beaten for revealing their names to strangers, especially male strangers that weren't part of their family. He had fit into that category.

He had been introduced to Sahar shortly after he arrived in the country. It had been a long time since he had deployed, but he was looking forward to the adventure. Once he had been processed and settled, he and his leadership met with the chief of staff of the Afghan

Air Force. The man had been short and wide with a weathered face, but he was an imposing man that someone wouldn't want to mess with despite his stature. The general's eyes were hardened from years of service and suffering in his country, but there was also kindness. Leadership had told him the general was a good man who wanted the best for his country.

Standing by the general's side was the most beautiful woman the sergeant had ever seen. She stood proud next to her father. Her head was wrapped in a stunning yellow shemagh, the traditional scarf worn by women in her country. He could not see most of her face, but her eyes were breathtaking. There was something about this woman that mesmerized him. She had dark, deep-brown almond eyes. The sergeant thought he saw wisdom there and maybe a hint of mischief. He couldn't stop staring at her. Even when he was introduced to the general, he continued looking at the beautiful woman. She wasn't introduced by name; she was simply referred to as his eldest daughter. This was customary in Afghanistan. She was there because she spoke fluent English and was therefore useful. He was thrilled when they told him he would be working with her as his conduit between the United States Air Force and the Afghan Air Force.

After their initial meeting, he had blown off the encounter, thinking he just wanted to be near a beautiful woman after what had happened with his wife. Eight months earlier, he had come home from base one afternoon much earlier than expected. He had wanted to surprise his wife because it was their fifteenth anniversary. He had stopped for flowers and bought her a stunning diamond necklace that was a bit more than they could afford. He had snuck into the house, wanting to surprise her. Then he had walked into their bedroom to find his wife being serviced by a young man half his age, and his heart broke into a million pieces. He loved his wife and thought of her as his best friend. He had thought everything was good between them, but apparently not. His military service had him working late hours, and he had been TDY quite a bit lately, which took him away from home. She had been complaining about being alone all the time, but he figured she knew what she was getting into when she married a military man.

Apparently, she was lonelier than he had thought. He had heard about spouses that took a lover when their husband was out in the field or away from home, but he had never thought that would happen with his wife. Now the divorce papers were filed, and they were waiting the customary ninety days for the divorce to be complete. It had all been put on hold with this deployment since he was out of the country. When he returned, he would be a divorcée. That concept seemed so foreign to him since he had always loved being married. They hadn't had kids, which he guessed was now a good thing, but he had always wanted a big family. But life doesn't always work out the way people want it to.

CHAPTER
FIVE

WHEN HE MET up with Sahar the second time, she took his breath away all over again. For this meeting, it was just the two of them. She smelled amazing. When they met in private, she let her scarf fall from her face to reveal full red lips and high cheekbones. He felt like a commoner next to her. She was statuesque and stunning. Her velvety voice mesmerized him. He thought he would get used to her as time passed, but it only got worse. He had fallen for her hard. He knew it was against his regulations and forbidden for her.

Nevertheless, they started to meet in private more regularly. The first time he kissed her, he melted into her body. Her lips tasted sweet and soft. He felt warm and safe in her embrace. They had been sneaking around at night seeing each other for months like two teenage kids. He simply couldn't get enough of her. Not just physically —he enjoyed speaking with her and hearing her views on the world. She was highly intelligent. He liked everything about her. He worried that he was falling for her because he was on the rebound, but still, it felt right.

One evening when they met, she was distant and sad. She wouldn't say why, but he knew something was seriously wrong. She told him she wouldn't be able to see him for a while. Something about her being sent to a school. It didn't sound true to his ears, but he figured it was her way of letting him down gently. She left him a gift and told him not to open it until the end of the next day. He was afraid to open it, thinking it was a goodbye letter or something to remember her by. He would never forget her. He put the gift in his tactical bag, knowing that at least he would see her the next day. Even though the others would be there, and he wouldn't be able to be near her, at least she would be there.

He and his team loaded up in the convoy and headed outside the wire. Overall, the times they had been outside had been relatively uneventful. As they drove, the feeling of sadness weighed on him as he thought about Sahar's departure. He knew it wasn't something that would last forever. They were from different worlds, but that didn't make the hole in his chest feel any less real. He knew his crew was looking forward to going home, but not him. Being alone in an empty house all the time sounded like torture to him. He wasn't good at being alone. He knew he would probably get used to it, but not any time soon.

They arrived at their location. It wasn't a place they had been to before. Their convoy pulled into a dusty lot. They were out in the open like sitting ducks, waiting to be shot at. The sergeant had a bad feeling about this. Most of the time he felt like an overprotective father, but in this case, the little hairs on the back of his head were standing on end. His gut was telling him to clear out—and he always listened to his gut. It had served him very well over the years.

He headed to the back of the Humvee to grab his gear when the entire back of the vehicle blew apart. It threw his body back with such force he couldn't breathe, and his lungs felt like they had caught fire. His head slammed into something hard and unforgiving.

CHAPTER
SIX

HE WOKE up with bright lights shining in his eyes and a sterile, sickly smell in his nose. He wasn't sure where he was at first. Every fiber of his being hurt. His head was pounding, and he couldn't see clearly out of one eye. He tried to remember what had happened and simply couldn't. He closed his eyes again and tried to take a deep breath, but a sharp pain pierced through his rib cage. "What the hell?" he said out loud.

Nurse Bonnie heard him from the hallway and popped her head in. She was a short, heavy-set woman with brown curls framing her full face. She smiled at him with kindness in her eyes. "Well, hello. We weren't sure you were going to wake up anytime soon. You had us worried."

"Where am I?" he asked.

"Oh, you don't worry about a thing, hon. You're in the hospital. We'll take good care of you."

"How bad is it? What happened to my team? Are they okay?"

She shifted her weight from one foot to the other and looked at the floor. "I'll go get the doctor for you. He can explain everything." She smiled at him and quickly walked away.

His head hurt so badly. He felt angry and disoriented.

A little while later, the doctor came to check on him. "Nice to see you awake. How are you feeling?" The tall doctor in a lab coat peered at the machines attached to his body.

"I've been better," the sergeant replied, and tried to smile but couldn't quite make it happen.

Dr. Sandoz peered at him through round, wire-rimmed glasses. His bushy eyebrows furrowed as he studied the man. The doctor looked more concerned than the sergeant would have liked.

"So, what's the damage, Doc?"

Dr. Sandoz took a step back and took a deep breath. "For starters, you were blown up. You have multiple contusions, three broken ribs, and significant trauma to your head. We were able to reduce the swelling in your brain, but we're not sure about the long-term damage. It's possible that you could suffer from long-term issues. Only time will tell."

CHAPTER
SEVEN

Fairchild Air Force Base - Present Day

LEAVING HER OFFICE, Mac shot Stanton a quick text to let him know she was heading over to the Spokane police station to meet with Romero. Her boss was with the prosecuting attorney, Captain Daniels, at the legal office to discuss the discovery and the evidence. He'd asked Mac to contact Romero and see if she could get an interview with him. Surprisingly, Romero had picked up on the first ring and said that he was available right then.

It was a short drive to his office in the middle of downtown Spokane. Mac cleared security and left her mace and Taser at the front counter with the intake officer. She was escorted back to a cubicle where a good-looking man sat.

Romero had bags under his eyes and looked worn down, but he was still attractive, or at least she thought so. *What is this, Hot Man Monday?* Everywhere she went, she kept running into good-looking men—or maybe it was just that she had been alone for so long and her libido was on overdrive. He wore worn-out jeans, cowboy boots, and a nice-looking button-down. She shook her head to clear her thoughts and plastered a smile on her face while making a mental note to go on a date with someone soon.

Mac walked up to his desk and asked if he was Romero.

He stood up with a big smile on his face. "Aww, you must be Mac! Most people call me Joe. Hudson said you would be stopping by to see me, but he never mentioned you were pretty or a lady." She gave him a sideways glance. "I apologize, ma'am; I tend to be a little forward."

She grinned at him. She liked him already. "My real name is Evelyn, but everybody calls me Mac because my last name is McGregor."

Joe smiled. "You don't much look like a McGregor."

"It's my dad's name; my mom's Latino," she said, smiling at his straightforward manner.

"I see why Hudson didn't elaborate. He and I go way back." She wasn't sure what Joe meant by that but figured she could ask Hudson later. His slight southern drawl made him sound like a southern gentleman. She thought it added to his charm.

"So, about the missing person's case you mentioned to Hudson," Mac said. "My client is the accused, and I want to see if there's any connection between the murder and disappearance of your victim."

Joe walked over to the cabinet and retrieved a plain blue folder. He sat back down and showed everything he had to Mac, which wasn't much. Again, she saw an amazing likeness between the two victims.

"So, what suspects do you have so far?" Mac asked.

"Not much, I'm afraid. She went missing in October. She's a prostitute, which is a very high-risk career, as I'm sure you know. She got picked up on a Friday night by a guy in a dark-colored pickup truck. No one saw the guy, of course, just the truck. The person in question picked up Abigail, our missing person, and no one has seen her since. What about your case? Any similarities?"

Mac thought about what they knew. It wasn't a whole lot. "All we know is, we found our suspect next to his wife's body covered in her blood...but that could be explained away. He says he found her that way, so we're not sure if he's guilty."

They batted information back and forth for a little while, figuring out the best approach. Joe adjusted his reading glasses. "Without any real suspects, my case is probably going to stay cold for a while."

Mac agreed that they needed to do some more searching. She still wasn't convinced the two cases were connected, though the women's similar appearances were uncanny. She had a feeling that there was much more to the story than what was right in front of them. She thanked Joe for his time and headed back to base. She was determined to find the truth.

CHAPTER
EIGHT

SHE PULLED into the parking lot of her building and was surprised to see a dark-colored sedan with a distinct *Security Forces Commander* insignia on it. She walked into her office, wondering what the commander wanted. It was probably about the case, him figuring out how to proceed with Johnson. Normally they worked through the prosecution, but leadership worked with the defense as well every now and again. She welcomed the leadership's involvement. If her office could get them on the accused's side, there was a much better chance of acquittal. She walked in to find the security forces chief and the commander talking with Captain Stanton. They were all joking and laughing about something to do with sports, which Mac had no interest in.

They all turned to greet her. "Hey Mac, how are you doing? It's been a while," Chief said with a warm smile.

She knew Chief from her time stationed at Holloman Air Force Base. He had been her mentor and had really helped her career a great deal. She had worked with him as a security forces augmentee, where a member of a different career field would fill in during security details. He had seen her potential and skillset with hand-to-hand combat and had taken an interest in helping her career.

"Hi Chief, it's nice to see you," she said with a smile. Warm thoughts about how he had taken her under his wing and helped her professionally, mentoring her through some emotional times, filled her mind. She liked him a great deal and considered him a big brother.

He had made a huge deal out of the fact that she was an expert marksman at the firing range. He even publicly recognized her for her professionalism and hard work. This was when she had still been working prosecution. He had given her a hard time when she moved to defense—or "the dark side," as he called it. When Chief had been ordered to Fairchild, she was thrilled, but she hadn't seen much of him since his arrival. The life of a chief could be a very busy one, she guessed.

Stanton cocked his head to the side slightly. "Mac—Johnson's leadership—is here to make sure he's taken care of."

The commander cleared his throat. "This is an open-and-shut case." He pointedly looked at Mac. "There's no sense in digging into this one any further since the evidence is crystal clear. I'm recommending Johnson get a psych eval and remain in pretrial confinement, so he won't hurt anyone else."

Mac just looked at him with her mouth slightly open. She couldn't believe the commander had already assumed he was guilty. Mac has some serious doubts about Johnson's guilt or innocence. In fact, their little visit today was making her question the facts even more.

The commander was a short, wide man who reminded her of a fire plug with a receding hairline, but he had piercing blue eyes that most people simply didn't argue with. He had a reputation for someone who always got what he wanted. He shifted his weight to one foot and pinned Mac with a stern look. "We want to get this taken care of and put this whole thing behind us as quickly as possible."

Mac understood that to mean he wanted to brush it under the rug so his squadron wouldn't look bad. She was sure that Johnson would disagree.

Chief walked up and put his hand on her shoulder. "Mac," he said. "We've known each other for years. If there were any doubt in my mind that Johnson was innocent, I would investigate every detail. If we find anything, we'll let you know, but all evidence points to him. Unfortunately, sometimes people just lose it. That is what happened in this case. Johnson came back and maybe found out his wife was having an affair. He was angry with his wife and ended up killing her."

Mac couldn't believe her ears. All she heard were theories that had no significant backing. They were speculating about the motive, and they were ready to condemn through prejudice. They certainly didn't want her office looking at the evidence.

Captain Stanton made eye contact with her but didn't say a word. They'd been working together long enough that he could tell what she was thinking. He gave her a pointed look, silently warning her not to say anything.

The commander and the chief had quite a bit of influence on the base. Even though they were only at the squadron level, they could still wield influence. The Area Defense Counsel's office reported to AFLOA—the Air Force Legal Operations Agency—outside the base's chain of command, but that didn't mean the commander or chief couldn't influence things to hurt the captain's or Mac's career. She knew Chief wouldn't do anything to hurt her, but she wasn't as sure about the commander.

That pissed Mac off. In what world did they think they could just come in and tell them how to defend their clients or how to do their job? It was way outside the scope of their authority. The reason their office reported to command off-installation was specifically to avoid situations like these. But here they were, telling them not to investigate the case, not to look into things. Clearly there was something that the SFS leadership didn't want them to know.

When they finally left, she looked at Stanton. "What the hell was that?"

Captain Stanton smiled. He liked her feisty nature and the fact that she always wanted to defend the underdog. "Okay, Mac, let's look at this logically. Why are they so hell-bent on ensuring our client goes down for the murder of his wife without fully investigating?"

She shrugged her shoulders.

"The only thing I can think of," Stanton said, "is that they're either getting pressure from higher-ups to make it all go away, or it's the bad press. Think about it: Security Forces are charged with protecting and defending the base, and one of their own is charged with murder. That looks bad. No, more than bad...it could completely destroy their reputation."

"How do you want to handle this?" Mac asked.

They discussed the case a little further and went over the information she had found out from Joe downtown. There had been nothing profound, just that dark-colored pickup truck picking up the missing woman, and Johnson didn't own a pickup truck. The two cases were most likely unrelated. Still, it still nagged at Mac how alike the two women looked. Their hair, the shape of their face, their dark, almond-shaped eyes were all the same. They could easily have been sisters.

"Clearly there's more to this case than what we're seeing. OSI is investigating. Let's see what they come up with, and in the meantime, we'll do some quiet digging. We have to tread carefully," he said, running his hand over the little bit of hair he had. "Let's not forget that our boss at AFLOA is friends with the SFS commander. That means he may be able to influence this case."

Mac thought about that. She knew that rank had its privileges. If colonels and chiefs were involved, sometimes the rules got bent, and innocent airmen could get hurt in the crossfire.

CHAPTER
NINE

HUDSON WALKED INTO THE GYM. He hoped he could get some sparring in after a long day. He walked into the sparring room and stopped cold; there stood the petite sergeant he had met earlier that day. What was her name again? She was facing off with a guy at least two to three times her size and doing quite well. She was using defensive tactics—leverage to compensate for her lack of strength and her small size—to her advantage. The larger man seemed slower and kept missing her. She was quick and landed a right hook directly across his chin. He shook it off but looked surprised. She swung her leg around and caught him directly in the midsection, knocking the breath out of him.

A guy walked up next to Hudson and whistled. "Wow, that woman has a lot of fury built up in that tight little body. She's sexy as hell but kinda frightening."

A grin crept across Hudson's face. "So, is she seeing anyone?"

"Not a chance buddy, you might as well give that one up. We've all been trying ever since she showed up, and she won't give anyone the time of day. She just comes to the gym, kicks a little ass, and then leaves. At first, we thought she was into women, but nope, a couple of them have tried too. Apparently, that one is simply off-limits. Fun to fantasize about, though."

Hudson gave the guy a pointed stare until he walked away.

Hudson went to the punching bag to start warming up. He was lost in thought when he heard a loud smack. He looked over to see the big man that woman had been sparring with laid out flat on his back. She stood over him, hands raised, bouncing up and down in a crazy victory dance. She reached down and offered her hand. The size difference between her and her sparring partner was almost comical. He wondered if the big guy had let her win, but somehow, he didn't think so. He watched her help her opponent up off the mat. The big man shook her hand and walked away. Hudson knew it was twisted, but the fact that she could possibly kick his ass really turned him on.

Mac was stretching and getting ready to leave when she looked up to see Agent Vivian Ross. Mac smiled, knowing that Agent Ross would know exactly what was going on in the Johnson case. "Hi Viv," Mac said, coming up to greet her.

"Don't even start with me, Mac," Vivian responded by way of greeting. She was a tall, good-looking, no-nonsense blond woman who was always about business. In her world, you had to be. People were always trying to get information from her about cases. Mac had only seen her let her hair down once during a girls' night out. It had been quite something to watch. Ever since then, they had been friends even though they were on two different sides of the fence.

It was clearly OSI's job to find evidence to support the prosecution of a case. Every once in a while, though, it turned out that the evidence they found also helped the defense counsel. They were supposed to be unbiased and simply look for the truth of what really happened, but as everyone knew, politics and the good ol' boys club muddied the waters. Viv worked in a predominantly male career field; she had to deal with the constant alpha male. Mac had met most of them. Some of them rose to the level of narcissistic personalities. There was definitely a great deal of testosterone in both their worlds.

Mac looked at each case, knowing that there were always three sides: what *he* said, what *she* said, and what *really* happened. "Come on, Viv, we get to see the evidence when you're done anyway," Mac argued.

Viv's forehead wrinkled, and she gave Mac an annoyed look. "You know perfectly well that I can't share details about an ongoing investigation, even with you."

"I know, I know," Mac said. "Just do me a favor and really look closely at this one. Something fishy is going on. Johnson's leadership basically threatened us today and told me specifically not to look into the case any further."

"Yeah, they probably just want this to go away because of all the bad press." Vivian rolled her eyes. She hated all the political crap that came with her job.

"Maybe," Mac said, "but I think there's more. I think someone in that squadron is trying to hide something. I have a feeling in my gut."

"You and your gut need to leave the investigation to OSI. We know what we're doing. Don't go sticking your nose where it doesn't belong."

Mac raised an eyebrow.

"Okay, I give," Viv said. "We'll dig into the case and leave no stone unturned. I promise." She turned and walked away without saying goodbye.

As Viv drove home that night, she thought about what Mac had said. It didn't make sense—well, not entirely—that Johnson's leadership didn't want his defense looking into his case. That was one of the key factors to a good defense counsel. They were the ones who had to make sure the accused saw a fair trial and that all the facts were heard, not just the ones the government wanted the jury to hear about.

Agent Ross took her job very seriously. She saw things from a very black-and-white viewpoint. Her soon-to-be ex-husband had filed for divorce because he said she was married to her job and wouldn't rest, even for him, until she had all the facts in the case.

CHAPTER
TEN

VIV PULLED into the driveway of the little cottage she would soon receive in the divorce settlement. It was a great place to unwind, which she often needed to do. So many people had told her that she needed to relax and not be so intense. She dropped her gear by the front door, then went to shower, change, and grab a glass of good wine. She sat out on the back porch listening to the little stream that ran through the back of her property. It made a gurgling sound as it rushed by with ice creeping along the edges. The frozen forest surrounding her felt calming.

She walked over to the back door to turn on the space heater and liked how the old boards creaked under her feet. She loved it out here, but in the middle of March, it was freezing. She sat back down on the swing and wrapped her blanket tightly around her cold body and put her toes next to the heater to stay warm. Transfixed by the water running beneath her open deck, Vivian thought about the case and all the unanswered questions.

Many things about this case didn't make sense to her. It didn't make sense why Johnson would kill his wife. The couple of times she had seen them together, there was no doubt he loved her, but things weren't always what they seemed. This job had certainly shown her what people were capable of. She had even been a little jealous of the couple—all her own relationships always fell apart. She now found herself embedded in a messy divorce. She would never discount what people were capable of, but there was always a reason for their actions. Sometimes, when people were deployed, they came home different. It was an unfortunate part of military life and would be an easy explanation for Johnson's behavior, but she still needed to figure out the why.

She was lost in thought when she felt his hand on the back of her head. She hadn't even heard him come in. Normally the old creaky wood on the back porch would have tipped her off, but he was stealthy despite being such a large man. She assumed it was because of all his combat training over the years. Sometimes he would sneak up on her and she wouldn't even know he was there until he was standing right next to her. At first that had unnerved her, but now she had grown accustomed to it. They'd only been seeing each other for a couple of months, but everything was going well so far.

Okay, so there were a few things that weren't going well, but she really liked him overall, and he seemed to have a strange hold over her. She couldn't seem to say no to him. She was strong in every other aspect of her life except when it came to him. One major downfall was that she couldn't share the relationship with anyone because he was so much higher-ranking than her. Now more than ever, they couldn't be open about it because of the Johnson case. She would never want anybody to think that she would skew the evidence one way or another simply because she was having a relationship with this specific someone. It just wasn't the way she did things.

She smiled up at him.

"How was your day?" he asked.

She cocked her head to the side. "Pretty good overall. I saw Mac at the gym today." She thought she saw a flash of anger pass across his eyes but figured maybe it was just the shadows on the back porch.

"Oh really," he said.

"Yes, she told me something very interesting. She said Johnson's leadership was threatening her not to investigate the case. You wouldn't know anything about that, would you?"

He gave her a disarming smile. "That isn't what we meant. We were just coming there to tell her that we had it covered, and we were going to take care of Johnson."

"What do you mean, you're going to take care of Johnson?" Vivian asked suspiciously.

"Aww, see, that's what makes you such a great agent. Always suspicious of everyone, even me. That's also what hurts relationships. Remember, we talked about this. Open communication is the key. No secrets and no accusing each other of things we didn't do," he said pointedly. "What we meant is that we're going to make sure he gets a fair trial, and there's no reason for her to worry about it."

"That isn't how Mac told the story," Vivian said.

"Well, in this case, my dear, I believe Mac is confused."

She thought about that for a little while. Maybe Mac had taken it the wrong way. Sometimes Mac was a little intense. Hell, sometimes Vivian was intense herself. What was she thinking? She had finally met a good man who understood her. Regardless, she had to learn to trust someone, and this man had been good to her. He was helping her through a tough time. Her anxiety often got the best of her. She forced herself to relax.

He shifted his weight behind her and said, "Don't you worry about a thing. I have this handled. Everything's going to be just fine." He knelt and kissed her full on the lips, and soon she forgot all about the Johnson case. There was something about him that was off-limits and kind of dangerous. She really liked that about him. She was always about following the rules, but this was the one thing she had allowed in her life that broke them.

It wasn't like their relationship was the definition of fraternization, but it was close. Under the Uniform Code of Military Justice, fraternization was when two people had an unprofessional relationship between an officer and an enlisted. In her case, someone could view this as an unprofessional relationship because it could directly negatively impact good order and discipline.

In this case, she was seeing someone outside of her organization, but it could be viewed as improper because he was involved in the case she was currently investigating while being in higher leadership. That meant he could have direct influence on the case, either positively or negatively. Not to mention that she was still technically married, and adultery, regardless of which party is married, was also against the UCMJ.

Viv liked that everyone in the military was held to much higher standards than in the civilian world, though sometimes that made life complicated. In the civilian world, no one really cared who slept with whom. If you were found to be doing something wrong, as long as it wasn't criminal, then normally you just got fired, not prosecuted.

CHAPTER
ELEVEN

HE PICKED her up off the swing and took her into the house. Even the way he made love to her felt off-limits; he was rougher than what she was used to. He carried her into the bedroom and threw her onto the bed, ripping the blanket off her as he went. He roughly removed her old t-shirt and sweats. She wasn't wearing a bra or panties underneath. He stood there looking down at her, not saying a word. His chest heaved up and down and he growled softly like a hungry beast. She could see his erect penis pressing against his pants. She began to move toward him, but the look he gave her made her stop.

He slowly removed his clothes while he was still looking at her with those dark eyes. Then in one swift move, he flipped her onto her stomach, pressed her into the mattress, grabbed her hair, and entered her from behind. It happened so quickly that she didn't even have time to react. He was hurting her. She was still dry when he forced himself inside her. She tried to enjoy herself, but it just hurt. His oversized shaft slammed into her, and he pulled her hair back so hard that she thought he was going to tear it out. He was growling like a wild animal. Tears started running down her face.

There had been rough sex before, but not this rough. They had even played with a little S&M and bondage recently, but it had been mutual.

This didn't feel mutual. It was very one-sided. She thought maybe it was her fault for making him angry and asking about his conversation with Mac. He pulled hard on the back of her hair, thrust himself deep inside her with a guttural sound, and was done. She lay on the mattress face-down and didn't move. He got up off her and, without a word, went to take a shower. She stayed still, not knowing what to do.

Once she heard the sound of the water change as he stepped into the shower, she peeled herself off the bed and walked to the bathroom. She looked at herself in the mirror and wondered what the hell that had been. Maybe it was nothing, just a little rough sex, and he had just gotten worked up. It wasn't like he had hit her or anything. *That would have been a deal-breaker,* she thought to herself. She was bleeding between her legs a little bit, but that sometimes happened because he was so big. He normally took that into account when they made love, but this wasn't making love. It had felt wrong. It was animalistic, primal, and most certainly done only to please him. She decided that she would just put it out of her mind and not think about it.

She quickly cleaned herself and put on an oversized t-shirt. She crawled into bed and pretended to sleep. The sound of his feet made her heart race as he entered the room. She felt the bed shift under his weight. He wrapped his arms around her, and it was everything she could do not to stiffen. He whispered in a low voice, "Sorry babe, I hope I didn't hurt you." With that, he rolled to the other side and went to sleep.

For a while, she simply listened to him sleeping. No matter how hard she tried, sleep would not come. Every time she drifted off, visions of him grabbing her by the hair and pinning her to the bed crept into her thoughts. In her dreams, he wasn't the man she knew. He was a vicious beast with black eyes. There were no whites, just completely black eyes, and that low growl from earlier. She finally slept for a couple of hours.

When she woke up, he was gone. There were flowers left on her kitchen table with a card from him apologizing for being so rough. She smiled, thinking about how lucky she was for finally having a man who knew how to say he was sorry when he knew he had done something wrong. Her soon-to-be ex-husband never apologized for anything. In all fairness, he had never had rough sex with her like that, but then again, it was vanilla at best with her ex. Their sex life had lacked all passion and feeling. At least with this new one, things were hot and sexy most of the time, though certainly a little rougher than she liked.

CHAPTER
TWELVE

MAC SAT cross-legged on her couch wearing an old t-shirt and leggings. The weekends were her favorite; they allowed her time to decompress and think. This weekend she was on call, so she had to be up at a decent hour. For once the early hour was welcomed because it granted her time to look further into the Johnson case. She had found it wasn't just the missing person's case in Spokane—it turned out that Idaho also had a similar missing person's case, and a murder. She felt it in her gut that she was on to something but couldn't quite figure out how to connect the dots. There were a lot of similarities to the cases but a lot of differences as well.

In the Spokane case, the young lady was a prostitute, which could had been enough to put her in the path of danger and make her case unrelated. On the other hand, one of the missing women in Idaho was a dental technician, and the murdered woman had been a nurse at a hospital. The only connection to each of the cases that she could see so far was that they all looked very similar to one another. Printed pictures of all the missing person's cases and the one murder case were spread out in front of her. What was the connection? It was nagging at her but felt somehow out of reach.

Two of the cases reported a dark-colored pickup truck near the location of the missing women, but no one had a license plate number or any other information to report. It just said it was a dark-colored pickup truck. Interesting, but that could simply be coincidence. All the women were age twenty-two to thirty. They all had medium to long dark hair and almond eyes. They all had a petite to medium build, and so far, the cases had all reported the ladies being kind or approachable. She combed through all the ladies' social media sites but didn't find anything particularly interesting. There was no connection between any of them.

Mac started pacing around the room, trying to think what she might be missing. It was easy enough to get from Spokane to Idaho. It was only about a forty-five-minute drive from the base, depending on where you were at and where exactly you were headed. If the killer had base access, he could have easily killed in Idaho, Spokane, *and* the installation. She just wasn't sure if she was shooting in the dark or if the cases were connected. Her gut told her there was more to this than what she was seeing, but what?

Staring intently at the pictures, she started wondering about Zonira's sister in Coeur d'Alene. Zonira's sister was all over her Facebook page, and she had a striking resemblance to Zonira. If there wasn't such a distinct age difference, Mac would have probably thought they were twins. If her hunch was right, there was a good possibility that Zonira's sister might be in danger. She looked at the time and wondered if she should drive out to meet this sister.

CHAPTER
THIRTEEN

MAC WAS PACING around the room, thinking about how her day might play out when her phone rang, interrupting her thoughts. It took her a minute to realize it wasn't her personal cell phone; it was the on-call JAG phone. She laughed at herself, thinking how silly she was. Of course, it was the JAG phone. No one called her cell phone regularly—not because she didn't like people, but simply because she didn't have many friends. She tended to put up walls between herself and other people because of her past. "Intimidating" was a word some people used to describe her, which made no sense to her. She really had to get past these trust issues of hers. She decided she wasn't going to dwell on it.

"Area Defense Counsel's office, Sergeant McGregor speaking. How may I help you?"

"Is this Mac—I mean Evelyn—I mean Sergeant McGregor?"

Mac smiled when she recognized Hudson's voice. He had a very distinct baritone that went along with his large physique. "Yes, this is Mac. What can I do for you?"

"Well, this is Sergeant Hudson. I mean, you can call me Gavin. Sorry to call you on your work phone. I just didn't know how else to get ahold of you, and this is the number Command Post has listed for you. I was just wondering if you were busy?"

Mac smiled again. "I was just working on the Johnson case, so I guess I'm busy, and I'm on call...but other than that, I'm available."

"That's perfect," Hudson replied, his voice rising an octave. "I was wondering if you'd want to get together for some lunch or dinner or something and maybe go over the Johnson case."

Mac hesitated a moment too long.

Hudson took a deep breath and said, "Don't worry, it's not a date or anything. There's just something about this case that's not sitting well with me, and I was hoping that we could discuss it. I knew Sergeant Johnson and Zonira pretty well. It just doesn't seem like something he was capable of."

He paused for a moment. When Mac didn't respond, he continued, "My buddy from downtown said he was very impressed by you. I was wondering what it was you two talked about."

She laughed. "He was, was he?"

"So, what do you think, Mac? Give me a chance. We can just bat this thing around, and if you don't like what I have to say, you just kick me out. In the meantime, I figure you have to eat."

"True," she said, "I'm always hungry. I eat constantly."

Hudson was a little surprised by that since she was pretty small, especially compared to him. "So, what sounds good to you?"

"How do you feel about going for a drive? I know a great place in Coeur d'Alene, and there's an errand I'd like to run while we're out there."

"Sure," Hudson said.

"Perfect. Do you mind picking me up in an hour?"

CHAPTER
FOURTEEN

HUDSON'S TRUCK pulled into the drive on time and, seconds later, she heard him lightly knock on the door. Out of habit, she looked through the peephole and saw him looking back at her. She unlatched the security chain, undid the deadbolt, and opened the door.

There stood Hudson, wearing an old pair of blue jeans and a tight black t-shirt that stretched across his large chest and biceps. She could actually see the outline of his abs through his shirt. She caught herself staring a little too long, but who could blame her? He looked down at her and smiled, and her heart thumped even louder in her chest. *Get ahold of yourself. What's wrong with you?* she berated herself silently. She smiled back and told him she just needed to grab her jacket.

His eyes followed her as she walked across the room. He enjoyed the way her tight jeans fit and how her hips swayed when she walked. She slipped on her jacket, and he found he enjoyed the view from the front as much as from the back. He looked away, trying not to stare. He figured she was used to men looking at her butt; he didn't want her to feel uncomfortable around him. The scent of honey and vanilla surrounded him as she walked past.

Mac stopped short. Her breath caught slightly. In front of her house sat an old, dark-colored pickup truck. It made her pause for just a moment.

Nope, she had to trust her instincts. There was nothing about this man that seemed threatening or that he could be capable of murdering anybody. None of her instincts were screaming at her, and that had served her well so far. Physically he could obviously do some damage, but there didn't seem to be anything about him that was threatening.

He walked around to the passenger side to open the door for her. That surprised her. These days, men usually didn't act much like gentlemen, especially in the military where she was expected to be one of the guys. She thanked him and climbed into the passenger side of the pickup. The entire truck smelled like him. It was a lovely woodsy scent. She found it quite pleasant.

On the way there, Mac laid out what she had discovered about the case so far and her theory about Zonira's sister possibly being the next victim. They batted the idea back and forth for a while, trying to spot a connection between the four cases.

Hudson told her about how he knew the Johnsons. "We were stationed together in Kadena AB, Japan. I was Johnson's supervisor, and occasionally our families would socialize during squadron events."

Mac's ears perked up when he mentioned their families—as in, he had *had* a family. She found herself more disappointed than she wanted to be and couldn't help but ask, "So you're married?"

"I used to be. We were planning on having kids and everything. I really thought we were going to last...but you know how it goes in the military. So, I deployed and came back to find her with another man. She was actually pissed when I beat the shit out of him." He made an angry grunt. "Can you believe that? The only reason I even found out was that I returned early."

He shook his head in disgust, then said, "That's the only scenario that makes sense to me where Johnson could have killed his wife. We talked when he got back. He told me all about how he and his wife were planning on starting a family. Not that she couldn't have been seeing someone on the side, but there's no evidence to support that theory."

"I couldn't imagine walking in on my spouse cheating with another person, especially after being deployed. The last time I went to the sandbox the only thing that kept me going was to be home in my nice warm bed. Having that destroyed would be a heavy blow."

Hudson took a deep breath and got a far-off look in his eyes. "Though the thing is, I could have killed him. The other guy, I mean. When I came home early and found them like that, in our bed... There was a long time after that day when I thought about doing that man bodily harm."

"I can only imagine. I mean, how despicable can you possibly be to come into another man's house and sleep with his wife while her husband is deployed and fighting for the very freedom that he enjoys? That's about as slimy as it gets!" Mac said.

"My point is that I could have never hurt her. No matter what she did to me or how badly she hurt me, it was always easier to hate him and imagine hurting him without acting. But back then, I still loved her. A man can't just turn that off. That's how I think Johnson felt about his wife. He was crazy about her. If it were a simple affair then he would have gone after the other guy, not his beautiful bride."

Mac thought about this. She had never been married, and she figured she probably never would be, though she hoped to be in a relationship one day if she found the right person. She was daydreaming about Hudson when she realized he was looking at her. She smiled at him shyly and cleared her throat. "How long ago did all this happen between you and your wife?"

"Almost a year and a half ago. It hurt like hell at first, but now things are better. After a while, I realized that we weren't right for each other after all. I know that sounds like I'm just making myself feel better, but after the marriage ended, I realized that I'd been blind to so many things about her that wouldn't have worked between us over the long run. I found out after we broke up that she never wanted to have kids. We had talked about starting a family, but she said she'd lied about it to keep me around." He ran his hand through his dark hair with a tired look on his face. "Anyway, I don't want to bore you with the details. How about you?"

Mac frowned, and he found that he missed her smile almost immediately. "I don't have anyone in my life. Just never came across the right guy. Don't get me wrong, I tried once or twice, but things just didn't work out."

Hudson nodded his head in understanding. Mac was an interesting woman. He had never come across anyone quite like her. She was long, lean, and beautiful but didn't seem to have any idea the effect she had on people, especially him. They lapsed into silence for a while. It was strange to him how comfortable he was with her even though they didn't really know each other.

CHAPTER
FIFTEEN

THEY CROSSED into Idaho not far from Coeur d'Alene. "So, where do we find Zonira's sister?" Hudson asked.

"She lives on the outskirts of town in one of the older neighborhoods. Her name is Ali Ahmad. According to my research, she lives alone and is working her way through med school. She rents half of a duplex from an elderly woman." She put the address into her GPS on her phone and the voice started spouting out directions.

They pulled down East Foster Avenue. The street was lined with huge, beautiful trees that reached out and touched each other at the top like an archway out of a fairytale. The branches blocked out some of the sun, casting elegant shadows over all the old homes. Mac was mesmerized. She had never been to any place in Coeur d'Alene other than downtown and had no idea the neighborhoods were this breathtaking. It felt like they were driving into a different world.

They stopped in front of a cute little one-story duplex surrounded by more trees. It was old but looked like it had been well maintained, with a manicured lawn and trimmed bushes. Someone clearly took pride in the place. They got out of the truck and walked up the old stone walkway. Some of the stones were a little loose but the walkway was still in decent shape. Mac guessed the house had been here for the better part of a hundred years because of the stone pillars and old-style construction, but there had been some upgrades done to the place.

They walked up and knocked on the door, but no one answered. They waited one minutes and knocked again. It was late afternoon by then, and there was no telling where Ali was or when she would be back. Mac hadn't been able to find a place of employment for her online, so this was going to be their only stop.

The other door to the little duplex creaked open and a small elderly woman stepped out. She had puffy bluish hair piled on top of her head. Her body swayed a little when she looked up at Hudson. Her tiny frail arms held on to her old knotted-up cane. "Wow, you're a big one!" She smiled a toothy grin of teeth that were clearly not real. "I'm Granny Sans. What can I do for you fine folks?" Her voice shook as she spoke, but her eyes were clear and full of wisdom.

"Ma'am, I'm Mac, and this Hudson. We're looking for the woman who rents the other side of your home."

Granny Sans grinned up at them. She couldn't have been taller than four foot ten. "Those are some awfully strange names for such a good-looking couple."

Mac thought about correcting her comment about them being a couple but figured it didn't matter. "Actually, I'm Evelyn, and this is Gavin, and we're looking for Ali Ahmad."

"Oh yes, lovely girl. Now come inside out of the cold and let me make you some coffee. I just baked some fresh cookies, don't ya know. They're piping fresh out of the oven. Come, come inside, will you?" she said, grinning.

As they followed her into the house, Hudson had to duck his head to clear the doorframe. Mac assumed he had that problem almost everywhere he went. The inside of the house was a little dusty but nicely decorated and smelled like fresh-baked cookies along with what she imagined a normal grandma's house should smell like. All the furniture was old, comfortable, and well-maintained. There was a stunning floral print with butterflies wallpapered on one wall and a small kitchen just the right size for Granny to bake cookies in.

"Well, sit down, sit down." Granny handed them two piping-hot cups of coffee in oversized mugs and disappeared into the kitchen.

Mac took a sip and was surprised to find how strong it was. She knew that if she drank the whole thing this late in the day, she would never sleep tonight. They both sat on the worn-out couch; it was small, and their legs touched. Mac could feel the heat coming off Hudson's body. *Wow, he smells nice.* Sitting this close to him made her realize just how much bigger he was than her. She kind of liked that. It made her feel warm and safe in his presence. Mac looked up at some pictures on the wall leading into the kitchen as a way of distracting herself. "Are these pictures of your family?" she inquired.

Granny popped her head out of the kitchen. "Oh yes, yes, I have three grandchildren. Their names are Joetta, Clara, and Byron. They are the cutest little buggers. They visit me sometimes, and recently gave me this sweater as a present. I always keep candy in my bag just in case they stop by. Would you like some?"

Gavin and Mac noticed two very fluffy Persian cats walking in-between the old woman's legs for the first time. Mac was surprised the cats didn't trip her up and make her fall. It was interesting that she didn't see any hair on the furniture.

Granny caught Mac staring at the cats. "I know what you're thinking, but I just love cats. It's nice to have some company when you're old like me." She smiled softly, looking down at her cats.

She finally came into the small family room with a massive plate of delicious baked chocolate chip cookies and sat on the couch facing Mac and Hudson. The cookies looked amazing. They both picked one up; Mac took a bite and almost melted. She had never had a chocolate chip cookie this good before. "Granny, these are amazing! Thank you."

Granny smiled back at her. "Now, what can I do for you two fine folks today?"

"We're trying to locate Ali Ahmad," Mac told her again.

"Oh yes, she's a sweet girl, lives next door...but she's not home right now."

"Would you happen to know where she is?"

"Well, let me see here. What time is it?"

"Almost sixteen hundred hours—I mean, four p.m.," Mac corrected herself. After being in the military for so long, she caught herself referring to military time even when around civilians.

"Oh, I see, I see… So, um, what day is it today?" Granny asked.

Mac smiled. "Granny, it's Saturday. Do you happen to know where Ali would normally be on a Saturday night?"

"Oh yes, yes. Awful business, I tell you. Such a smart girl. She's going to be a doctor, don't you know?"

"Yes, ma'am, we did know that. What we need to know is where we can find her. What do you mean by 'terrible business?'" Mac asked.

Hudson sat next to her, quietly letting her handle the interview. Mac appreciated him letting her take the lead.

Granny sat there for a while with her face all scrunched up in concentration. She was such a sweet little old lady; Mac hated the thought of causing her any distress. Granny finally looked up at them with a sad look in her eyes. "She's working at that awful place down-town to pay her way through college. I really hate knowing she's out there doing that. She's such a sweet girl, and I have become quite fond of her. Would you go check on her for me?"

"Of course, we will," Mac replied. "Where's she working?"

"Oh, for heaven's sake, my memory is just not what it used to be. Um, let me think here." Granny paused for what seemed like a long time. "Oh my, is Ali in some kind of trouble?" she finally asked.

"No Granny, Ali is fine. We just need to ask her some questions about her sister," Mac said.

"Oh yes, yes, that poor girl. She was always coming to visit Ali. Sometimes I would mistake Zonira for Ali. They looked so much alike. How is Zonira doing?"

Mac was caught off guard for a moment, unsure how to break it to the sweet old woman that Zonira was dead. Mac took a deep breath, but Hudson spoke up first.

"Ma'am," he said, lowering his voice to a softer baritone, "I'm afraid Zonira passed away. We're here to make sure Ali is doing okay."

"Oh." The woman lowered her eyes to stare at the old beige carpet. "Does Ali know?"

Hudson nodded. "She should have been officially notified earlier this week."

"Oh, poor girl, she must be devastated. I was off visiting my grand-babies and just returned home this morning. I had no idea. That poor girl, she should have called me. I would have come home to be with her." A small tear escaped from her eye and rolled down her wrinkled cheek.

"She probably didn't want to worry you," Hudson said.

"I see, I see," Granny finally said, straightening slightly. "You should be able to find Ali at the State Line place later tonight. I have no idea where she is right now, but the poor girl is probably off somewhere grieving for her sister. No one should have to go through that. She's a dancer, don't ya know. That's how she pays her way through school. Ballet, I think, but I'm not really sure. I just know she makes enough money to pay her rent and bills, and..." She trailed off. "Did I tell you that my little Ali is going to be a doctor?"

"Yes, ma'am. Thank you for your hospitality. You've been very helpful," Mac replied.

They stood to leave and saw Granny had drifted off to sleep; she was snoring softly on the couch. They quietly put their mugs in the kitchen sink. Mac really liked Granny and hated to leave without saying goodbye, but she didn't want to wake her either. It surprised her how quickly elderly people could doze off. Mac pulled out one of her business cards and wrote *Thank You* on the back and laid it in her hands. They pulled the door shut behind them, careful not to make any noise.

CHAPTER
SIXTEEN

THEY CLIMBED BACK into Hudson's truck. "What's the State Line?" Hudson asked.

"It's a strip club in Post Falls, Idaho." Mac was pleased that he hadn't known what it was.

"Do you think she'll be working tonight, especially since she just lost her sister?"

Mac thought about it for a few moments. "I have no idea, but currently it's our only lead on finding her. It's worth a try. Why don't we grab some food and walk around for a bit? The State Line opens at three p.m., but the girls don't usually start going on stage until later. You can actually get a buy-one-get-one-free lap dance between fifteen hundred and twenty-one hundred hours."

Hudson raised an eyebrow and grinned. "And how do you know so much about this place?"

"It's not what you think. That place is where many of my clients have gotten into trouble. I've had several assault and drug cases, and a few drunk and disorderly conduct charges. I've been there several times to verify case details and evidence for my clients." She left out the part where the manager mistook her for a woman wanting to audition as a dancer and tried to offer her a job. When she declined, he'd tried to persuade her with more money and a top position, all without even finding out whether she could dance.

"Where do you want to go eat?" Hudson asked. "I know it's early for dinner, but I'm starving."

"I know a place called Honey off Sherman Avenue. Are you familiar with the area?"

Hudson shook his head. "Afraid not. I haven't been out to eat in a long while and certainly not in CDA."

"No worries," Mac said. "I'll show you the way. It's one of my favorite restaurants, and we've already talked about how much I like to eat. I prefer to eat earlier. It helps my digestion."

They found their way to the restaurant and parked a few streets away. It was chilly out but not too cold to walk. Mac shivered involuntarily.

Hudson looked down at her. "Would you like my jacket?"

"No, I'm fine, thanks. I'm always cold. I think I may have been born without a heater."

As they got closer to the restaurant, the amount of foot traffic picked up around them. People were walking from store to store. Couples going out on dates. Parents with their children running around their legs asking for ice cream before dinner.

Hudson smiled warmly. He had always wanted a family of his own. It just wasn't in the cards for him.

Mac noticed his smile. "What are you thinking?"

"Oh nothing, just daydreaming."

They walked into Honey and were greeted by a pleasant dark-haired woman who quickly sat them in a back booth. Hudson looked around at the interesting décor with honeybees on the walls and a strange-looking, huge stuffed bee head attached to the wall. The place had character, no one could deny that. Mac ordered something called "Devils on Horseback" as an appetizer.

"What on earth is that?" Hudson asked.

"You'll like it, promise," Mac assured him. They both ordered the apple cider pork chops.

The food arrived, and the portions were huge. Hudson thought it was a good thing he'd brought his appetite because there was no way Mac was finishing all her food. To his astonishment, she downed half the appetizer followed by her entire dish. He enjoyed watching her eat. She took each bite slowly, making sure she got plenty of flavor on her fork, and chewed slowly, sometimes closing her eyes to enjoy the savory flavor of the meal. She breathed deeply with a satisfied grin once they had finished.

"So, would you like to walk this meal off and get some ice cream?" she asked.

He wasn't sure where he was going to even fit the ice cream. "I'm always up for a little something sweet after a great meal." Even though he was full, which was no small feat, there was always room for a little ice cream. He ate an average of 5,000 calories a day to maintain his weight, and when he was training, he would eat even more. It was a bit of a nuisance, having to constantly plan his meals and never feeling satisfied. On the other hand, he figured his approach was better than watching what he ate or dealing with weight problems.

They went to a small shop on the corner that served ice cream out of a little window. They had all kinds of strange names for their ice cream, but it was delicious and creamy. They walked for a bit longer, eating and window shopping. They enjoyed each other's company as the evening wore on.

CHAPTER
SEVENTEEN

THE NIGHT WAS cold as they climbed back into Hudson's truck. He noticed Mac was shivering and cranked up the heat. It didn't take long to make it back to I-90 and head over to the State Line. They pulled into the parking lot.

Hudson was surprised to see a plain-looking one-story building that was tan and drab-looking. There weren't any neon signs, just a big black-and-white sign plastered to the side of the long building that said *Showgirls* on it. From the outside, the place looked more like an old warehouse, not a club. They walked in to find a fully stocked, lit-up bar. In the middle of the room was a large stage with a pole lit by blue and orange lighting.

They took a seat in one of the booths. Hudson ordered a Fat Tire beer, and Mac ordered a diet root beer. Hudson raised an eyebrow. "What, you don't drink?"

"Not often," Mac replied. "I have my reasons. Plus, if you have a few beers, I can drive you home if you need me to. I don't mind being the designated driver."

"No need, I'm only having one, and we aren't here to party."

They asked one of the waitresses if Ali Ahmad was working tonight. She was standing in front of them in a tight pair of short shorts, high heels, and a little red tank top. Her blond hair was curled nicely and draped around her shoulders. She had a pretty face and kind eyes. Mac wondered how people ended up working there. She wasn't a prude, but she couldn't imagine all these strange men gawking at her.

The waitress smacked her gum, bringing Mac back to reality. "Yeah, Al is up next. If you want, I'll let her know you want her after she's done."

"Thank you," Mac replied, but was a little uncomfortable with the waitress's choice of words. Mac smiled at Hudson nervously. He seemed completely relaxed, just looking around the room at the people coming and going. There were certainly quite a few older men, some younger ones too. They came in all shapes and sizes. There were even some women there that appeared to be with their husbands. Mac wondered what they got out of it and figured she knew the answer: these girls did all the work to get their men turned on, then they got all the attention afterward. Of course, it could be another reason; they could simply like girls too. Either way, she found it fascinating to study people, and thoroughly enjoyed people-watching. They were tucked in the corner away from the stage where they could observe the others without being seen.

Except a man had watched them come in together. *What are they doing here?* he wondered. He was sitting in the opposite corner out of view. He didn't think anyone could see him in the back, but he felt nervous anyway. He was here to see Ali. He knew Ali was Sahar in disguise.

Did they know about him? He felt paranoia grip his mind. He became fidgety, and the muscles tightened along his neck and shoulders. How could they possibly know? Why were Mac and Hudson together? Were they tracking him? No, no, they couldn't know. Maybe they were just here on a date? That seemed weird to him and didn't feel right. He had been waiting all night to see Ali, and he wasn't ready to walk away. He slid farther back into the booth to avoid being seen. He took several deep breaths to calm his nerves, and there she was.

The lights went out in the club. One huge light over the stage turned on, bathing the stage in a soft glow. Ali stood there with her back to everyone. She was breathtaking. She wore strappy black platform heels that made the muscles on her strong legs pop. She was tall and lean and wore a little black dress that hugged her curves. Her long, curled dark hair hung down her back, meeting her small waist. Everyone in the club went silent, staring at her. Music filled the room. Mac didn't recognize the song, but it started out slow and sensual.

Ali slowly turned to face the crowd. She was absolutely stunning with an exotic look. Hudson and Mac sat there mesmerized.

At the other end of the club, he stared too, unable to take his eyes off her. She *had* to be the one. She was the one he'd been looking for. He sat back in his seat, pleased with himself. He would be with her soon.

The waitress returned to Hudson and Mac's table with their drinks and informed them that Ali would be over as soon as she was done with her dance.

"Thank you," Mac said.

Hudson leaned toward Mac while they watched Ali dance and said, "If I were obsessed with exotic beauties, she would be at the top of my list."

Mac agreed. "Yeah, she possesses the same victimology as the other girls, but she's definitely the most stunning of the group." Mac felt slightly uncomfortable as Ali began to strip out of her dress. She almost felt like she was invading her privacy somehow, even though she was stripping in a public place. She couldn't help but wonder how Ali had ended up here. From what she knew of her, she was a highly intelligent woman. Clearly, it had to do with going to school for her doctorate. Maybe this was just a means to a better life for her. It wasn't like she was selling her body for money. *She's just showing off...impressively,* Mac thought.

After Ali finished her dance, she came over to their table. He watched from the other side of the club. What were they doing talking to Ali? They had no right to be near her. She belonged to him and only him! He took deep breaths, trying to control his anger. His therapist had told him to try counting, so he sat and counted. He knew he had to be patient with her, just like her sister on base.

Once upon a time, he'd thought Zonira was the right one...but she hadn't been. He watched them. As his heart rate started to return to normal, it became clear to him that he would have to eliminate Mac. He had known Mac for years and knew she would never give up. She was the only one involved that worried him. He thought her smart, capable, and dangerous. Hudson could be controlled, but Mac was a wild card. He couldn't have her ruining his plans. It was unacceptable.

CHAPTER
EIGHTEEN

ALI LEANED FORWARD toward Hudson and asked if he would like a lap dance. "Umm, n-no," Hudson stuttered.

"We just want to ask you a few questions if you have a moment. It's about your sister," Mac said helpfully. She saw the pain in Ali's eyes. She hated to do this to her, but they had to know more about what was going on.

"There's a room in the back that's quieter," Ali said. She turned on her heels and headed to the back of the club. Mac and Hudson followed.

It was a small room, not much bigger than a walk-in closet. A vinyl bench lined two sides of the room, and there was a center area for the ladies to dance. Mac and Hudson sat on one bench while Ali sat on the other. Mac tried not to think about what had been done on that bench. "I'm helping defend Zonira's husband," Mac said. Ali looked at the floor for a long time. "What can you tell us about your sister?"

Ali took a deep breath. "My sister and I came to this country when we were very young. Our parents worked hard to secure our citizenship and make a life for us. We grew up in New Mexico. Our father worked multiple odd jobs in Las Cruces. It wasn't a glamorous life, but it put food on the table. Our mother waited tables and helped wherever she could. They were really good people." A tear slipped from the corner of her eye.

"Our dad got involved with some bad people. He was just trying to provide a better life for us, but with only a work visa, he couldn't get anything above minimum wage. He came home at night so tired he could barely stand. Then, one day, he was approached by a man who offered him a lot of money to deliver packages. My father later found out that he had unwittingly become part of the drug business and transported uncut cocaine. He became paranoid about our safety. He had always been overprotective, but this took it to a whole different level. Shortly after that, our mother was diagnosed with cancer. My father couldn't walk away from his situation because he needed the money to cover our mother's medical bills. We didn't have any insurance, and it was very expensive to get treatment. No matter how many specialists we went to, they just couldn't save our mother. She died a year and a half later. Six months after that, our father was killed during a drug raid."

Hudson and Mac nodded in silent encouragement for her to continue.

"Zonira was seventeen at that point, and I was fifteen. She worked to keep us going. She always made sure I was doing well in school. She finished high school and worked odd jobs but couldn't pay the rent. She finally found a good-paying job stripping in one of the Las Cruces clubs. That's where she had met her husband. He was fascinated with her at first, but the more he came around…well, eventually they fell in love. She was so excited when he asked her to marry him. She felt it was a new start for us. By then, I was about to graduate high school, and she wanted me to have a better life.

"Terrell Johnson is a good man. He had no problem with me tagging along in their new life, but obviously, it wasn't meant to last forever. I wasn't allowed on base because I'm not a US citizen, so in New Mexico we stayed off base. Shortly after they got married, he got orders to come here. They were offered a house on base that would save them a ton of money. I told her I would be fine. I was a grown woman myself by then and needed to figure things out on my own, and well, here we are...or here I am." Ali looked down and took a deep breath, trying to keep her composure.

Mac touched Ali's hand. "I know this is hard for you. What can you tell us about Zonira's life with Terrell once they were married? How was their relationship?"

Ali averted her eyes, and then finally spoke in a quiet voice. "You have to understand, Zonira was a wonderful woman with a heart of gold, but she hated being alone. Shortly after we got here, Terrell got orders to deploy. It was strange. He wasn't supposed to go anywhere because he was still in training, but somehow, he ended up on the next rotation. Anyway, Zonira did well at first. She came to visit me every week. She seemed to be keeping herself busy. She was trying to find a job, and she enrolled in school. I was so proud of her.

"I was a little worried because she kept talking about a man that kept coming around to check on her. She said it was just how the military worked. When your husband is away, I guess they assign someone to check in on the spouse, but how she described this guy gave me the creeps. He had been pressuring her, saying something about it being good for her husband's career. She said it was nothing to worry about... I guess I should have worried more."

Mac leaned in closer to Ali. "Do you know who this man was?"

"Unfortunately, no," Ali said. "Zonira described him as older with dark hair. She said he was higher up on the food chain. That struck me as odd because Terrell is just a low-ranking guy. Why would a high-ranking person be checking in on Zonira? She also mentioned that she got the creepy feeling that she was being watched. You know...that weird sensation where you can almost feel someone's eyes tracking your every move, but then you look around, and nobody's there? She didn't tell me outright, but I think she might have slept with this older man. Zonira wasn't easy, but she could have been pressured into it, especially if this man was threatening her husband's career. She wouldn't tell me the last time I pushed her on it, and I got the feeling there was more to the story than what she was telling me."

"Thank you for your time, Ali," Mac said. "You've been extremely helpful. We're very sorry for your loss, and we're very concerned about your safety. We have reason to believe that the man who murdered your sister may still be on the loose."

Ali smiled. "That's sweet of you to worry, but I can take care of myself. I pack mace and a Taser everywhere I go. Most of the time I conceal carry, but certainly not in this outfit." She grinned.

Hudson was impressed. He hadn't expected her to pack heat regularly, though he shouldn't have been too surprised considering where she'd come from and how paranoid her parents must have been about the girl's safety. It wasn't too odd to be carrying since both he and Mac had guns on them. He had just assumed that military types were the ones who always carried, not regular civilians.

"If you think of anything else, please call me, and stay safe." Mac handed her a business card.

"Thank you," Ali said and got up off her bench. She was very tall in her platform shoes. Mac wondered if it was hard to balance on those things, but Ali made it look easy.

"Ali." Mac stopped her as she was about to leave. "Is there any way you could leave town for a bit, just in case?" Mac was asking as a last resort. Ali was an easy target working nights, and in a place where anyone could blend in.

"No, I won't run. Not from a coward like that. If he did kill my sister, then he took the last of my family. I hope he comes for me so I can get the satisfaction of putting a bullet between his beady little eyes. I've survived worse and won't let a scumbag like him scare me off," Ali said, tilting her chin up in defiance.

Mac had to respect her strength and determination, but it did nothing to quiet the knot growing deep in the pit of her stomach. Ali glided toward the door and was gone.

Mac and Hudson sat, processing the information. "So, who do you think the older guy could be that was hanging around Zonira?" Hudson asked.

"Not sure, but it's our first solid lead, and it tells us it was likely a military guy," Mac replied. She started thinking about how many men surrounding this case could meet that description. She had just described a large number of men on the base: tall, Caucasian, and with dark hair. Hell, she was sitting next to one of those right now—not that

Hudson's hair was black, but it *was* brown. "High-ranking" narrowed the list a little, but the definition of high-ranking was relative. Zonira's husband was a senior airman—an E-4—so she felt that a technical sergeant or E-6 could be considered high-ranking in relation to her husband. It really wasn't much to go on.

CHAPTER
NINETEEN

MAC ARRIVED at work the following Monday morning. She was tired and having a hard time staying focused. She had spent the remainder of the weekend going over the case file with Hudson. They had made plans to head back to CDA after work to talk with the investigators about the missing dental technician and the murdered nurse cases. Joe had already set up the meeting for them.

She'd enjoyed Hudson's company much more than she wanted to admit. It reminded her of how lonely she was at times. She shook off those thoughts and tried to focus on the case. All evidence still pointed to Senior Airman Johnson being his wife's killer. There was no forced entry to the home, which meant the killer had had access. The only DNA and fingerprints found at the scene were Terrell Johnson's. He might have had a motive to kill her if he'd found out that she was sleeping with the older man. The murder was brutal and vicious, which logically pointed toward a crime of passion. Johnson might have a good temporary insanity defense. She would have to run it by Stanton.

She walked in to find Stanton deep in thought. He looked up, and she saw the worry in his eyes. It looked like he hadn't slept much. She sat down in front of his desk and waited for him to tell her what was going on. He sighed deeply, trying to figure out what to say. She saw him looking at her with deep concern, and that worried her.

"Okay, boss, you're scaring me. What's going on?" she asked, thinking the worst but never suspecting what was coming. "Did something happen to Ali?"

"Who's Ali?" Stanton asked. "And no, it has nothing to do with the case."

"Ali is our victim's sister," she said.

"Oh," Stanton replied. "I don't know how else to say this except to just give it to you straight: You've been implicated in a drug-trafficking ring on base."

That was not what Mac thought she would hear. Not in a million years would she go near drugs, especially with her family history. Mac didn't know what to say. She sat there with her mouth open, and then she began to feel anger boiling up in her. *How dare they!* "Did they say who reported me and if they have any evidence?"

"Not that I know of. Unfortunately, I'm not able to work on your case due to a conflict of interest. I've arranged for you to see Captain Bennett Kibble. We went to law school together. He's the best of the best and will get to the bottom of this as quickly as possible. In the meantime, I can't have you working on any cases."

Mac didn't know what to say. She was completely dumbfounded and angry. She clenched her hands into tight fists. "Boss, you have to believe me. I had nothing to do with 'drugs' or a 'drug ring.' However, I get the feeling someone is trying to get rid of me. I've been looking into the Johnson case further, and I think someone feels I'm getting too close to the truth."

"Take a deep breath. Don't worry, we'll get this figured out. Tell me what you know," Stanton said.

She took several deep breaths. It took a little time, but eventually, her breathing regulated, and she started to calm down. She had an unblemished career with multiple awards and had never been accused of anything like this before. She felt violated and betrayed by her Air Force. After being part of this community for most of her adult life and honorably serving her country, she was disappointed, to say the least.

Another deep breath and she began to detail the facts of the case, including the other victims downtown that bore a striking resemblance to their victim, and her suspicions. Then she told him about Ali and what she knew of her. She admitted most of the evidence on base still pointed to Johnson, but there were a lot of different coincidences that didn't line up. Mac didn't believe in coincidences. She wanted to know who the higher-ranking mystery man was that was hanging around their victim.

"Good work, Mac. Great fact pattern. What's your theory on the case so far?" Stanton asked.

She sat back in her chair, fiddling with the tip of her hair. "My gut still tells me that Johnson is innocent, but currently I have no direct evidence to support that theory. I believe a killer is targeting young women that bear a strong resemblance to our victim. I don't think Zonira is the first, and I don't think she'll be the last. My gut tells me that Ali may be next on the list of victims. I think if we dig deeper, we might find that there are other, earlier victims out there that we don't know about."

Stanton thought about what she said. Deep lines of concern creased the sides of his eyes. "I agree that there might be something to your theory of a serial killer...but how did he gain access to base?"

"Well, they could already have had access to the base, or the killer could be a military member. Ali told me about a guy that kept checking in on Zonira. She got the feeling that Zonira had done more with him than just socialize, and that he may have threatened her husband's career to get her to cooperate. She described him as an older, higher-ranking man. I want to find out who this man is. It might shed some light on what was going on with Zonira. It may also give Johnson a motive and help the prosecution with their case against him. Ultimately, if Johnson did kill her because he found out she was cheating, we could go for a temporary insanity plea."

Stanton thought Mac had one of the most intriguing investigative minds he had ever seen. He had learned during their time working together not to ignore her gut. He had always encouraged her to go to law school, but she had chosen psychology instead and was currently studying for her master's degree in criminal psychology. She had a knack for figuring out how people thought and what made them tick.

She almost always knew when one of their clients was lying and was able to gently pull the truth out of them without offending the client. It was a true gift and would have made for one hell of a lawyer.

"Mac, you understand as well as I do where this puts us. If we can get the charges against you dropped then you're back on the case, but until then...there's little we can do."

"Does this mean I have to be relocated out of the office until further notice?" Mac asked.

"That's what is recommended per normal protocol. AFLOA is suggesting you be assigned to the chaplain's office until further notice," Stanton replied. "If it helps, everyone is rooting for you, and most don't believe the charges against you. I hope you know that I'll stand by you through this until we figure it out." Stanton ran his hand through his hair as he often did when he was troubled.

"Thank you," Mac replied. "I truly appreciate your support. I know I'm being set up; I just have to prove it." She squared her shoulders with a determined look in her eyes. "Now, start from the beginning and tell me everything you know and who it is that's representing me so I can get things moving."

Stanton smiled. "I figured you wouldn't take this one lying down. But as I said earlier, I'm being stonewalled. I have no information, but I'm sure Kibble will get the evidence soon enough. I warned him that you would want to be fully involved, and he said he welcomed your thoughts and would share all the evidence he gets his hands on."

"Thank you very much for taking care of me."

"I am so sorry you're dealing with this."

"What do you have to be sorry about, boss? It's not like you set me up or something."

"No, that's true, but if you weren't investigating the case and looking into things, then you wouldn't be in this situation."

"No worries," Mac replied. "We'll work this out."

Mac went back to her desk to call Kibble and start the discovery process. When she dialed his number, the phone rang several times. She realized her heart was beating quickly. She focused on calming herself. It would do her no good to get all riled up. That could cloud her judgment and her ability to analyze. The call finally went to voicemail, and she heard the low, booming voice of Kibble asking her to leave her name and number, and he would get back to her as soon as possible. Somehow, she took comfort in that deep tone, but she wasn't sure why. She left her information and went to log in to her system.

She could get into the main platform, but her access to her database —where they kept all the case files—was blocked. She walked back into Stanton's office. "Boss, I can't access the case files or look anything up. Do you know if my profile has been blocked?"

"Afraid so," Stanton replied.

"Shit, that's going to slow me down," Mac huffed. "So, how soon do you need me to clear out?"

Stanton looked down for a minute. "Sorry, Mac. They're sending over a paralegal to take your spot in about an hour. You're due to report to the chaplain's office at eleven hundred hours. You're welcome to take your computer with you so you can stay up on emails and keep in contact with Kibble if that'll help."

Mac undocked her computer and put it in her bag. She was lucky to have a mobile workstation that allowed her to work from anywhere. There were pros, but there were also cons because she found she worked more this way.

After the shock and anger of the situation began to subside, a determined calm washed over her. Getting angry would only cloud her judgment. She was certainly known to have a bit of a temper but now was not the time. She steadied herself and started packing everything up. She was about to put the case file concerning the Johnson evidence in her box when Stanton walked in.

"I'm sorry, Mac, I can't let you take that with you," Stanton said apologetically.

"Oh, of course," Mac replied, and handed him the file. She loaded everything into her bag and a box and headed for the door. She left most of her things behind, thinking optimistically that she would be back at her desk before long. Probably. She was also a realist and knew that sometimes, once the prosecution and the investigators had sunk their teeth in, it didn't really matter if you were guilty or innocent. It only mattered what they could prove.

Stanton opened the door for her. "Mac, please let me know if there's anything I can do to help. Kibble will take good care of you. He's a good man, and he knows this means a lot to me."

"Thank you, sir. That's all I can ask for at this point. I'll keep you posted as things progress. Take care of yourself and give Emma and the kids a hug for me. I hope to see them again soon," Mac said—and with that, she was gone.

CHAPTER
TWENTY

MAC CHECKED in with the chaplain's office. Chaplain Bastion was sitting in his office when she arrived. Mac knew him well. He was a nice man with kind eyes. His uniform was sharp and crisply pressed, but underneath was a kind soul who always had time to help people no matter how busy he was. Mac had referred many of their clients to the chaplain's office for counseling in the past. She had even seen him a few times for guidance and counseling.

It was one of the only places on base other than her office that had complete confidentiality unless there was a threat of harm to self or others. She wasn't the type to harm herself, and she certainly wasn't the violent type unless you were talking about her sparring partners—but that was different. Most of her opponents didn't get hurt, and both parties knew ahead of time that someone might experience a little pain. It was part of how you became a better fighter. Life had thrown much worse at her, so hurting herself had never crossed her mind. Plus, she'd lost someone that way once and would never put the people around her through that kind of pain. The only proper approach in her mind was to conquer her inner adversary.

Chaplain Bastion looked up and smiled. "Well now, if it isn't Mac! How have you been?" Bastion said in his low, soothing voice. He always had a calming effect on her that she couldn't quite explain. She sat down across from him. His desk was messy and littered with papers. He smiled at her warmly. "To what do I owe the pleasure of seeing you today?"

Mac was surprised. "Um, they didn't tell you?"

Bastion smiled, and the lines along his eyes became more pronounced. Mac realized that she had never seen him angry or even distraught. She always knew him as possessing the same calm demeanor he had right now. "Oh yes, well, they told me some things, but I want to hear them from you. Now, start from the beginning, and we'll get to the bottom of all of this."

Mac took in a deep breath and held it for a moment and then leaned back into the comfortable leather chair on the other side of his desk. He came around and sat opposite her. She slowly let the air out of her lungs and then began to tell him everything. Occasionally, he would ask questions or comment, but mostly he just listened. She even talked about Hudson. "I really like this man," she admitted.

"That's not an easy thing for you to admit," Bastion replied.

"I know, but this man makes me feel safe and, well...never mind."

The corners of Bastion's mouth curled into a smile. "You know that's not how this works. You tell me everything, and I help you work through it."

"I know, I know, but I've only known him for a little while, and it seems weird to me to feel this way about him. When I'm around him, I feel like I'm home. Crazy, right?" Mac exhaled, staring at her feet.

"That's not crazy; it's how you feel. Barring your emotions is never healthy," Bastion replied.

She told him all about their weekend together and what they had found out about the case. She felt surprisingly better about the situation when she was done, but she wasn't sure why. "I feel like I'm missing something big about this case. It seems to be hiding just out of reach, but I know I'm getting close. If I wasn't, then someone wouldn't have gone to all this trouble to frame me."

"That's interesting. How do you feel about the situation, and what are you going to do about it?" Bastion asked in a low voice.

"Well, I'm going to keep working the case and figure out what the hell is going on!" Mac said through clenched teeth.

"That's smart, but what if the person who you feel is framing you comes after you?"

"I'll just have to deal with that when it happens."

CHAPTER
TWENTY-ONE

WHEN AGENT VIVIAN ROSS came to work that morning, she felt terrible. Her boyfriend had threatened to leave her. They had been fighting all weekend about the Johnson case and Mac. She knew a little bit about Mac's past and felt certain she couldn't be guilty. Admittedly, she wasn't exactly sure why Mac was so against drugs, but she knew it was about her family. She sat in her car for a few minutes trying to clear her mind. She hadn't slept much and knew she didn't operate well without sleep. Some of her coworkers could sleep very little during a case and then catch up when they finished, but her cognitive abilities declined significantly when she didn't get enough sleep. Her boyfriend, who worked in Security Forces, thought she was letting her friendship with Mac cloud her judgment. He had a way of making her question herself. Even if she knew something was missing in the evidence, he was always able to sway her to see it his way.

However, this time she wasn't so easily swayed, and he had gotten so angry that he'd left mid-argument. She tried calling him, but he was ignoring her. He had a talent for silent treatment, and that was the one thing she couldn't stand. It made her feel helpless as if she had unfinished business. Now she just kept playing the argument over and over in her mind, obsessing about how she could have handled things differently so as not to make him so angry. She always felt so guilty when they fought, and he was so good at making her feel like the entire thing was solely her fault. He could really get under her skin.

The OSI office was tucked behind the base post office of all places. It was out of the way on purpose so suspects and witnesses could come and go without anyone knowing exactly why they were there. It could be because they were getting their mail or answering questions or being interrogated. That was the beauty of the location. The building was old like most of the buildings on Fairchild Air Force Base, but overall, the red brick exterior was in good condition. They had renovated her office space several years back, making it look fairly new and modern on the inside.

She walked past the front entrance and scanned her credentials to gain access. There were multiple offices inside the building. She walked into her tiny office in the corner and dropped her bag on her military-issue standard brown desk. It wasn't a bad desk. She had received it as a hand-me-down after her boss received a new one. It was way too big for her office, but she liked having the space to spread out her case files.

Her coworker popped his head inside her office, pulling her out of her thoughts. "Good morning," Agent Green said.

"Good morning," Viv replied distractedly.

Agent Green was a tall, gangly man with bony features and a thin, skeleton-like body. He had blond hair cut in typical military fashion—high and tight—and a very young face. She always teased him that he needed a sandwich, but she knew he ate a ton and still couldn't gain any weight.

She looked up at him, welcoming the distraction. "So, what do you think about these cases?"

"Who would have thought Mac would get tangled up in the drug trade? I mean, I know we have drug rings on base and all, but I never suspected Mac would be involved," Agent Green said.

Everyone knew Mac; she was like a bulldog when it came to investigating her cases. Especially when she thought one of her clients wasn't guilty or there was missing evidence. She would launch her own investigation and leave no stone unturned. She was the best defense investigator Viv had ever met—not that "defense investigator" was an official title—but there was no other way to describe Mac. She had made the OSI on base look bad a few times by finding evidence they had missed and giving it to her boss to present at the court-martial.

Viv felt bad for Johnson because he could really have used Mac in his corner. If Viv ever found herself accused of anything, she would want Mac on her defense team. All of this just didn't settle well with Viv. She knew you couldn't argue with the evidence. Facts were facts, and that was that, but there was a gray area in every case. No matter how Viv felt about Mac, the facts couldn't be changed, and she had to remain impartial to evaluate the case properly.

She returned her focus to Agent Green. "Let's bat this thing around a bit. What do we really know about these cases?"

Agent Green went and grabbed his case files. "Well, in the Johnson case, we know he was found covered in his wife's blood. We also know he was in shock, which was confirmed by the emergency response team. We know that his DNA was all over her and the house, but that's to be expected since he was her husband. We also know his finger-prints were on the knife, though he claims he picked it up and moved it aside when he found his wife. We don't have a clear motive, though I'm sure if we went digging, we could find one. Many people in the military have relationship issues, and monogamy in a relationship is hard to find. Did you know that over sixty-four percent of Air Force marriages end in divorce? Maybe she was cheating."

"Let's just stick to the facts of the case as we know them," Viv responded. "Okay, so is there anything else that we know to be fact in that case?" She was writing everything he said on a large whiteboard in their conference room.

"Nope, that's all we know to be factual at this time. However, we all know that, statistically, uxoricide—the killing of a spouse or signifi-cant other by the husband or male partner—is extremely common among murder victims. It's statistically more likely to be the husband than some random person."

"This is true, but the current facts can all be explained away by the defense. We have no motive, no evidence that Johnson had a history of being violent with his wife, or anyone else for that matter."

"Though he did receive a LOR for shoving a guy in a bar down-town," Green said.

"A letter of reprimand?" Viv said. "What for?"

"Allegedly a guy slapped his wife on the ass, which makes his actions there pretty understandable. Otherwise, he has no derogatory data, no unfavorable information file, nothing. Johnson has served his country honorably up until now. He was even recognized during his deployment for ingenuity and professionalism by his general. I'm not sure what the story is on that one, but not many people get recognized, and certainly not by a ranking general as a first-term airman on his first deployment."

Viv drew a line down the middle of the board and put Mac's name at the top on the other side. "Okay, so that's what we know about Johnson. What do we have on Mac?"

Green read through the report, then said, "Not much, I'm afraid. According to evidence, she was seen with some known drug dealers off base. There's a photo of her accepting a package from Jose Valdez, one of the lead drug dealers in Spokane. She also has base access and has met with several military members who are under investigation for drug use and, in some cases, drug distribution. So far, we have no evidence that she's in possession of drugs. The base legal office is looking at getting a search authorization for her home off base. She was recently subject to a 'random' search of her vehicle at the front gate that turned up nothing."

Viv tilted her head to the side and raised an eyebrow.

"Don't look at me," Green said. "I didn't put her under investiga-tion. They just assigned me to the case file."

Viv exhaled. "So, what you're telling me is, we have no concrete evidence against Mac other than that she's been seen with people that are either known or suspected of being in the drug trade. Her main profession is to defend people suspected of committing crimes, which could be why she was meeting with these people. She could have simply been collecting evidence for her case."

"I agree with you, but that's way over my head."

"I'm not aggravated with you, Green; I just don't understand how such circumstantial evidence can suddenly be accepted as fact. Something doesn't feel quite right here, and I don't know what it is." Viv hit the wall in frustration.

Their boss walked into the room. He was an intimidating man with broad shoulders and a wide face. They joked that he looked like a side of beef with a buzz cut. He was heavily into bodybuilding and took his fitness regime very seriously. Viv liked to work out, but her boss put her to shame. He ate clean and religiously. He always stayed on schedule no matter what was happening with their cases. Even if they were sitting in a meeting with their chain of command, he would somehow work in time to suck down a shake or eat some chicken to make his muscles remain large. She knew most women liked the way her boss looked, but Viv thought he was too big and a little unnatural looking. His uniform screamed under the strain of his biceps, and his shirt looked a few sizes too small.

Viv didn't care what people said about him. She felt he was nice to her most of the time and always ruled fairly on issues under his command.

He walked into the room and looked at the whiteboard with Viv's notes written out. He read through what she had and nodded his head in acknowledgment. "Okay folks, good work, now package it all up. A different unit is investigating the case," he said in a commanding voice that left little room for discussion. Green and Viv looked at each other, puzzled. "I need your reports, files, everything you know about the two cases on my desk by the close of business today."

"Yes, sir," both Green and Viv responded.

When their boss left, Viv asked, "What the hell is going on here?"

Green shrugged his thin shoulders. "Beats me, but we better get moving." He walked back to his office to start writing his report.

Viv was left staring at the lack of evidence in front of her. She shook her head in disgust as she wrote her own report. Later, when she dropped it off in her boss's office, he pinned her with a determined stare. "Agent Ross, when I say you're off both cases, it means you are not to look into them, contact anyone involved with them, or so much as accidentally run into anyone involved on base. Do I make myself clear, Agent Ross?"

"Yes, sir, crystal clear," she responded. "But sir, can I ask why?"

"That's on a need-to-know basis, and right now, you don't need that information," he said sternly but without malice. "I know you have a vested interest in Mac's case, and you guys are friends, but this one has to be off-limits, at least for now."

"Understood, sir." Viv did an about-face and left his office.

CHAPTER
TWENTY-TWO

MAC LEFT Chaplain Bastion's office with a promise to come back and help him with whatever he needed tomorrow. She was technically assigned to him for the time being and wanted to make sure she wasn't taking advantage of his kindness. But for now, she was headed to the gym to clear her head and blow off some steam.

She walked in to find one of her favorite sparring partners stretching on the mat. "Hey Greg, how's it going?"

He looked up at her and shook his head. "I can't believe you, Mac. I expected better from you."

"Greg, you can't honestly think I'm guilty of whatever they're accusing me of now. Someone is setting me up."

Greg had a sad-puppy-dog look about him. He was an average-looking man, but his eyes always made him come across as morose. He appeared older and wiser than his years, and she had always liked hanging out with him. Not that she had spent a lot of time with him—they mainly just sparred—but when they did spend time together, she enjoyed his company. "According to you, maybe, but from what I hear, they have some ironclad evidence against you," Greg said.

"'Ironclad' my ass! How could they possibly have solid evidence when I'm not guilty of anything?" Mac said, her voice rising. People in the gym were staring at her.

She turned around to grab her bag, only to find Hudson staring at her. She knew what he thought just by the disappointed look in his eyes. He didn't say a word. He just walked past her with his head down and didn't look back.

People always disappointed her. That was probably why it had been so long since she'd been involved with anyone. Every time she let her heart become vulnerable, it ended badly, or at the very least that person would disappoint her. Clearly, she was on her own again.

She told herself it was a good thing there was no one to get in her way now. The evidence would lead to the truth; all she had to do was follow where it took her. Maybe she could call her sister for help.

Her eyes scanned the gym. People who had been staring at her now looked away. She decided she wasn't going to let them push her out of her own gym. If they thought she was guilty, then so be it, but that didn't mean she was going to hide in a corner somewhere.

She analyzed all the details of the case as she ran and then lifted some weights. The longer she worked out, the better she felt. Eventually, she went over to the punching bag and put on her gloves. The muscles in her back tensed as she prepared for the first punch. Once she got started, she felt she couldn't stop. It felt so good to let out all her anger and frustration. She felt betrayed and let down. It hadn't been the first time and certainly wouldn't be the last, she suspected. But the more she hit the bag, the more determined she felt. Her gut told her that if she figured out Johnson's case, it would also lead to her name being cleared.

Where to start was the question. Who could frame her with that much evidence—or at least get OSI to investigate with merely circumstantial evidence? It would have to be someone who was higher ranking and had access to restricted files. As she hit the bag and sweat streamed down her skin, she thought through the possible suspect list. He or she would have to be trustworthy and have access to sensitive material. The suspect was likely male. While studying the criminal mind, she had read that a female serial killer was uncommon but not impossible. She tucked that fact away for the moment.

The evidence surrounding the man who was hanging out with Zonira was interesting. What did she really know about him? Not much, unfortunately, except that he was an older man who was higher ranking. Unfortunately, "older" was a relative term. The victim and her sister were in their twenties. She remembered thinking when she was that age that forty seemed old. Ali had said they'd found it odd that the person checking in on Zonira wasn't close to being the same rank as her husband. Ali had described this man as having dark hair. That was a little helpful but not much. There were a lot of men on base who had dark hair. Many military men looked older than their years because of the pressure-cooker environment that many of them operated in, so he may have been younger than he looked.

She started running through all the different men who fit the profile, but there were just too many. She would have to figure out a way to narrow it down. There was also the possibility that the killer was a civilian and had somehow gained access to the base, or that the murders were unrelated, and Johnson actually did kill his wife.

Her head was spinning with all the information. She hit the punching bag a couple more times, lost in thought, not realizing that people were still staring at her. Some of them just stole glances at her while others blatantly stared. Hudson was still there and looked up when she stopped punching the bag.

Mac walked over to Hudson and pinned him with a steely glare. "I know you think I did something wrong, but I didn't," she said.

"It doesn't matter," Hudson replied. "I can no longer be around you until your name is cleared."

"It matters to me what you think," she said in a low voice.

"I'm not sure what to think. All I know is that I've been told they have solid evidence against you and that you've been removed from the case."

"Is that enough for you to turn your back on me?" she asked, lowering her eyes to the ground.

"You don't understand, Mac. I can't be around you right now no matter what I think or feel." Hudson exhaled deeply, then looked into her eyes. "Look, Mac, I like you, but this puts me in a tight spot. If I help you in any way, it could mean my career."

Mac raised her voice. "Yeah, you think this puts you in a bind. How the hell do you think *I* feel about it? The whole world is turning against me. My career is in the toilet. People who have known me for a long time have the audacity to question my innocence. Even if the charges are somehow dropped, you know people will always wonder if I simply got lucky or got away with it somehow."

"Calm down. They have some pretty solid evidence that you've been running drugs from downtown. I can't discuss this with you, but it's pretty big. Look, I've gotta go. Watch your back… If you're being set up, they're doing a great job." Hudson looked at her one last time and then walked away.

CHAPTER
TWENTY-THREE

HUDSON TRIED to shake off the feeling that he was walking away from his future. His legs felt heavy, and he was torn between what he knew and what he felt. This felt wrong to him, but he had seen the evidence. There was no way to fabricate that kind of evidence, or at least not that he knew of. He knew better. He had seen people thrown under the bus for much less. Someone could have fabricated the evidence, but he had no way of finding out. His career meant a lot to him, but he hated to admit that Mac was worth the risk.

Who was he kidding? He wasn't going to throw away his career over a woman he had only known for a short while. Plus, if she was involved with drugs, that was a deal-breaker for him. When he turned twenty-one, his younger brother, who had been only eighteen, had gotten mixed up in drugs. Hudson had done everything he could to get Michael off the stuff. He had even paid to have him go to one of those special rehab clinics, but as soon as his brother got out, thugs got ahold of his little brother. He remembered being deployed when his mom called and got through to his commander. His commander and first sergeant had driven out into the field to pick him up.

He had been devastated. They sent him home early to attend Michael's funeral. He never shook the feeling that it was his fault. The look of pure pain and sorrow in his mother's eyes nearly brought him to his knees. He knew if he hadn't left for the military and just stayed home to help his mother look after his younger brother, then he would still be alive. He would never forgive himself for that.

CHAPTER
TWENTY-FOUR

THE MAN PACED around his living room. He was very happy about the way the day had gone. Mac was out of the way. With Agent Ross off the case as well, he could finally relax. He sat down on his old brown leather couch for a few minutes, but he was too revved up. He needed to see her soon. He had to possess her and make her his, but it wasn't time yet. He took a deep breath to steady his emotions. He closed his eyes, focusing on the dark space there.

He tried to rest, but all he could see was her beautiful face and the way her lips had felt when she kissed him. Then his mind flashed to the afternoon when she had given him a gift full of explosives and he lost two men. They had been good men. He didn't see them when they died because the bomb knocked him unconscious, but he hoped they hadn't suffered. Losing them felt like he had lost his own children.

He felt anger boiling inside him. He wasn't able to stay calm the way he used to. Now the simplest things would set him off, and he had to focus on maintaining control over his emotions. He still couldn't believe that she had given him the bomb of her own free will. She was special and wouldn't have done that to him. He missed her and wished he could hold her again. There was such a turmoil of mixed emotions running around in his head. Sometimes he wanted to hunt her down and make her pay, but he knew it wasn't her fault.

Deep down, he felt that if he could control her, he could stop her from hurting others. He knew he was obsessed with her and wanted to do everything he could to keep her from blowing anyone else up. He ran his hand through his hair again, trying to control his anger. He got back up and began to pace.

The house was old and creaked under his feet when he walked. He liked the solitude it provided. He went to the back room, where the old washer and dryer sat in the corner. Cobwebs hung above his head and in the corners. He lifted the loose board that was hidden on the other side of the room. Inside was a small metal box that held his many treasures. He slowly removed the box, carefully walked back into the living room, and sat down in the old leather couch. The key to the box was deep in the pocket of his blue jeans. He dug for it and slowly inserted it into the box.

He stopped and stood up. He thought he had heard something—or maybe not. Still, he walked outside and checked the perimeter of the house, carrying his box with him to safeguard it. There it was again. A sound, very faint in the distance. *Are they coming for me?* he wondered. He slowly walked the property, making sure to stay invisible, keeping his metal package close. Making sure to stay silent, he could feel a rising panic and hypervigilance taking charge, making him respond to the smallest of sounds. He walked the perimeter of his home three times. Always three times, once counterclockwise and twice clockwise. He stopped to check his traps at quarter intervals. Everything was in place.

He took a deep breath and listened to the forest. It was quiet until a small rabbit jumped from behind the house. The man jumped at the sound and pulled his loaded Glock that he had tucked in the back of his pants and shot at the rabbit. His hands were sweating and his eyes wild until he realized what had invaded his property. He started laughing hysterically. It didn't sound like him, even to his own ears; he sounded demented and manic, like an insane person's laugh. He had to pull himself together. He had a job to do and people to protect. If she was left unchecked, who knew what kind of damage she would inflict on other innocent people?

She's in Afghanistan, a voice in his head told him. No, she was here.

He had seen her, and she had to be stopped. He was the only one who could stop her. It was his duty to serve and protect. He thought he had her last time, but then she reappeared at that nasty strip club. That woman would go to any lengths to deceive those she was ordered to hurt. He personally knew the burden of orders. She was just following orders; it wasn't something she wished to do. It wasn't her fault that she was a pawn in the enemies' game, but she still had to be stopped. This was war, after all, and there were casualties in war. He just hated that it had to be her. He missed her soft touch every single day, but he still couldn't forgive her for blowing up his team. At least he had survived, but some of the others hadn't, and for that she would have to pay, no matter who had forced her into it.

He looked at his surroundings one last time, quietly listening for enemy soldiers approaching. Satisfied that he was alone for now, he walked back into the house, listening to the familiar creak as he walked across the front porch and opened the door that was held in place by a few old, rusty hinges. He locked the front door with all three deadbolts, a chain lock, and a door lock. He went to each window in the one-story house and checked to ensure they were secure. The locks were in place. He checked his motion detectors to make sure they were active then unlocked his phone to check the perimeter cameras and make sure they were all operational.

Finally satisfied, he sat back down on the old leather couch and set the box in front of him. The key was still there where he had left it. He felt relieved that no one had stolen it, and that he hadn't lost it while checking the perimeter. He knew he was paranoid, that people wouldn't come to steal his key, but he couldn't calm the nagging feeling. He always checked three times. If he had checked her package, that explosion would have never happened. But he was a fool. He had trusted her. He had loved her. But she had changed that, and he couldn't go back.

The pictures of her had developed nicely in his darkroom. He had taken several pictures of her at the strip club and when she had taken a walk in a park while talking to the old lady she lived next to. They were good pictures. She was beautiful and would go nicely in his collection.

He opened the book to her page and meticulously placed each picture in its place, making sure they were just right. Once he was done, he stood up and went to each door and window to recheck them three times. He rechecked the security system, motion detectors, and cameras. Everything was still in place.

He opened his book at the beginning. There she was. The first one was so beautiful and serene; he touched the first picture of Sahar. He ran his hand up and down the picture, remembering what she felt like.

He found himself becoming aroused. He slowly turned the page. The same woman looked back at him with dead eyes. He ran a finger over the lock of hair he had attached next to her picture. His heart quickened, and his breathing became low. He slowly pulled his penis from his pants and began to stroke. He turned to the next page, and there she was again. She was slightly different but once again alive and beautiful. He ran a finger across her picture, slowly looking at every inch of her. He turned the page to see her mutilated body spread out on the floor of a house on base. He started rubbing himself harder and faster. He hadn't meant to make her bleed like that, but when he had, he'd felt such excitement. It made him feel more alive than he had ever felt before. He leaned back into the couch, remembering the feel of her warm blood on his hands. The look in her eyes as her life slipped away. Just the thought of her dying in his arms made him ejaculate. He laid back and closed his eyes, satisfied and spent.

CHAPTER
TWENTY-FIVE

HUDSON PACED AROUND HIS HOUSE. It was an older house tucked down an old dirt road. He liked the solitude it provided. He ran his hands over his head as he paced. He had let himself do something he'd promised he would never do again: he had let himself have feelings for another woman. After it had ended with his wife, he thought he would be better off alone than putting himself out there again like that, vulnerable and just waiting to get hurt. But there was always an exception to every rule, and Mac was the exception. She kept creeping into his thoughts when he didn't want her to. She crept her way into his dreams, and it made him feel lost and alone when he woke up. He knew Mac was something special, but he couldn't get past the drug thing. What if she was innocent? What if she had been set up, that the person they were hunting felt they had gotten too close? Anything was possible.

The phone ringing interrupted his thoughts. He exhaled audibly when he saw his mother's number on the caller ID. He really didn't want to answer the phone. She always wanted to know when he was going to give her some grandbabies. "Hi Mom, how have you been?"

"Oh, just fine honey, how are you? How is that young lady you've been hanging out with?" his mom asked.

Hudson exhaled deeply. He had mentioned Mac the last time he had talked to her, and she obsessively latched on to the idea that he and Mac were an item and that she would have grandbabies soon. "She's fine, I think."

"What do you mean *you think*? You mean you don't know how your own girlfriend is doing?"

"It's not like that, Mom. We aren't together. We were just investigating a case together," he said, trying to sound as convincing as possible.

"Right. That is *not* what I heard in your voice the last time we talked. You're excited about this young lady. You like her, and you're avoiding getting close to her. Just because that good-for-nothing ex-wife of yours did you wrong doesn't mean that you must be alone for the rest of your life. It's just not normal. You're a good man, and she would be lucky to have you. Now you march over to her house and tell her how you feel before it's too late and she goes off with some other young man."

Hudson hated how well his mother knew him. "I'm not having this discussion with you right now. I appreciate your concern, but I'll figure things out on my own time. I have to go. I'll call you later. Love you, Mom."

Hudson quickly disconnected before she could argue. He loved his mom and had a lot of respect for her, especially how much strength she had shown after they lost his younger brother, not to mention the hell his father had put her through. He would do anything for her, but he really hated when she had him pegged.

CHAPTER
TWENTY-SIX

A SHORT TWENTY-MINUTE drive from Hudson's place, Mac was also pacing around her house, looking for different ways to get out of this mess. She had added everything she knew about the case to her board. It was filed neatly with a prostitute, a dental tech, a nurse, a military spouse, and Ali, who might be the next victim. She had downloaded pictures of all the women off their social media followed by pictures of all the potential men that could be involved with the case. She eliminated the younger ones and the ones with light hair.

She stood and stared at her board, trying to figure things out. She had pictures of Zonira, Abigail, Lilianna, Elise, and Ali with a synopsis of what was known about each of them. The two sisters were clearly connected, but there didn't seem to be a connection with the other women except for their appearance.

Mac needed help. She was stuck, and there was only one person she could always count on. She had placed a request through her sister's handlers for her to contact Mac as soon as she was able. Lola was in hiding and being protected by some very powerful people due to her family history. Her younger sister was a brilliant hacker who could find information on just about anyone. She was amazing, and Mac really missed her.

She was the only person on earth that Mac truly trusted. She had to be careful though because she didn't want anyone to find Lola. Currently, she was in a safe house somewhere overseas in an undisclosed location that even Mac didn't know about. They were only allowed to talk every few months just in case someone was tracing their calls or had found Mac and was watching her. Mac felt they were safe for now because she had changed her name and joined the military. If they found her, she always felt she could escape to the safety of the base. She began to worry. It had been over twenty-four hours since she had requested to talk with Lola over the secured network.

The victims kept creeping into her mind as she paced the room. She was wearing comfortable sweatpants that hung loosely on her hips and an old college sweatshirt with warm socks on her feet. She was always cold and could never seem to keep her feet warm enough. Her doctor had told her it was perfectly normal for a woman who didn't have much body fat to be colder. It didn't help that in Washington there were only a couple of months of warm weather before it was time to bundle up again. She often forgot to eat when she got wrapped up in a case like this. Her appetite diminished even further when some asshole involved her personally. That had only happened a couple of times previously, but it really messed with her stomach.

She moved on to the list of men she had compiled with their pictures. She had the Security Forces chief, whom she had known for years and couldn't imagine ever doing anything so violent. He had always been very kind to her and even protective, making sure her career was going in the right direction. She had met him when he was still a master sergeant. To this day, she still wasn't sure why he had taken an interest in her, but she appreciated all he had done for her. On the other hand, he had clearance and was involved in the case. He drove a dark-colored truck and he had dark hair.

Next was the Security Forces commander. He was an older man as far as the military was concerned, age forty-one, and he had dark hair. He also had access to the victim on base and was involved in the case. He did not drive a dark truck, but he had access to them.

The next person on her list of suspects pulled at her heartstrings. It was Hudson. She had become quite fond of him. He was a kind and gentle giant. He had to be one of the biggest men she had ever come across, and he made her feel safe. She liked the way he talked to her and cared about what she thought. They had really hit it off until he had turned his back on her. Just thinking about their exchange at the gym made her mood darken further. She understood, kind of, but it still hurt. She had hoped he would believe in her and stand by her, but who was she kidding? He barely knew her. They had only been spending time together for a short while. Even though there was a connection, he didn't owe her anything. She wasn't entirely sure she would have responded any differently if the tables were turned and he was the one being questioned.

She was pacing the floor deep in thought when her DOD mobile classified phone rang. Lola's security detail had secured the phone for Mac so they could communicate without their calls being traced or hacked. The only time it rang was when her sister was calling.

She grabbed the phone off the end table, not wanting to miss the call. "Lola, is that you?"

"Well, hello to you," her sister's sweet, spunky voice said over the line.

Mac sighed in relief. "It's so good to hear from you, Lola. How are you?"

"Oh, you know, same ol', same ol'. Nothing really new in my world. The goons are having me hack new systems all the time, and I just get to sit here following orders like a little puppet."

"I know it's not fun, sis, but at least you're safe."

"Oh yeah, like a mouse surrounded by cats." Lola giggled. Mac smiled, missing her sister terribly. "So, enough about my glamorous life, what's going on with you? You wouldn't have contacted me if it wasn't serious."

"What? I can't just call to talk with my little sister?" Mac said, trying to sound offended.

"You know what I mean. Don't play coy with me. We don't talk because we never want them to find us. So, what's so damn serious that you needed to reach out?"

"Sometimes I wonder if all of this is really worth it. We can't even talk regularly. I miss you, Lola."

"I miss you too, but it's too late for all that now. We made our choices, and that's that. It's much better than how things were, and we can't change the past. Overall, they treat me well, but I know it's because I know too many of their secrets." Lola laughed. "They'll never let me go."

"I know," Mac responded.

"What can I do for you on this fine day?" Lola asked again.

Lola was on the beautiful island of Guam. The ocean was breathtaking, and the people were kind and good-hearted, but she never lost sight of the fact that she was a prisoner. She had chosen this life when she had escaped the family, but she never thought it would end up like this. She'd thought it would be exciting and glamorous to work for the government. They contracted her out to the CIA, FBI, and other government agencies that needed her specific skill set. She knew she needed their protection, but it certainly came at a price. She could hack into any system. There really wasn't one she had come across that was outside her abilities. She even could check on her sister by hacking into other people's camera systems.

Lola was escorted everywhere she went and not given a moment's peace, except when she decided to fool around with one of the guards and they would do special favors for her. Sometimes she wondered what it would be like if she met the right man and started a family. Live a normal life, or something like that. She had never known normal before, so she figured it was something like the stories in the books she read. She was a romantic at heart and wanted to one day find the perfect man. That certainly wasn't going to happen in Guam. So, for now, until she could find a way out, she could at least help her big sister.

She shook off the pity party and focused back on Mac. "Okay, spill the beans. I've seen you with that tall, dark, and handsome. Is he good in the sack?"

"You certainly haven't lost your spunk," Mac said with a smile. "For your information, I'm not sleeping with him, and his name is Hudson."

"Well, why the hell not? I haven't seen you with a man in what seems like ages. A girl has needs, you know. If you don't get some soon, you'll shrivel up and become an old maid."

"I appreciate your concern but stop spying on me and you won't have to worry about my sex life or lack thereof."

Lola laughed. She had an amazingly loud, boisterous laugh that always made Mac smile. "Never going to happen! So, what can I do for you? Please tell me you want me to set you up with a sexy male escort! Now that would be fun."

Before getting down to business, Mac decided to turn the tables on her sister. "What about you, Lola? Do you have a new man in your life?"

"Nah, I'm just running around here in outfits that would make most working girls blush. Teasing my guards and making them want me even more," Lola responded casually like that was completely normal. She had taken more after their father than their mother. She was short like Mac, and they had the same almond-shaped eyes, but that was about where the similarities stopped. Mac was curvy with dark features and took after their mother—a mix of Puerto Rican and Latino—whereas Lola took more after their father with her long, curly red hair and pale, porcelain skin. She was petite and cute but still had the right curves to attract plenty of attention. She always reminded Mac of a pixie fairy with an attitude.

"Why am I not surprised," Mac laughed. "Lola, I'm in a little bit of trouble, and I could really use your help."

"Anything, you know that," Lola responded.

"Thank you. So, I've been accused of being involved in a drug ring." Mac paused to let that sink in. "I've been tracking a serial killer, or at least I think he's a serial killer, and one of the suspects is a guy I really like."

"Oh, that's all? Boy, when you step in the shit, you really go deep," Lola chortled.

"Seriously, I need you to do some digging. I'm not sure what I'm up against, and to be honest, I'm kinda freaking out here. I worked hard to create this new world, and I would like to keep it. I'm not sure if I can handle starting over again, and certainly not in the outside world. I'm protected in the military. I know I'll have to face that one day, but I'm just not ready yet."

"Calm down, sis. You know I'll help you. We'll figure this out together. Send me everything you have, and I'll get back to you as soon as I can."

"Thank you, Lola. I appreciate you more than you know," Mac said, and hung up the phone.

It had always struck Mac as odd. No matter what, Lola always sounded relaxed and at ease in any situation. Mac assumed it was just her way of protecting herself, but she also knew she herself was a worrier, especially when it came to Lola. They had always protected each other when they were kids. Mac had taken the brunt of it to protect Lola, but her sister hadn't gotten out unscathed. She thought about Lola all the time and worried about her constantly. At least under government protection she would be safe, or at least Mac hoped she would be. She thought about her all the time and wished things could be different.

CHAPTER
TWENTY-SEVEN

MAC WASN'T one to sit around and let the world handle itself. She called Joe Romero to ask if there were any new updates on the prostitute case.

"Hi, Mac, it's good to hear from you. I thought you had forgotten all about me," Joe said in his slow southern drawl.

"Hi Joe, it's good to hear your voice. How have you been?"

"Better now that you called," Joe said.

Mac smiled into the phone. "Joe, I was wondering if you had anything new on your missing working girl."

"Oh, I'm hurt, darlin', you're calling me about a case? And here I thought you were just calling because you liked me," Joe pouted.

Mac blew out an exasperated breath.

"Okay, okay, I give," Joe said. "Nothing on this end. I've had several new cases lately, so that one kinda went on the back burner, to be honest. Why are you askin'?"

"There have been some new developments in our case. I was wondering if you would mind if I went downtown to talk with some of Abigail's associates?" Mac left out the part about the new development that she was now suspected of being in a drug ring.

"Sure but be careful down there. Those girls are tough, and their pimps aren't very pleasant either. Call me if you get into any trouble."

"Sure thing, Joe, thank you," Mac replied and hung up.

Mac drove to Sprague, where Joe had told her that Abigail used to work. She was in an old pair of form-fitting jeans and a short trim-cut leather jacket. Her hair was pulled back into a ponytail, and she wore no makeup. She wanted to blend in and not look threatening, but most importantly, she certainly didn't want anyone to think she was one of the working girls. It was getting late, and most of the girls were mulling around looking for a prospective "John" so they could make their money for the night.

Joe had told Mac to look for a tall woman that liked to wear animal print. She walked up and down the street. There were multiple girls and some not-so-friendly-looking large men sitting off in the shadows, watching. Mac assumed they were the pimps Joe had warned her about. They eyed her up and down with a hungry look in their eyes. She felt a shiver creep up her spine and quickly moved on. She instinctively touched the gun strapped to her side for comfort.

Her eyes scanned the street and finally spotted Latifa down the next block. Joe had told her that Abigail and Latifa were roommates and looked out for each other. Mac thought they made for an odd pair of friends. Abigail looked like an exotic young woman who played the innocent girl, and Latifa was a beautiful tall woman with smooth cocoa skin who was larger than life in more ways than one. She had wild hair that exploded off her head in all directions, and true to Joe's word, she was dressed head to toe in animal print.

Latifa looked at her as she approached and gave her an appreciative look up and down. She let out a low whistle. "Damn girl, with a body like that, you could put JLo to shame. And that olive skin of yours! Don't tell me you're a working girl. Shit, you'd put me out of business!"

Mac smiled and tried not to laugh. No one had referred to her that way before. "Nah, I was just wondering if I could ask you a few questions?"

Latifa looked her up and down again with her head cocked to one side. "Are you the *pooo*lice?" she drawled.

"No, not at all. However, I am investigating a case on base. I work for the defense counsel and want to ask you about Abigail."

Latifa lowered her eyes at the mention of Abigail. "I sure do miss that girl," she whispered in a low voice.

"Would you mind if I ask you a few questions?" Mac asked again.

"Nah, I guess not. Business is kinda slow today anyway."

"Could I interest you in a little dinner while we talk? My treat."

"Well, now that's an offer I just can't refuse. Plus, I always do better work on a full stomach. Makes me less cranky with the customers and all." She flashed a mischievous smile that lit up her eyes.

"I know a diner right up the street," Mac said as she started walking. It was cold out, and the wind was whipping through her hair. Latifa's wild hair bobbed up and down as she walked in her heels. The cold wind was creeping through Mac's clothes. Latifa was wearing much less than she was, so she had to be freezing. "Don't you freeze out here in the wintertime?" Mac inquired.

"Nah, we usually aren't out here that long when business is good. When it ain't, we just slide into one of the doorways to get out of the wind. It ain't that bad really. You kinda get used to it after a while."

They turned the corner and approached a small diner that was open twenty-four hours a day. It looked old and run down from the outside, but Mac knew the food was delicious. It was owned by a retired military guy and his wife. Their kids often worked as the wait staff and bussed the tables. They were good people and fantastic cooks. The restaurant hadn't taken off the way they had hoped, but Gerald, the owner, loved to cook and loved talking to people even more. They walked in the door and heard a little bell ring.

Gerald stuck his head out of the kitchen. "Hey Mac, how you doin' hon? It's been a minute. I thought you mighta found a better place to eat."

Mac smiled. "Hi Gerald, it's nice to see you too, and that will never happen. You serve the best food in town."

"You know it. Can't beat my comfort food. Who's your friend?"

"This is Latifa. Do you mind if we take the table in the back?" Mac asked.

"Go right ahead, hon, you take whatever table you want. I'll send someone over to take care of you in just a sec."

Latifa and Mac settled into one of the back booths. The leather was a deep red color that had cracked in several places. The tabletop was weathered, and the seats worn, yet Mac always felt welcome and at home here. It was a safe place where people didn't judge. They always had a smile and kind words for her every time she visited.

"Thanks for agreeing to talk with me, Latifa. What can you tell me about Abigail?" Mac asked.

"Well, not much, I'm afraid. I know she didn't date much. The job tends to do that to you. It's hard having a real relationship with someone if you're turning tricks, you know. Most guys that want to date us have mental issues or are just plain freaky. She certainly kept some regulars around, though. She played the young, innocent girl routine to a T. It was impressive to watch. That girl could get men to buy her just about anything. They all wanted to *save her* from this life."

"Did she have anyone recently that was creeping her out a bit?"

"As a matter of fact, now that you mention it, she had a guy—or at least I think it was a guy—that tucked his truck down the side street and kept watching us. I wasn't sure if he was watching her in particular, but he sure did give us all the creeps, and then on the night she went missing she climbed into that same truck." Latifa shook her head. "I know this kind of thing happens, but that young one was a good girl. She really had a chance to get out and make something of herself. I really care for that girl. If there's anything I can do to help you find her, you let me know."

"Thank you," Mac replied. "Did you see anything that made the truck stick out? Could you see the person behind the wheel?"

Latifa shook her wild hair back and forth. "Nah, I could only make out the silhouette of what looked like a large man. He didn't have plates on the front of the truck or anything, so I don't know."

"Do you remember what color it was?"

"It was dark blue, maybe black. Not sure. Sorry I can't tell you more."

The waitress came over after a bit, and they ordered their food. Latifa ordered the steak and baked potato, and Mac ordered a hamburger and fries. The food came out quickly, and both ladies dug in like they hadn't eaten in days. It was mouthwatering. The meat was juicy and tender with just the right amount of seasoning.

Latifa moaned softly. "Now that has to be one of the best meals I've ever eaten. How is it that I work just up the street and didn't even know about this place? I'll have to pace myself. If I overeat here, I won't fit into my clothes anymore...and that's an issue in my line of work." She chuckled.

"I hear ya," Mac said. "I love coming here, but my job frowns on me gaining weight. I have to pass a physical fitness test every year. If I gain weight, I also have to buy new uniforms, and that's expensive."

They fell into a long silence as they finished their meals. Mac felt the conversation wasn't going to offer any additional information, so she asked for the check.

After paying and leaving a tip, both ladies walked back onto the cold street.

"One more thing, Latifa...did Abigail have any problems with her pimp or a handler?"

Latifa smiled sadly. "Yeah, we all have problems with them, but they would never damage the merchandise. They take a cut from our earnings, and Abigail was one of their best earners. They would have been crazy to hurt her. She was worth too much."

"What about you, Latifa? Are you planning to get off the streets one day?"

"Oh, I don't know sugar, this is all I've really ever known. I ran away when I was just a kid because my stepdad was taking turns with me. So, I'm not really sure what else I would do with myself." Latifa didn't seem sad about it, just resigned to the way life was.

Mac nodded her head. "If you think of anything else, please give me a call." She handed her a card. They walked back to where Mac was parked. "Take care of yourself and let me know if you ever want to change things. I might know a few people who could help you out."

"Thanks, I'll keep that in mind. You take care of yourself and watch your back. There's a lot of evil out there."

CHAPTER
TWENTY-EIGHT

FRUSTRATED, Mac headed for her house. She had hoped Latifa would know more, but she only confirmed what Joe had already told her. There had to be more out there, but she just couldn't put her finger on it. Her thoughts kept running over what they knew about the case, like a spin cycle set on repeat. She drove down her street lost in thought when she realized the lights were on at her place.

She veered her SUV off to the side of the road and watched the house. She knew she hadn't left the lights on. The only light she ever left on was the porch light. She always kept her house secured and locked up tight.

She killed the engine and quietly slipped out of the driver's seat. Keeping her body low to avoid detection, she crept up to the side of the house, pressing her body close to the garage. She stopped and listened for any sound, controlling her breathing before moving forward. Peering around the corner of the garage through the front windows, she saw no one. Her heart almost stopped when she heard a rustling in the bushes behind her until a cat came slinking out and ran past.

Okay, okay, get a grip, Mac told herself. *Whoever broke in is probably already gone.*

She moved closer to the house. Keeping her body low, she made her way to the side window where the breakfast nook was. It gave her an unobstructed view of the living room and kitchen. Every light in the house appeared to be on. Her breath caught in her throat when she looked in and saw complete destruction. The place was a complete wreck. Her heart sank as she saw all her belongings thrown about. *They're just things, they aren't important*, she tried to convince herself. She clenched her fists and wanted badly to hit something. She felt an overwhelming need to make someone else feel as violated and angry as she was.

Mac steadied herself and then retrieved her phone from her back pocket. She swiped the phone to find Joe's number and called. He picked up on the second ring. "Joe, this is Mac. Someone broke into my house tonight," she said, angry at the way her shaky voice came across.

"Are you okay?" Joe asked.

"Yes, I was out talking with Latifa. I wasn't home, but they trashed my place," Mac said, trying to keep control of her emotions.

"Have you gone inside?"

"No. I don't see anyone in the house, but I haven't checked."

"Good. Go back to your car and wait for me to get there. Send me your address."

"Okay, thanks." Mac was normally more pig-headed and would check herself, but this had rocked her, and she also wasn't stupid. If the killer was still in her house, she didn't want to go in and confront him. He was clearly capable of doing all kinds of nasty things, and he preferred to prey on women, which was not in her favor. Plus, she needed to get the police report on the incident for the insurance anyway. She quietly walked back to her car and waited.

There was no movement, and her house was silent. Normally she really enjoyed the quiet little street she lived on. It was an older one-story home with a brick front and pillars surrounding the porch. She always thought it looked like a little cottage out of a fairy tale. She had neighbors, but most of them were quiet and kept to themselves. She sat there in her car in the dark, waiting. It only took fifteen minutes for Joe to show up. She was surprised to see Hudson pulling up right behind him.

Her heart skipped a beat. She wasn't sure how she felt about Hudson at the moment. She felt betrayed by him, but at the same time she knew he didn't owe her anything—but it still stung.

All three of them got out of their vehicles, nodded their heads in acknowledgment, and advanced toward the house in silence. They looked at each other but said nothing. As they got closer, they all pulled their guns in anticipation of the pending threat. Mac's pulse quickened as they approached. It was clear the lock had been picked. The intruder had left scratches around the keyhole, leaving no doubt it had been messed with. Mac kicked herself mentally. She had meant to install better locks on the house and had just never gotten around to it. She had also meant to install a security system and that hadn't happened either.

Joe opened the house, slowly looking around. Hudson came next, followed by Mac. They went in different directions as they entered, checking the house room by room, yelling "clear" each time they had secured a room. The house had been ransacked and looked like a tornado had come through. On the surface, it didn't appear anything was missing. The intruder was long gone, but he sure did leave a mess in his wake. He had even emptied her pantry—not that she had a ton of food—but the food she did have covered the floor. Thankfully, the intruder had left her fridge alone, and she wouldn't have to replace that. It was something to be thankful for. He had gone through her drawers and ransacked her bedroom. He'd even stripped the sheets off her bed. She took a deep breath. It was going to be a long night, but she had to clean it all up or she just wouldn't be able to sleep.

"Can you tell me if anything is missing?" Joe asked as he began taking notes. He was going from room to room, taking pictures and making notes of what he found now that everyone's adrenaline had gone down and the house was clear and relatively safe for the moment.

"Not anything that stands out," Mac responded absently, looking around. She was shaking slightly but didn't want to show her fear. She had learned a long time ago that showing fear was a form of weakness. On top of her deep-seated trust issues, she also had a hell of a time showing her emotions. She always internalized them.

Hudson came around the corner with a little multicolored kitten in hand. "It sure does look like they did a number on your place," he said. He was stroking the kitten's head. The little furball looked completely at peace against his strong chest. Mac thought it would feel good to be cuddled up against his chest too. He walked over and handed her the kitten. His woodsy scent invaded her sinuses. It calmed her almost immediately. "I didn't know you had a kitten," he said, pulling her back to reality.

"I don't. He must have wandered in from outside somewhere," Mac said. The kitten was purring against her chest.

"Any idea who might have done it?" Hudson asked.

"No, but someone is trying to get to me. First, the false allegations about me being involved in a drug ring—which is complete bullshit—and now this. Someone is trying to knock me off their trail. I don't know who it is, but I'm sure as hell going to find out," she said angrily.

Joe walked up. "What do you mean *drug ring*? I wasn't told about any drug charges against you."

"They're UCMJ charges on base. They are investigating me under Article 112a, wrongful use, possession, and possible distribution. They have absolutely no evidence, but someone wants me off this case and badly. I can't even work in my own office because of the investigation. They assigned me to the chaplain's office."

"I see," Joe said. "Anything I can do to help?"

"Nah, it'll blow over as long as they didn't actually plant evidence or anything. I've been through worse. I can handle it on my own. Thanks for asking, Joe," Mac said pointedly, looking at Hudson.

"Mac, this guy could really be dangerous," Hudson said protectively, trying to show he was also there to help.

"Yeah, and I can handle myself. I'm sure you wouldn't want to put your precious career in danger." Mac instantly regretted her choice of words.

Hudson lowered his eyes. "I'm sorry, Mac, I didn't know what to think. Honestly, I still don't, but it certainly looks like you're being set up...or at least someone is trying to do you and your career a great deal of harm."

"Don't be too hard on ol' Hudson," Joe said. "He has a bit of a nasty history with drugs."

Mac raised an eyebrow.

Hudson glared at Joe. "That was not for you to share."

"Are you an addict?" Mac asked bluntly.

"I wouldn't be wearing the uniform if I was, and you know it," Hudson responded. "If you really want to know, it was my little brother. He overdosed and died when we were young." His eyes filled with sadness.

"I'm sorry."

"Don't be. It was a long time ago."

Mac set the kitten down and started wandering around, picking things up off the floor. She was making a pile of all the clothes and bedding.

Hudson followed and started helping without saying a word. He picked up a pile of her clothes that had been thrown across the room and realized one of the articles was a silky pair of pink thong panties with a little lace triangle in the front. His mind immediately went to all kinds of inappropriate thoughts. He quickly dumped the pile of clothes in with the others that needed cleaning and cleared his throat. "So, what are we going to do about all this?"

Mac was about to respond and point out that "we" weren't going to do anything when Joe walked in. "Mac, I can have a patrol drive by your place. We don't have the manpower to keep someone posted here, but I can have someone do a drive-by on the regular."

"Thank you, Joe, but that won't be necessary. I'll be fine. I can handle myself. If this guy shows up again while I'm home, he'll get more than he bargained for," Mac said, squaring her shoulders.

Hudson was about to tell her what he thought about her last statement but decided not to push the issue until they had at least cleaned the place up a bit. He walked into her tiny home office. There were papers everywhere. He started picking them up and looking at them as he went. There were pictures and details of the victims they were looking into, and of Ali. Then he picked up a piece of paper that listed possible suspects and saw his name. He felt his temper flare.

At the top of the list, she had written what she knew about the predator. In dark letters, it said: *access, dark trucks, dark hair, older, motive.* Next to the word *motive,* there was a question mark. He took several breaths, trying to calm himself and see it from her point of view. He had three check marks next to his name which meant he met three of her criteria.

She walked into the tiny office behind him. He turned around and handed her the piece of paper with his name on it. He didn't look at her, just brushed past her and walked out the front door.

Joe walked in a few seconds later. "What the hell is wrong with Hudson?" he asked.

Mac said nothing but handed him the piece of paper.

"Oh," Joe said.

CHAPTER
TWENTY-NINE

HUDSON DROVE HOME FUMING. He hated that Mac had gotten under his skin. Why on earth did she think he was a suspect? He tried to calm down and think of it from her point of view. She didn't know him very well, and he really didn't know her all that well either. So why was it that his brain felt scrambled every time he was around her, and he wanted nothing but her? All he had wanted to do was hug her and make her feel safe. Take away that look of fear in her eyes—but no, he had to get pissy and stomp off like an overgrown child. What the hell was wrong with him when he was around that woman? He decided not to look too closely at how Mac made him feel and just focus on the case. If he could solve the case, then maybe he would have time to look closer at his feelings.

When Hudson got home, he paced back and forth, feeling restless and uneasy. His home felt safe and secure. He couldn't imagine how Mac was feeling after her entire home had been turned upside down. He ran his hand over his head and took a deep breath. He slammed his fist against the wall. He hated the fact that she got to him the way she did. He walked into his small bathroom and splashed water on his face. There was only one thing he could do: he had to go back and see her. He went to his bedroom with the worn comforter on the oversized bed. The California-king-sized bed was the only thing that would fit his frame. He would miss sleeping in comfort tonight, but she was worth it. Hopefully, her couch was more comfortable than it looked.

Hudson pulled up in front of Mac's small house and quickly crossed the front lawn, looking around for any movement. He saw nothing. He thought about doing a perimeter check but thought better of it without letting Mac know he was around. She already had him on her list of suspects. It would not do him well or win him any favors if she thought he was the one snooping around her property. He walked up to her door and knocked with three loud raps on the door. He heard her mulling around inside. He squared his shoulders and stepped back from the peephole so she could see him.

She hesitated and then, without opening the door, asked, "What do you want, Hudson? It's been a really long night, and I have a lot to do."

He took a deep breath. "I'm sorry for storming out earlier. I saw your suspect list. I understand you were just being thorough in your investigation. I get that I meet some of the criteria as a suspect. I'm here to prove to you that I shouldn't be on that list. If you'd let me, I would like to sleep on your couch just in case the intruder comes back."

Mac exhaled loudly—not because she was frustrated but because she felt vulnerable around him. She looked through the peephole again and saw his broad chest and strong arms waiting there patiently. Thoughts of how long it had been since she had been held—how good that sounded at the moment with what was going on—flooded her brain. She slowly opened the door and removed the chain that hung between her, and Hudson then stepped aside, letting him pass. He had an overnight bag in one hand and his uniform on a hanger in the other. She thought it was comical how much bigger his uniform was compared to hers. It looked like a giant's uniform.

When he walked past her, he caught the faint scent of vanilla and honey again. He loved the way she smelled. It threw his mind straight into the gutter, dreaming up all kinds of inappropriate thoughts. Now was not the time. He was there to keep her safe, not maul her like a crazed teenager, though the thought had merit.

"Can I get you anything?" Mac asked. Hudson hung his uniform on the doorknob so he wouldn't look like he was wearing a garbage bag the next day and set his bag down. She took in an even breath and then exhaled slowly. This man was standing in front of her in sweatpants and an old t-shirt, and he still took her breath away. It should be illegal to look that good.

Hudson bent forward and slipped off his shoes. He looked up to see her staring at him, and a small, sexy grin crossed his lips. "Do you like what you see?"

"Not going to happen, Hudson. I have enough issues without bringing the likes of you into my life."

Hudson looked offended. "What's that supposed to mean?"

"It means I'm not exactly in a position to start any kind of romantic relationship right now, and I am certainly not in the market for one. That crap just brings trouble," she responded more forcefully than she meant to.

Hudson stood to his full six-foot-six height, and she had to strain her neck to look him in the eyes. "Mac, I know you've been hurt, and you have some major trust issues, but I hope with time you'll learn to trust me," he said in a low voice.

"You have to understand, there's been a lot going on. In one short week, I've had my home and career violated, and I did nothing wrong other than investigating a case. I want you to know that I've had nothing to do with drugs and never will. My family has an ugly past with that stuff as well. I won't ever get mixed up with it. It destroys people and families." She looked down and blew out a low breath.

Without saying another word, he wrapped his arms around her in a warm embrace. There was nothing sexual about it, but the feel of his huge body against hers sparked a flame that she wasn't prepared to deal with. He felt warm and safe and smelled amazing. Electricity coursed through her, and she knew she wanted more. The stress immediately drained from her body as she snuggled into his chest. She stayed there for a while, just enjoying the sensation.

Hudson slowly pulled away from her. "I like you a great deal, Mac. It's been a long time since I felt anything for a woman after my ex-wife. I would like to explore this once we know you're safe. Right now, I think it would cloud my judgment. I have a hard time thinking clearly when you're around." He wore a mischievous smile on his lips that reached his eyes.

Mac stayed quiet and looked at him.

A concerned look came across his face. He cleared his throat. "I mean, if you're interested in exploring a relationship with me," he said quietly.

She liked that he felt off-balance around her. It made her feel good and confident. But it also told her that he was serious and not just trying to get in her pants. She put on a stern look. "I don't know, Hudson, you can be a pain in the ass sometimes, and I'm not the easiest person to be around either."

Hudson smiled again. "I'll take my chances. Now let's get this place cleaned up and get a little sleep so we can function tomorrow."

CHAPTER
THIRTY

JOE'S PROMISE TO check in and have some of his patrols do drive-bys and even Hudson sleeping on her couch did little to help her sleep. Every time the wind blew, or the house creaked, she would jump awake, and it took her too long to get back to sleep. She tiptoed out to make the morning coffee and almost laughed out loud at the sight of Hudson. She'd felt awful for him because he barely fit on her little couch, his arms and legs dangling uncomfortably off the edge.

Mac arrived at the chaplain's office feeling exhausted, and a little rattled. She was sucking down her second cup of coffee and not looking forward to the day. After her house had been destroyed, she hadn't slept at all. Hudson's sleep on her couch had helped, but now she couldn't get rid of the image of him standing in a towel outside her bathroom that morning. He'd stepped out because he'd forgotten the t-shirt that he wore under his uniform. His body was muscular and toned in all the right places. She went around the corner with her cup of coffee and couldn't even speak. *That man really should come with a warning label, for crying out loud.*

Now, she sat at the extra desk they had given her to use. She felt like she had no purpose. Chaplain Bastion had stopped by earlier to see how she was holding up, but he really didn't have anything to keep her busy. She answered some emails and forwarded the ones she could no longer help with to her boss. She began searching the internet for clues to what she had missed. With limited information access, she really couldn't do much.

Mac closed her eyes, took a deep breath in, then blew it out, trying to maintain her composure. She had to think. What other angles could she explore? She looked at Abigail's Facebook page, trying to figure out the links between Zonira, Ali, Abigail, Lilianna, and Elise. She had a sinking feeling that there were more women out there, but she just didn't know where to start. There had to be some clue as to who was behind these missing or murdered women. She just had to stay focused.

She was concentrating, lost in thought, when a voice behind her made her jump out of her skin. Mac turned around to see the Security Forces chief standing behind her. "Good morning, Mac. What are you up to?"

She shrugged a shoulder up and down. "Just passing the time," she said, rolling her eyes. "Until they figure out that I'm not guilty of this crap."

"I heard all about it," he responded in his deep, gruff voice. He had dark features and a broad chest. He stood proud in his uniform. She was keenly aware that he fit most of her main suspect criteria, but she also saw him as big brother and could never imagine him hurting anyone, especially women. To Mac, he had always seemed so kind and respectful, never frazzled or upset, just even-tempered.

"How about a run?" he asked.

Mac gave him a disappointed look. "You know how much I hate to run."

"Yeah, but you have a lot going on, and it'll clear your head."

"Fine, if you insist…but we're going at my pace, not yours. Deal?"

She went into the ladies' room to change into her running clothes. Really, she had nothing better to do, and maybe discussing things with her longtime mentor would help clear her head a little. Right now, it just felt like she was spinning her wheels.

They started a slow jog down the sidewalk in front of the chaplain's building. It was cold out, but the sun was still shining down, casting a slightly warm glow over them.

"So, what are you going to do about this?" Chief asked.

"I really don't know, but I have to do something. Someone is out there trying to ruin my career. They tossed my place last night trying to scare me off."

"Are you okay? Is anything missing? Did you file a police report?" Chief fired questions off in quick succession.

"Yes, I did all that, but nothing was missing. They just trashed the place."

"I see. Is there anything I can do?"

"Not that I can think of," Mac responded.

"So, what do you know so far?" Chief asked.

Mac went through everything she knew, going into detail about each woman involved and that she suspected there were other victims she just didn't know about yet.

He looked down at her inquisitively. "I thought you were pulled off your caseload altogether. Mac, you could really get yourself into more trouble here. You have a stellar career. I know you want to solve this, but if you just step back and let the investigators work it out then the evidence will show what really happened," Chief said flatly, pinning her with a stern expression.

Always the big brother, she thought. "You and I both know that's not the way this always works. If it did, I'd be out of business. Plenty of good men and women in our wonderful Air Force have been wrongfully accused of a crime. Look at Johnson. He's still sitting in pretrial confinement for killing his wife, and he only has half his defense team at work. We've seen members who have had to deal with punishments that were disproportionate to their crimes. In this case, I'm absolutely, one hundred percent not guilty, and I'm not going to sit around twiddling my thumbs waiting for some jackass to figure out they're wrong," she said with fury in her eyes.

"Okay, okay, but don't say I didn't warn you. I'm just worried about you and your career. I don't want to see things getting any worse."

He had a good point. Maybe she shouldn't be pushing, at least not publicly. Staying under the radar was a much better idea.

CHAPTER
THIRTY-ONE

SHE STOPPED by the gym for a quick shower, then walked back into the office. Her body ached from the run and exhaustion as the rest of her day dragged on. Hudson texted her, asking how her day was. Her response was only half true when she said she was fine. This situation had knocked her off balance. Her pride always got the best of her, and she hated when someone questioned her integrity. Her strength, dependability, and honesty were the things she was most proud of. She never wavered outside the lines. It was against her nature to break the law. She had worked with enough military criminals to know that wasn't the type of life she wanted to live. She was very thankful she had escaped her own family's criminal empire, and never wanted to go back. That was a part of her life she tried hard not to think about. Even though she had escaped over thirteen years ago, she still found herself looking over her shoulder, waiting for one of *them* to show up.

Her phone rang, bringing her back to reality. She didn't recognize the phone number on the caller ID. Even though it was her personal cell phone, she always answered the same way—in her line of work she was always on call, so she never knew. "Good afternoon, this is Technical Sergeant McGregor. What can I do for you?"

"Hi, this is Zachariah Ward from the CDA police department," said a slightly high-pitched voice across the line. "Joe Romero said you would be stopping by to look at some of our case files a few days ago, but then we didn't hear anything else from you."

"Yes, thank you for following up. We had some things come up here and didn't get the chance. Is there any way you could send me the case files?"

"Sure can. What are you guys looking at on your end?" Zack asked.

Mac gave him a rundown of the case with Abigail and Zonira. "We also suspect our next victim might be Ali Ahmad. She's the sister of our second possible victim. My theory is that our guy is killing women who all share similar looks. Zonira and her sister Ali could have been twins if not for their age difference."

"That's an interesting theory," Zack said. "Our dental technician, Mrs. Lilianna Broadsmith, went missing approximately four months ago and has yet to show back up. Her husband has been calling me every day, but we can't find any trace of her. She hasn't left any financial footprint, and no one has seen her. She went to work and then to a yoga class; that was the last time anyone saw her. We haven't found any witnesses or leads. It's like she simply fell off the face of the earth."

"Was there any video surveillance around the yoga studio or outside of the nearby stores?"

"Nothing," Zack responded. "No traffic cameras in the area. The studio she was at was in a rural area that didn't see a lot of traffic. It was on her way home from work. So, we aren't sure if she had been stalked and abducted or simply had an affair and ran off with another man. It happens, you know."

"Yeah, it does. Can you send me everything about her? What about the nurse?" she asked. "What do you have on her? It sounds like a pretty grizzly scene from what Joe tells me."

"Yeah." Zack took a deep breath. "Her name was Mrs. Elise Morrison. She was married with two small children at home. It was kinda weird too. It almost looked like the person who killed her had strangled her, revived her, and then had intercourse with her while stabbing multiple times throughout. Then he re-dressed her in clothes that didn't belong to her. We're not sure why. Normally if it's a sexual sadist, the killer likes to stab the victim while they're still alive as a form of sexual release, but we're not sure if that was the case here."

Mac had studied cases like that and agreed that this killer had some interesting characteristics. If there was, in fact, one killer. She still wasn't one hundred percent convinced the cases were related. "So, Zack, tell me, what did the women look like?"

"Well," he said, hesitating a little, "they were both very beautiful and kinda looked alike, but certainly not identical. They both had long dark hair, medium tan skin, dark eyes, not tall, and were subjectively attractive."

"That sounds similar to our victims," Mac responded. "Is there any way you guys could check in on Ali Ahmad? She works at the State Line strip club. She may be his next target. If these cases are related, then it only makes sense that Ali would be on this guy's hit list."

"No problem, I'll go check on her myself this evening. What's her address?" Zack asked.

Mac rattled off the address and thanked him for his time. She wrapped up for the day and headed for the house, hoping that the case file would be in her inbox by the time she arrived home.

CHAPTER
THIRTY-TWO

MAC HAD TEXTED Hudson to let him know she had more information. He texted back that he would wrap up and meet her at her place with some dinner.

She felt on high alert as she walked up to her house. The fatigue was starting to sink in after not sleeping or eating enough. Before entering, she did a perimeter check and looked inside all the windows. Anger flared at the person who had taken her security away. She wanted to feel safe, but now all she expected to find was a boogeyman waiting for her. It was ridiculous. She hoped to find this bastard soon so her life could go back to normal, plus she desperately needed some sleep. The exhaustion was making her even more paranoid, and that didn't help anything.

Her door was still locked when she checked it. Relief swept over her, but she still kept her gun drawn as she walked from room to room —even checking inside the closets, the bathroom, and the pantry—to make sure no one was there. She went back to the front door and locked it just to be safe.

She stepped into her room and slipped out of her uniform. She was standing there in her uniform t-shirt and black socks when she heard Hudson's knock. "Just a minute," she hollered toward the door.

He stood on the other side waiting patiently with their dinner in hand. She walked up and checked the peephole just to make sure it was him. She opened the door and stood before him in her socks and t-shirt but nothing else. She smiled at the look on his face. "Wow," was all he said.

Mac laughed and smiled wickedly. "What? You get turned on by uniform socks?"

"No," he said in a low, sultry voice. "I get turned on by you."

She smiled at him shyly and walked away, swaying her hips. "Well, in that case, I'll go put on my old-man sweatpants. That should really do it." She smiled back at him while walking into her room. She came out a few minutes later wearing a worn-out pair of sweats and a threadbare t-shirt that was see-through in certain spots.

Hudson tried not to stare, but she looked amazing. Who was he kidding, she looked amazing in anything—but he'd promised to leave her alone until they got to the bottom of the case, after which they could figure this thing out without all the stress and distractions. Plus, he didn't want her to do something she would later regret just because she was feeling vulnerable.

Mac walked into the office to see if the file from Zack had come through yet.

"I hope you like Chinese food," Hudson said as he put the food on the kitchen table.

"One of my favorites," she hollered from the office. "Thanks for picking it up." She booted up her computer, waited while her email loaded, and was happy to see the requested file waiting for her in her inbox. She printed two copies for them to review after dinner. Then she turned around and collided into Hudson's chest, not realizing he had been standing behind her. He reached down and wrapped her in his warm embrace. Her sister called this the "hug factor." She always said you knew he was a good man if he could give a good, warm hug and make the world seem like a better place. *Boy, does Hudson have a nice hug!* He was strong and smelled amazing. She could feel the heat of his skin warming her.

He pulled away, lowered his head down, and touched his forehead against hers. "Are you hungry?"

"Yes," she said, "but we should probably eat first." She grinned.

He laughed in his deep, sexy baritone. "With that kind of talk, we're both going to get into trouble." He reluctantly turned away and sat down at the table. The old wooden chair creaked under his large frame.

They ate in relative silence, listening to the sound of the printer humming in the background. Mac sat down and took a bite of her food, savoring each morsel. He loved watching her eat. It scared him a little how many things he liked about her. As he sat there staring at her, he honestly couldn't think of one thing he didn't like, at least not yet. But these were feelings he wasn't sure he was ready to experience yet, so he pushed them aside.

After dinner, they went into her tiny office and quickly realized it was too small to work in. They carried all the papers to the living room and spread them out across the floor. They took each case file and the pictures that went with them and started putting them in order. There were four women they knew of so far that were either missing or dead and one potential victim.

"The first missing woman is Abigail," she said and taped Abigail's picture to the whiteboard she had dragged out of her office. Under Abigail's picture, she wrote her name and that she was a working girl. "She was last seen October of last year."

"Okay," Hudson said. "What else do we know about her?"

"Not much, I'm afraid. She didn't appear to have any family in the area, and she was working in a high-risk career field. Really, anything could have happened to her. She's had no traceable financial activity since she disappeared, but if she's running from someone then she could be working cash-only since her profession primarily peddles in cash. There's been no activity on her cell phone or her social media accounts since October of last year."

Mac finished writing notes about Abigail and then placed the picture of the next woman a few inches to the right. "Okay, so this is Elise Morrison, and she's a nurse. Her body was found approximately two months after Abigail went missing," she said while writing the information below the photo.

Hudson read from the file. "She's married and a mother of two. She was found in a hotel room with multiple stab wounds, and ligature marks on the neck, and she had been sexually penetrated. The guy must have worn gloves and a condom because they found no DNA or fingerprints on the body, but of course, she was in a hotel room, so there were multiple DNA and fingerprint samples on the comforter and around the room. She had also been re-dressed after being stabbed." Hudson stopped reading. "That's a little weird. It shows remorse like he's trying to cover up what he did to her by dressing her."

"Zack from the CDA police department also said that her body was posed," Mac said, and wrote down the details under Elise's photo. "In Elise's case, her husband has a rock-solid alibi. He was in a business meeting at the time of her death that multiple people can attest to. Since Elise worked night shifts, he would sometimes have dinner meetings while the nanny watched the kids. It says that the CDA police department is still looking into the possibility of him slipping away from the meeting to kill his wife, but that doesn't seem likely. The timing just couldn't be possible.

"Next up is Lilianna Broadsmith, who went missing two months after Elise," Mac said.

Hudson picked up Lilianna's missing-person file and read it to her. "Okay, so Lilianna was also married but had no kids. She was a dental technician. She was last seen at her yoga class. She never arrived back home, and there's been no sign of her afterward. She hasn't used her credit cards or an ATM. Her husband says she's a fighter and very resourceful. Her vehicle was found abandoned down the street from her home with no signs of a struggle. They processed the vehicle, and there were no other fingerprints except for Lilianna and her husband. Her husband remains a suspect in her abduction."

"Then there's Zonira Johnson," Mac said, "who was murdered only one month after Lilianna's disappearance. That's an impressive acceleration if we're dealing with the same person."

Hudson picked up the file on Zonira and began to read. "Zonira was found in her home in base housing. Her neck was also broken. It appears that he was strangling her and applying too much pressure, crushing her larynx. Her body sustained multiple stab wounds. The medical examiner's report says that she was alive during the stabbings, and then her neck got crushed. She wasn't re-dressed or posed. This could be because something interrupted the perp. Her husband was found screaming and holding her dead body when the police arrived. Obviously, his DNA and fingerprints are everywhere. The evidence against him isn't looking good. He has no alibi for the day. He said he was fishing and spending some alone time in the woods. The base investigators found that odd since he had just recently gotten home from deployment. Why didn't he want to spend time with his wife on his day off?"

"Not sure, but his wife was going to visit her sister," Mac said thoughtfully. "I do know everyone is different. Sometimes I need my alone time to get my head straight. Maybe he just wanted to go fishing, and she didn't like fishing. It could be as simple as that." Mac wrote Hudson's question under Zonira's name.

"The last woman we fear may be a future victim—or is at least part of this—is Ali," Mac said. She went to the end of their timeline and placed Ali's picture up on the board. "So far, what do we know about Ali?"

"Well, we know she's single and an exotic dancer by trade."

"Okay." Mac wrote that information below Ali's name.

"She's the sister of the last victim who was murdered only eighteen days ago," Hudson said.

"Wow, it's only been eighteen days? It's amazing how much your world can get turned upside down in such a short amount of time."

Hudson nodded his head in agreement and pressed forward. "We suspect Ali may be the next target, but we have no evidence to support it. She lives alone and is resourceful and tough like Lilianna. We also know she's attending college to become a doctor, which she has in common with the nurse. They're both in the medical profession."

Hudson and Mac stood back to look at their timeline. "Okay," Mac said. "What links these women together?" She drew a line under the pictures of the women and started another list titled *commonalities*. Under the heading, she wrote *dark hair, almond eyes, olive skin tone, exotic look, high cheekbones, full lips, average-to-small build*.

Mac stood there, chewing on the end of the dry-erase marker. Finally, she asked, "What do you think, Hudson?"

He stood back and studied the pictures of the women carefully. "Um," he said absently, "I don't want to scare you, but all these women look a lot like *you*."

"I guess a little." She shifted uncomfortably and quickly changed the subject. "So, what do we know about our killer?" Her mind wasn't ready to accept that she looked like these women, especially because she already felt like she had a target on her back. Clearly, this guy had her in his crosshairs. She had to figure out who he was before he got the chance to kill again, for both her own safety and Ali's.

"We know he drives a dark-colored truck, but that's a lot of people on Fairchild and in Spokane. We believe he is part of Fairchild, but he could also be someone who has a contractor's badge or was sponsored onto the base," Hudson said.

"Ali said that her sister was somehow involved with an older, high-ranking man with dark features. That could be nothing...but it could also be the key."

"True. Is there anything else we know?"

"Nothing concrete," Mac said. "We know that these types of killers normally can't stop killing even if they want to. The fact that he shows remorse for some victims leads me to believe that he's repeatedly killing the same woman. We need to figure out the 'why.' What's his trigger?"

"He clearly knows how to cover his tracks," Hudson said. "He hasn't left any physical evidence that we're aware of, which leads me to believe that he's organized and meticulous and has probably been killing for a while."

"He could have police or military training in crime investigation and evidence collection since he seems to know exactly what the crime scene techs are looking for," Mac offered.

They sat there looking at the board. "Okay," she said. "So, we know the person who did this would have to be big enough to overpower a woman without her struggling or making a huge scene as long as we're assuming he also took Abigail and Lilianna. It appears that he was able to abduct these women without anyone around them noticing. The two murder victims didn't have defensive wounds. So, what does that tell us?"

"Well," Hudson responded, "he could have subdued them in some way. Maybe chloroform or a strong sedative? It's also possible that he's someone the women trusted and willingly went along with."

"True. I think that's everything for now," she said, absently playing with her long dark hair.

Hudson exhaled beside her. "We're both exhausted. Let's call it a night and look at this fresh in the morning."

She laid her head on his shoulder, and he leaned back, running his fingers through her hair. They were both so tired. The stress and anxiety running through them over the last several days was wearing them down.

Before long, they were both fast asleep on the couch. Hudson stirred at about 0200 hours in the morning. The lights were still on, and Mac was snuggled up beside him. Her neck was at an unnatural angle, so he slid out from underneath her and gently laid her head on the couch. He walked over to the wall and clicked off the lights. He stared out the window, wondering if someone was watching them. He didn't see anyone.

Stretching his long arms and rolling his neck, he listened to his spine grind and pop from sleeping sitting up on the couch. He was going to pay for that in the morning, but for now they both needed some sleep on an actual bed; otherwise, they would be too tired to solve anything. Hudson walked over to the couch and gently picked her up, doing his best not to wake her. He took her into the bedroom and gently laid her down. He hoped like hell that she wouldn't get angry with him, but he needed some solid sleep. He took off his shirt but left his pants on and lay next to her. For the first time in a long time, he fell fast asleep and slept solidly.

CHAPTER
THIRTY-THREE

MAC WOKE the next morning to her alarm going off with Hudson's arms wrapped around her. She quickly silenced the incessant thing and snuggled into his arms. She felt so warm and safe. It was the best morning she had had in a long time. His amazing warm scent engulfed her and made her feel like she was where she was meant to be. She had never really felt this comfortable with other men; she'd always had her guard up.

Her reservations about relationships ran deep because of her upbringing. Her mother had treated her father with venom, beating him down until he'd had no other choice but to walk away. After he left, for some reason, her mother missed him terribly. She took in one man after another to fill his absence. They had been evil men who were abusive to Mac and her sister, but they couldn't hold a candle to the treatment their mother would dole out. Mac still wasn't sure what made her mother the way she was, but she was cold and calculated, and she used people as pawns in her quest for power. At least she and her sister had gotten away for now, but it left Mac with a guarded personality. It wasn't that she didn't want a relationship; it was just that she was anxious about trusting others. She had so many people in her life that had betrayed her or treated her poorly that she wasn't sure if she would ever truly let her guard down.

Hudson stirred beside her. He pulled her closer to his warm chest, and she could feel his arousal pressing up against her. She took in a deep breath, not sure what she wanted. She knew her body wanted him, there was no question about that with the hum of arousal pulsing through her, but it wasn't that easy. He nuzzled against her and kissed her neck. She softly moaned as a shiver ran down her spine. He whispered, "We better get going or we'll both be late for work."

She groaned. "Do we have to?"

"Afraid so," he said. He propped himself up on one elbow and stared down at her.

"What?" she asked.

"You're stunning."

Mac smiled a wicked little grin. "You're not so bad yourself."

He leaned down and pressed his lips against hers, devouring her mouth. She parted her lips, allowing his tongue to explore her mouth. He pressed up against her and groaned. His warm chest against hers was more than she could handle. He slowly pulled away. "I need to go hit the shower before we let this go too far."

Before she could protest, he stood up and headed for the door. She knew they had agreed to wait, but she couldn't remember why at that moment. She heard the shower turn on and lay there, imagining his wet body being soaked in the warm water. It had been way too long since she had been touched, let alone satisfied. Her resolve was quickly melting away. If he was going to keep hanging around, they were going to be in trouble. She wasn't sure how long she had been fantasizing about him when he hollered, "All yours!"

She padded down the hall into the bathroom. It was all steamed up, and she welcomed the warm water on her skin. She stood under the hot water for a while, just letting the stress of the last few weeks melt away from her body. Eventually, she got out, figuring it was about time to go to work. She towel-dried her hair and let it hang down her back, then wrapped another towel around her body. She hadn't brought any clothes with her, so she headed out into the hall where she was met with the amazing smell of bacon and pancakes. She peered into the kitchen and there stood Hudson in the tiny little space, humming as he cooked her breakfast. She couldn't help but smile. He glanced over and saw her looking at him, still in her towel.

"Good lord, woman, go put some clothes on before you make me do something I shouldn't!" Hudson said as he held out a large mug of coffee. She took a sip of the warm, soothing liquid. "I hope that's the way you like it. I was guessing. I thought I remembered you saying something about sugar and creamer."

"It's perfect." She took a few steps toward him with a sexy grin on her face. "I'll tell you what else I would like," she murmured as she got closer to him.

He grinned. "You're going to make me burn the bacon."

"I like my bacon crispy." And with that, she let her towel drop to the floor.

He stared at her, unable to say a word. He knew she was beautiful, but here she stood in front of him in all her glory. His brain completely shut down.

With a quick flick of the wrist, he turned the knob to the stove and walked over to her. Not saying a word, he pulled her into his body and lowered his head, kissing her deeply. His mouth felt warm and soft against her lips. Enticing and so much better than she'd ever dreamed of asking for, like pure heaven.

He pulled away slightly, putting his forehead against hers. "Are you sure about this?" he asked, running his finger along the line of her chin and tucking a strand of hair behind her ear. Even with her standing there, her beautiful body against his, he would stop if she asked him to.

Mac tilted her head slightly back and whispered, "Yes."

That was all the encouragement he needed. He slid his mouth down to her neck and began kissing. She was simply stunning, a bronze goddess with lush, beautiful curves that inspired all kinds of inappropriate thoughts. He wanted her in every which way he could imagine. Cupping her ass in his large hands, he lifted her off the floor. She wrapped her legs around him and he almost lost it. She arched her back, showing him how much she wanted him.

Her soft curves against his hard, chiseled body were almost more than he could stand. He hadn't been with anyone in so long. Not since his ex-wife. He wanted to take his time and make sure she enjoyed herself as much as he knew he would. He gently laid her on the bed and stood back to look at her beautiful body.

A sultry look crossed her face. "Do you like what you see?" she asked in a low, husky voice.

"You're perfect," was all he could say.

She smiled and leaned forward, stroking him through his pants.

He gently removed her hand. "Not yet," he said in a low voice.

"This doesn't seem fair," she pouted playfully. "You get to see all of me, touch me, play with me, but I don't get to do the same?"

He stepped back. "It's just been, well, a while…and I want to make sure you enjoy this as well."

"How long is 'a while?'" she asked with a smile.

"Over two years."

"I see. If it makes you feel any better, it's been a long time for me as well. Now, if you don't take off those clothes, I'm going to think you don't want me."

"You'll never have to think that," he responded. He quickly slipped off his pants and, with one quick gesture, pulled his shirt over his head.

Her breath caught. His body looked like it had been sculpted just for her. He was well-muscled and solid everywhere. She propped herself up on her elbows and looked at him longingly. "Now turn around and let me see all of you."

He smiled and slowly turned, wiggling his ass as he went.

"Now that is a nice view," she said.

He came over to the bed and lowered himself over her. He began kissing her neck again and slid his fingers over her hard left nipple, giving it a soft squeeze. She moaned and arched her back in response. He slid his mouth down to her nipple, cupping one in his hand and pulling the other into his mouth. She responded with a low grumble in her throat. If she kept making those noises, he was going to lose it. Keeping one hand on her full round breast, he moved down her flat stomach, kissing and caressing until he came to her soft mound. He went between her legs, softly kissing and licking, and ran his finger gently across her clitoris. Her sweet musky scent engulfed him. She started rocking back and forth as he slid his fingers inside her soft wetness, letting his tongue play over her until she closed her eyes and let out a throaty scream.

He slowly started working his way back up her body, stopping at her nipples to play with each of them in his mouth. "Tell me what you want," he moaned.

She arched her back and pressed her hips into him, inviting him in. "Yes, please, now," she pleaded. The urgency in her voice caused him to grow hungrier. Sensing his hesitation, she reached into the nightstand and handed him a condom.

He smiled down at her. As he slipped it on and slowly entered her, fire flashed through her veins. She gasped as a throaty moan escaped her lips and her eyes shut in ecstasy. He loved the way she looked at that moment. He felt her growing urgency beneath him. Her strong legs wrapped around him. The feel of her nails digging in his back was almost more than he could handle. She contracted around him, on the verge of explosion as his breath quickened and he erupted inside her.

CHAPTER
THIRTY-FOUR

THE MAN WAS WATCHING from the side window of Mac's home. His arousal intensified as he watched them play with each other. Mac was hot, but holy shit, he'd never imagined her body looked that good. He took a few deep breaths as he watched Hudson gather her up in his arms and cart her off to the bedroom for what he assumed would be some extremely hot sex. His imagination wandered to what it would be like when it was his turn. He thought about rounding the house to the bedroom window to watch the rest of the show but decided against it. The last thing he needed was for someone to catch him.

This is good, the man thought to himself. A sexy little love affair would be a good distraction for Mac. It would throw her off her game, hopefully. There was something about her. He knew he should just eliminate her but couldn't bring himself to do it. Plus, there was too much attention on the case. If he took her out, people would look harder at the cases, especially if authorities found all the information and case files in her home.

He sat on the wet ground feeling the cold seep through his pants as he waited for them to finish. *Maybe a suicide?* he thought. That could work. She had lost everything—her career, her reputation—and he could spin it to be even worse than that. But he still wasn't sure anyone would buy it, and certainly not the people who truly knew her.

Maybe he could leave them alone. He hadn't left any real evidence behind. Nothing that would truly point toward him. He had taken great care to shave his entire body and exfoliate to ensure he never left skin follicles or hair behind. He always wore a skull cap to cover his hair just in case. You never knew when a woman would get her hands loose and try to claw his skin or pull his hair. He would always wash them afterward if there was time. Except there hadn't always been time. He thought about those women, the ones he had possessed, but then there had been interruptions he hadn't counted on.

Abigail had been easy. She had willingly gone back to his cabin, granting him all the privacy he needed to enjoy her. Elise had been subdued easily enough, but he'd had only that nasty old hotel room to take her to. She had deserved better, but it'd had to do. He hadn't expected her. She had just appeared like a gift. When she'd walked past him on her way to her yoga class, he hadn't been able to resist. She was just too perfect. So, he rented a hotel room and enjoyed her there, but unfortunately, he couldn't take her home. Well, at least she had made a great addition to his book.

Lilianna was a fighter. He had really enjoyed her. She was feisty and defiant. Her will to survive had been more than he'd seen in a long time. He had considered taking pity on her, but in the end, he had to have her. She was resting peacefully in his garden where she belonged.

Then there was Zonira. Wow, that woman was something special and had almost convinced him that she was Sahar…but in the end, she wasn't. In his mind, they were all Sahar, until he realized they weren't.

He hadn't meant to kill her right there in base housing, but she had turned against him, and before he knew what had happened, she was lying there in a pool of blood. The force of the experience excited and scared him at the same time. He knew he had to control himself. Paranoia washed over him every time he thought about how that last one could come back to haunt him. *Was I careful enough not to leave any of myself behind?* he wondered.

His mind wandered back to the present. The two as a pair seemed to be getting too close for comfort. Hudson was a large opponent and would need to be dealt with. That one would be tricky. He was a strong presence in the community, both on and off base. People liked and respected Hudson, but he was getting tight with Mac and would possibly help her solve the case.

The man wasn't sure how to proceed, and then an idea began to form in his mind. He stood up and brushed off his pants. He had a little work to do.

CHAPTER
THIRTY-FIVE

MAC AND HUDSON ended up in a sweaty tangle of limbs, completely spent and satisfied. They lay there in each other's arms for a few minutes until their breathing returned to normal.

A phone rang. Hudson leaned over Mac's naked body to grab his phone out of his pants which were now piled up on the floor. He saw the Security Forces Chief's number on the caller ID.

"Hi Chief, what can I do for you? Yes, Chief, I'll be right in," Hudson responded in a crisp military tone.

Mac propped herself up on an elbow, listening to one side of the conversation. She knew they were both running late, but she just couldn't feel guilty about it no matter how hard she tried. She should send Chaplain Bastion a quick text to let him know she would need some extra time this morning. She liked the chaplain and didn't think he would care.

"What was that all about?" Mac asked after Hudson hung up.

"It appears I'm late and need to cover a few meetings for the commander." He grinned. "I can think of worse reasons to be running behind." He reluctantly untangled himself from her and headed for another shower. He quickly rinsed off again.

When he came back into the room, Mac was still lying there

fiddling with her phone. She felt him looking at her and started to squirm, feeling self-conscious. "What?"

Hudson blew out a low whistle. "I may never get used to you."

She smiled back at him. "Now don't start that, or we'll both lose our careers. I'm going to take a little extra time this morning to follow up on some leads. We have to get to the bottom of this so life can get back to normal."

"Fair enough. I guess that means I should get to work." He slowly put on his uniform and grabbed his keys. "Can I see you after work?"

She smiled. "Of course."

He bent down and kissed her and was gone.

Hudson was lost in thought as he climbed into his pickup truck and headed down the road. He never saw the man in the shadows watching him. He eventually pulled out onto Highway 2 and headed to the base. His truck quickly accelerated to sixty miles per hour as the large, powerful engine hummed. The speed limit was fifty-five, but Hudson figured it didn't matter if he went five over. No one ever seemed to care. His thoughts kept returning to Mac. He had never met anyone like her. She was strong, sexy, could defend herself, and didn't take shit from anyone. It was certainly a unique combination and very hard to find. She was like his own personal catnip.

On top of that, she could shoot. It was one of his favorite pastimes. He loved going out to the range to blow off steam. He couldn't wait to be near her again. Somehow over the last few weeks, she had become much more than just a woman he found attractive. She had found her way into his heart. He was becoming quite attached to her but needed to give it time, so he didn't scare her off. He knew she had all kinds of trust issues that he would have to get past. He thought about her beautiful smile and quick wit. He would do anything to keep a smile on her face.

Hudson found himself humming a tune with a smile plastered on his face when he heard a loud pop that sent his truck veering toward oncoming traffic. His heart rate accelerated as he tried to pull the steering wheel hard to the right, but that only made things worse, sending the truck careening into an uncontrollable spin. His body felt weightless as he went airborne; the huge truck flipped up on its side and rolled upside down. He smashed his head into the windshield before the airbag deployed and the truck finally settled back down on its side again.

———

The man passed the mangled truck and smiled. One less thing to worry about. Now the only threat was Mac. From the looks of the wreckage, Hudson would not be walking away. The man felt a short twinge of guilt but decided that people would just have to understand there were casualties when you were at war. It wasn't pretty; it was just the way it was. His main focus was to remain free until he could catch Sahar and stop her from killing others. No matter the cost.

CHAPTER
THIRTY-SIX

MAC TOOK another shower and looked over the evidence again. She put on her uniform and pulled her hair back into a bun. As she laced up her boots, she found herself lost in thought over the morning's events. *Wow,* that was all she could think. *This one is going to hurt when it ends.* She knew it couldn't last. Hudson was a good man. He was kind and made her feel safe, but she would have to let her guard down, and that was something she had yet to learn how to do. He had her rattled, and she really needed to go to work, check-in, and try to put together a good profile of possible suspects.

She didn't want to take advantage of Chaplain Bastion's kindness. He had been too good to her for that. Maybe, if he had time, she would sit down with him and discuss Hudson further. She really didn't know what to do about Hudson. He was the first man in a long time she liked hanging around with. He was smart, funny, and kind, and that body of his just wouldn't quit. Every inch of him was amazing, but the most impressive part of it was the sleep. She smiled at the thought. Last night was the first time she had slept through the night without waking up. Warmth filled her body at the thought of his protective arms wrapped around her. He was unbelievable, and she was terrified. Letting him in meant letting her guard down and possibly getting hurt, but she wasn't ready to walk away yet either.

She locked up her house and got into her little SUV. Nothing could ruin her mood, or so she thought. Humming to music as she drove, she worked her way through the neighborhood and then out onto Highway 2. The traffic on Highway 2 was backed up all the way to Craig Road. That was very uncommon. She rarely saw it jammed that far. She slowly pulled out in traffic, waving at the man who had let her in. Her vehicle slowly inched down the road. As she got closer, she could see emergency vehicle lights flashing ahead. "That must be a nasty wreck," she said out loud to herself. She remembered a recent accident that had backed up Highway 2 for over an hour. A motorcycle rider had collided with a large SUV. Needless to say, the rider didn't make it.

She sat back, waiting and humming along to a song on the radio. She was in the left lane so that she could drive onto the base when she got closer. There seemed to only be one vehicle involved in the wreckage. She couldn't tell what it was because the vehicle was so mangled, but her breath caught in her throat as she got closer. At first, it looked like any old pickup truck, but as she inched down the road, she could see the first sergeant diamond that adorned the back tailgate of Hudson's truck.

She couldn't breathe and found herself pulling in behind one of the cop cars. This couldn't be. She had just been with Hudson less than an hour before. The air seemed to be caught in her throat. She climbed out of her vehicle and started blindly walking toward his mangled truck.

A police officer intercepted her. "Ma'am, you can't be here. I need you to get back in your vehicle and clear the scene."

Mac didn't hear anything he said. She was pushing on the man blindly with tears running down her face. He was a young kid that looked like he had just come out of the academy. The young cop certainly wasn't prepared for this during his first week on the force. "Is he…?" Mac trailed off.

The young officer looked around for help to deal with the hysterical woman when an old GMC Jimmy pulled up behind the woman's vehicle. The young officer was grateful when he realized it was Joe Romero getting out from behind the wheel. He waved at Officer Romero and pointed down at Mac, who was still pushing on his chest.

Joe walked over and gathered Mac into his arms just as she looked up to see them hoisting Hudson onto a stretcher. They quickly loaded him inside the back of an ambulance. Her eyes grew wide in horror at the sight of the man she had just shared her bed with. His face had blood running down the side. He looked pale, but she could see his chest still moving up and down.

Mac took several deep breaths, trying to calm herself. "What happened?"

"I'm not sure," Joe admitted. "Let's follow him to the hospital and find out about his condition. Could look worse than it is."

"Um, I have to move my car," she said absently.

"I'll get one of the patrolmen to park it in a parking lot down the road. We can come back and pick it up later."

Joe tucked her into his old SUV and shut the door. He went over and handed the keys to one of the young patrolmen and asked him to take it to a safe place. He found out where the ambulance had taken Hudson and went back to his SUV. He found Mac sitting there with a blank expression on her face. The tears were no longer flowing. She had turned pale and was just staring ahead. "Are you okay?" Joe asked softly.

She nodded her head up and down. "Where did they take him?"

"He's going to Deaconess off of Fifth. If we head out now, we should get there shortly after he's admitted. Do you know any of his contact information?"

"No, um, we never really talked about that kind of stuff," Mac responded.

"I need to call his chain of command to make sure they're aware of the situation."

"And I need to let mine know where I'm going to be," she said. "The last thing I need on my shoulders is an AWOL charge. That would just top this week off beautifully."

Joe smiled sympathetically at her. "Hudson will be okay, Mac. He's a fighter. If anyone can pull through something like that, it's that huge doofus."

They fell into an uncomfortable silence for the rest of the ride to the hospital. Joe showed his credentials when they arrived and asked to be updated as soon as they knew something. Mac and Joe sat in the waiting room. She paced back and forth, unable to sit still.

"Do you want me to get you some coffee?" Joe asked.

"Sure, thanks," Mac said absently.

Shortly after Joe walked out of the room, a doctor came out from behind the swinging doors that led to the back of the hospital. He was a short, stocky man with large bags under his eyes. His balding head made him look older than she imagined he was. He had a grim look on his face that made Mac's heart stop. She tried to calm herself.

"Doctor, do you know the status of Gavin Hudson?" Mac asked and held her breath.

The doctor exhaled. "Yes, are you his next of kin?"

"No," Mac said honestly. "I'm a...friend. Joe Romero, the officer who's investigating Mr. Hudson's case, should be right back."

"Well then, I'm Doctor Peter Wilkinson. I'll be taking care of Mr. Hudson."

"Can you at least tell me if he's going to be, okay?" she asked with a desperate edge to her voice.

"He is..." The doctor trailed off as Joe walked up and handed her a coffee.

"Joe, this is Doctor Wilkinson. We were waiting for you so he could tell us how Hudson is."

"Nice to meet you," Joe said.

Mac looked at the two men impatiently. She cleared her throat. "Hudson's status?" she blurted.

"Yes, overall, he's going to be fine. However, he has a few broken ribs, a concussion, a dislocated shoulder, and a lot of soft tissue damage. It's going to take him a while to get back on his feet. He took one hell of an impact blow, but his airbag saved his head for the most part. We still don't know if there will be any lasting effects. Only time will tell. Preliminarily, it appears he'll make a full recovery. He's going to need a lot of care while he recuperates. Does he have any family in the area that we should call?"

"His mother, though she's not local," Joe offered. "I can give her a call and let her know what happened."

"Thank you, Officer Romero," Dr. Wilkinson responded. The doctor stood there for a few seconds looking at the two of them. "I have to ask…if this was a basic traffic accident, then why are you here?"

Joe had anticipated the question. "I'm friends with Mr. Hudson. I have reason to believe there may have been foul play."

"I see."

"We'll look at the truck as soon as we get it back to the police impound. Could you notify me if there's any change in Mr. Hudson's status?" Joe asked. He handed Dr. Wilkinson a business card.

"Certainly."

"Can we go see him?" Mac asked.

"Sure, but he needs his rest and is heavily sedated, so he may not even know you're here," Dr. Wilkinson replied.

They quietly walked into Hudson's room. The machines attached to his body monitoring his breathing and heart rate looked terrifying. There was an IV attached to his arm in the oversized bed they had him in. There were thick white bandages around his head and rib cage, and bruises and cuts everywhere, but at least he was breathing. Mac took comfort in watching his chest rise and fall. She sat down in the seat next to his bed and held his hand.

Joe quietly cleared his throat. "Mac, I'm going to go look at his truck. I get the feeling that this wasn't an accident. Hudson took good care of that truck. He's one hell of a mechanic and never lets things go. I can't imagine he would've missed something bad enough to cause his truck to malfunction like that."

Mac nodded. "I'll stay here with him. Let me know if you find anything. And Joe…thank you."

"What for?"

"For taking care of me, getting me here, watching out for Hudson. You're a good friend, Joe."

"You guys would do the same for me," he said and walked away.

CHAPTER
THIRTY-SEVEN

MAC PACED for a while and then finally sat in the uncomfortable seat in the corner of the room. She wasn't exactly sure what to do. There was very little she could do for Hudson except try and be there if he woke up. She settled in and started looking at her phone. After waiting for a while, she began to doze off, only to have her nap disturbed by a high-pitched beep. At first, she thought it was one of the machines hooked up to Hudson, but then she listened carefully and realized it was coming from her bag.

She reached down to root around in the bottom; it was like a bottomless pit in there. She really needed to clean the thing out. Eventually, she found the source of the annoying noise and quickly silenced the phone. It was her encrypted device that she used to communicate with her sister.

Lola had texted her: *I may have him. Call me.*

She quietly got up, not wanting to disturb Hudson, and walked out the door and down the hall. After some navigating through the maze of hallways, she found an exit out into a lush green courtyard. It was quite beautiful, with a small table and chairs in the center of towering evergreens and some skeletal-looking dogwoods. She couldn't wait until everything was in bloom again. Washington was such a beautiful place when everything came alive in the spring. As much as she hated the winters here, she absolutely loved the spring and summer. It was still cold outside, but the sun managed to peek through the clouds.

Lola answered on the first ring. "Hey Sis, how's it going?"

Mac made an unladylike sound.

"That bad, huh?"

"Yeah, pretty bad, actually. Hudson—that guy I've been working with and, well, kinda seeing—he was in a car accident this morning shortly after he left my house."

"Wow, that's not good. How is he?" Lola asked with concern.

"He'll survive, but he's going to be a little beat up for a while," Mac said. "So, what do you have for me, Lola?"

"I'm glad to see nothing ever changes. You're all business."

"You know I didn't mean it that way. I just have a sinking suspicion that Hudson's truck was sabotaged, and it wasn't just a mechanical malfunction. Joe, the cop I've been working with, said that Hudson is meticulous about maintaining his truck. Do you think I'm being paranoid?"

"Not really, it looks like someone *has* been watching you. I caught a figure outside your house this morning via your neighbor's security camera. I couldn't get a clear view of him through the trees, but there was definitely someone there."

Mac's heart dropped. "Do you know what time exactly?"

"It looks like he showed up at about oh-seven-hundred hours and left sometime around oh-eight-twenty hours. As far as I can tell, he followed your boyfriend's truck out onto Highway 2. I couldn't see them after they left your place. I'm still searching for another video from traffic cameras or storefront security along the highway."

"Okay, okay, that could be our guy." The first thing that slipped into Mac's mind was what they had been doing during that time. That time window meant whoever had been watching the house had gotten quite a view. She felt self-conscious but would have to deal with that later. Right now, she had a murderer to catch. "Did you get any pictures for me?"

"You insult my skills, dear sister. Of course, I have pictures, but I'm afraid they're not very clear. I'm still looking at surveillance from some of the other locations we know he's been. For now, I just have the pictures from your place. It might give you an idea of who he is, but I'm not sure. It's certainly not clear enough to run through facial recognition software."

"You're the best. Thank you. How are you holding up out there?"

"Oh, you know, same same, though I have been hearing some rumblings about the family. I'll fill you in when this is all over with. Watch your back. This guy you're after seems like a nasty character. I know you can handle yourself, but don't let your guard down."

"Um, I gotta go," Mac said abruptly as she watched the SFS chief walk toward her.

"Are you okay?" Lola asked.

"Yeah, I just gotta go. Call me when you find something more. Thanks, Sis, I owe you one. Take care." Mac hung up before Lola could say anything more.

Mac slipped her phone into the inside of her jacket so Chief wouldn't see it. No one knew about Lola, and she wasn't about to share that information with anyone. Not even Chief. She took a deep breath and then walked back into the hospital, plastering a smile on her face that reached nowhere near her eyes.

"Mac, I've been looking all over the place for you!" Chief said. "The nurse said you were here with Hudson. I didn't realize you guys were close. I'm sorry this happened. Do you know what malfunctioned on his truck?"

"No idea, but the accident was horrible, and I'm pretty sure the truck was totaled," Mac said, relieved that Chief didn't inquire about her relationship with Hudson any further.

"Has anyone notified his family?"

"As far as I know, Officer Romero called his mother, but I'm not one-hundred-percent sure."

"I see. Well, thank you for being here for Hudson. How did you find out about the accident so quickly?"

What is this, the Spanish Inquisition? Mac wondered. She cleared her throat. "I passed the wreckage on my way to work this morning and recognized his truck. I just wanted to make sure he was okay."

"Smart thinking. We have to make sure we take care of our own,"

Chief said. "Now, let's go back up the stairs to see how he's doing. The commander is up there waiting."

They started walking back through the maze of sterile, cold hallways to Hudson's room. During their walk, Mac filled Chief in on what she knew of Hudson's condition.

"Wow, that's unfortunate," he said. "It'll be a long healing process for him, but we're very pleased he'll be okay. How long did the doctor say he'll be out of commission?"

"Not sure," Mac responded. "Only time will tell."

They walked back into Hudson's room and her heart sank at the sight of him all over again. She just couldn't wrap her mind around how one minute he was in her arms, and the next he was in a hospital bed with a bunch of machines hooked up to his body.

The commander walked up to her and shook her hand, thanked her for being there, then excused himself to talk to the doctor. An awkward silence fell across the room as they looked at Hudson lying there unconscious.

"Well, there's nothing more we can do here," Chief said. "Make sure you keep checking in so my people have accountability for you."

"Yes sir, I know. I already let Chaplain Bastion know where I am and why."

"Good to hear, Mac. I know this will turn out okay for you. Just keep your head down and wait for the storm to pass. I'm here for you if you need anything."

"Okay, Chief, thank you," she said, trying to smile. She was thankful for Chief's support but was starting to feel less sure that everything would work out. Things were getting out of hand.

Chief seemed satisfied and headed for the door. She liked and respected Chief, but she was relieved to see him go. She needed some quiet time to focus and get to the bottom of this.

The clock on the wall ticked audibly as she waited to ensure she was alone, and they wouldn't be coming back any time soon. Once she felt secure, she pulled her laptop from her backpack and opened her email. Inside she found a message from one of Lola's many Gmail accounts. That girl had more aliases than anyone she'd ever met. If

Lola ever decided she wanted to disappear, Mac knew she would likely never find her again.

That worried her. She hoped Lola was doing okay and not just putting on a front. She missed her other siblings as well, but they weren't as close. The difference was, they had picked their side, and unfortunately, they had sided with their mother. She wondered if her father was still out there somewhere. She sure hoped so.

The internet connection at the hospital was slow, and it seemed to take forever for the email to load and the PDF file her sister had attached to open. It said nothing; it just had pictures attached. This didn't surprise Mac. Her sister was cautious about what she said across the open internet. If anyone ever found her, it would not be good.

The photos finally loaded on her computer. Lola was right. The photos were grainy. She couldn't make out many details about the man who had clearly been watching her home. As far as she could tell, he was a taller man with what looked like a muscular build. He appeared to be doing something to the passenger tire of Hudson's truck. She wondered if that was what had caused him to crash.

She brought up the second picture and maximized it on her screen. It was a shot of Hudson's truck leaving her driveway and heading down the road. In the background, she could see the side of the stalker's head but couldn't make out any details. She flipped to the next photo to find the man walking away from her house. Mac assumed he was headed to his own vehicle somewhere outside of the camera's view. There was something familiar about the way he stood in the picture, but she just couldn't put her finger on it.

CHAPTER
THIRTY-EIGHT

AGENT ROSS and Agent Green were sitting in the OSI office going over files late Thursday afternoon. Things were not going well. Viv could smell a mixture of burnt coffee and male testosterone in the air. She was one of the few women in OSI. Most of her coworkers were alpha males with something to prove. It had taken her a while to prove herself, but she was finally at a place where her coworkers and boss respected her abilities. It hadn't been easy. She'd always felt she had to be twice the agent of her male counterparts, but overall, she enjoyed her work. She felt it was challenging and rewarding in many ways.

This week felt different. They had been told to leave the Mac and Johnson cases alone without explanation. That didn't settle well with her. If nothing else, she was determined and diligent to a fault. She was used to being able to see a case from start to finish. It didn't make any sense that they weren't allowed to investigate those cases. They had handed off cases to other agencies before, like the FBI, but they had never given up cases that were clearly in their jurisdiction.

"What do you make of all this?" Viv asked Green.

She liked Green. He had always treated her well. It didn't seem to matter to him that she was a woman. He never treated her any different. Of course, you never knew what people were really thinking, but he had never shown her anything less than respect.

"Oh no you don't. We have our orders," Green replied.

Green wasn't a risk-taker; he was a by-the-book kind of guy. He liked the rules, which was why he liked the military. There were Air Force instructions that told him how things were supposed to be done. As long as he followed his guidance and did as he was told, things seemed to work out okay. Internally, he acknowledged that he liked to color inside the lines, and he was a little strait-laced—okay, maybe more than just a little.

He looked over at Viv. She was amazing. Not only was she a risk-taker and confident in her decisions, unlike him, but she was absolutely beautiful. Her no-nonsense personality and the fact that she never took shit from anyone really turned Green on. He knew it wasn't a good idea to try and date a coworker. He could hear his dad's words in his head: *"Never get your honey where you make your money."*

Green smiled at the memory, but his father had never warned him about a woman like Agent Vivian Ross. Even the way she moved was exotic to him, and he couldn't stop thinking of her day and night. She knew nothing of his feelings. He couldn't handle that kind of rejection, certainly not from her. He would rather just fantasize about what it would be like to be with her. To worship her. To make her his. It was safer that way, and for now, that worked for him.

He wore a goofy grin plastered across his face until he realized Viv was standing next to him. He inhaled, trying to focus.

"Excuse me, Green, but I think the orders are bullshit. What the hell is this? Do they think we're incompetent, or just stupid? Where do they get off taking our case away from us like that?"

Green watched her pace around the small space like a caged cheetah. "I just want some answers," she continued. "We're here to make sure that the right people are prosecuted and that the right evidence is put in front of the members in a court-martial, and now we're being told to *stand down*?"

"I get your frustration," Green said, "but there's nothing we can do about it. We could both lose our careers."

Green was right. She could lose her career. *But what 's a career worth if it's packed full of lies and people going to prison for crimes they didn't commit?* As far as she could see, they had circumstantial evidence against both Johnson and Mac at best. Everything they had at this point could be explained away. She hoped a good defense attorney would poke enough holes in the cases to make them go away with an acquittal, but she knew there were no guarantees, especially if they didn't have conflicting evidence to prove their client's innocence.

She studied Green, who sat at the other end of the little office space they shared. She tucked a strand of blond hair behind her ear. He was a good agent, but he wasn't about to put his neck out on the line to help her. If the evidence was there, then fine, but her gut told her something was wrong with this picture, and she wasn't about to sit around waiting for somebody to pull their head out of their ass. It just wasn't in her personality. Her mind was made up.

Viv knew Green had feelings for her. It was obvious in the way he stared at her with that goofy look on his face. She thought it was sweet but was far from interested in him. He just wasn't her type. "You're right, Green. I'm going to investigate the other drug case that was assigned to me. Apparently there's a possible drug ring out in the Aircraft Maintenance Squadron."

"That is a great idea. Do you want some company?" he asked hopefully.

"No, I'm good. I'm just going to head out there and look into a few things. I'll be back shortly."

Green looked disappointed as she grabbed her keys to walk out. "Be careful," he called after her as the door shut behind her.

CHAPTER
THIRTY-NINE

THE MAINTENANCE SQUADRON was on the other side of the base. She hadn't lied to Green, but she fully intended to determine whether maintenance knew about Mac's involvement. They were one of the busiest squadrons as far as troops getting into trouble for one thing or another. They were all very familiar with Mac and her ability to get charges reduced or dropped by finding holes in the government's evidence. Her clients loved her, and the leadership and prosecution respected her even though they weren't thrilled that she kept poking holes in their cases. One of Mac's clients had reportedly said she was involved in the drug ring—Viv was going to talk to that person to find out what was going on.

She walked into the maintenance building and started looking for their first sergeant. She figured it would be best to notify him before interrogating one of his troops. She found Master Sergeant Lee Crawford sitting behind an old beat-up desk. Viv always thought he resembled a large dildo with big ears. He had a large, round head that was smooth as a baby's butt. His blond eyebrows and pasty white complexion gave no variation to his features.

He'd always been a bit of an ass, and to say she wasn't a fan of his would be an understatement. His office was decorated with awards, certificates, and degrees. He had a bit of a narcissistic side. There wasn't much of a family presence in the office, but that was fairly common in the military. The divorce rate was extremely high in the military and especially in maintenance. Maintainers worked days, nights, mids, weekends, and deployed, often taking them away from home. That could wear down even the strongest of relationships, and it sometimes opened the door to infidelity which led to divorce.

"Good afternoon, Sergeant Crawford. How are you doing today?" Viv asked. Crawford didn't acknowledge her at first; he simply kept plugging away at his computer. She waited patiently.

Without looking up, he finally said, "What brings you here today, Agent Ross?"

"I'd like to talk with Senior Airman Alex Pratt. He's part of an investigation that I'm conducting. I wanted to let you know that I'm here to follow up on a statement he made so I can verify some facts and circumstances."

"Fine," he said. He clicked away at his computer a few more times. "Senior Airman Pratt is part of Alpha Flight. You can find him in Bay Two."

"Thank you, Shirt," Viv said, and headed out to the hangars. She had been there many times, investigating a variety of cases. Military people often found themselves in a lifestyle where they worked hard and played hard. Not necessarily a bad thing, but sometimes they played a little too hard and ended up in trouble, which was precisely why she had a job.

As soon as Agent Ross exited Crawford's office he stood up, looked out to make sure no one was in the hall, and closed his door. Then he picked up the phone and dialed a number from memory. He didn't want to call from his cell phone and leave a record.

"Hey, it's Crawford. Agent Ross just left my office. She's questioning Pratt. You said you wanted to know if anyone was poking around. She said she wanted to verify some details about his statement."

"Did you give her any information?" the man at the other end of the line asked.

"No, sir, I just sent her over to talk with Pratt. Nothing more."

"Good work. Thank you for keeping me informed."

The man hung up before Crawford could say anything else.

CHAPTER
FORTY

THE HIGH-CEILINGED hangar sprawled out in front of her, smelling of dust, JP8, fuels, and other chemicals. At the perimeter of the large open space that led out to the flight line were the offices. The office space wasn't in much better shape. The furniture was old and worn out but comfortable. They had a place for the maintainers to hang out on breaks.

Viv walked into the flight chief's office. "Hi sir, I'm Agent Ross from OSI. I'd like to see Senior Airman Alex Pratt. Is he available?"

She had never met the man who sat behind his desk. His wide frame and full, round face didn't depict the fitness standards of the military. She absently wondered how he got away with it. With his rotund gut, it was unlikely he could pass his PT test. His pants bunched up underneath his gut and his uniform shirt was draped on the back of his chair, so she couldn't see his nametag. The brown t-shirt that stretched across his belly was stained and dingy and looked like he hadn't changed out of it all week.

"Hello, 'Agent Ross from the OSI.' What do you want with my guy?" he asked in a gravelly voice.

"He made a statement. I'm here to verify the details."

"Well, he's in the tool shed and won't be done for another twenty minutes or so. You want me to let him know you stopped by?" He smiled in a failed attempt at friendliness.

"No, I'll wait. Thank you."

The flight chief rose and strode up to her. The pungent smell of body odor and grease rolled off his skin and assaulted her nostrils. She tried her best not to recoil from the smell. She took a few steps back, not wanting him to get too close. "Suit yourself," he said, looking her up and down. "You can wait out there until he comes back. You get fifteen minutes with him before he has to have tools ready for the next launch."

"Thank you," Viv responded.

She could have reminded him that he had no right to impede her investigation but decided to play nice for now. Her desire to get away from him outweighed her need to school him on the rules. Most people underestimated her because she could easily pass for a Sunday school teacher with attitude. No one ever guessed she was an OSI agent.

Agents rarely wore their uniforms. There were several reasons for that, but mostly they didn't want their rank and information known when interrogating someone who outranked them. It could undermine their investigation by improperly influencing a situation. Viv used this to her advantage and dressed professionally, which made her come across as intimidating. She'd been told that she was a little scary.

She settled into the worn-out seat in the break area and pulled out her government laptop to check emails while she waited. Only ten minutes passed when a gaggle of young airmen came storming through the door that led to the flight line. They were all joking and talking loudly. She stood to get their attention. Instead, they kept horsing around, not noticing her until she cleared her throat.

They all looked in her direction expectantly. She clearly didn't belong in their world with her hair pulled back in a perfect bun and her clean face and hands. They were all covered in grease, dirt, and sweat. They reminded her of little boys that had just come in from playing in the mud.

One of the young airmen stepped forward. "What can we do for you, ma'am?"

None of the young men had their outer uniform shirts on, so she couldn't tell which one was Pratt. "I'm looking for Senior Airman Pratt," she replied curtly.

"Oh, um…" The young airman looked down at his feet. "That's me, um… What can I do for you?"

"I just need to ask you a few questions."

His pack of buddies quickly moved away. They didn't want anything to do with her. Viv thought the kid couldn't be any older than eighteen. His short curly hair was in a military cut. His hands and part of his face had grease on them, typical for his career field. His job was technically crew chief, which loosely translated into "aircraft mechanic."

"Is there a quiet place where we can go to talk?" Viv asked him.

"Of course, ma'am, follow me," Pratt responded. He led her down a hall and into a cramped conference room with an oversized table. The chairs were old and frayed in multiple spots, but it would do the trick. She took a seat opposite Pratt, who was looking around the room like he needed an escape route.

Viv smiled at the young man, trying to make him feel at ease. "Alex, I'm Agent Vivian Ross with the OSI, and I'm not here specifically to investigate your case, but I do want to discuss the statement you wrote. Would you be okay with that?"

"Um, I guess so."

"I do have to advise you of your Article 31 rights. These rights were read to you when you made the original statement. You signed here showing that you understood those rights." Viv showed him the statement with his name and signature in the block acknowledging as much. "Do you still understand these rights as they've been explained to you?"

"Yes, ma'am," Pratt responded.

"Would you still like to talk with me today without your attorney present?" Viv asked for clarification; she was strict about following the rules when it came to airmen's rights. She had seen sloppy work get cases dismissed. As far as she was concerned, her mission today was to get to the bottom of both the alleged drug ring in maintenance and the charges against Mac. A "kill two birds with one stone" kind of thing.

"Yeah, I'll talk."

"Could you explain to me in your own words what you wrote in this statement and why?" Viv asked, specifically being vague. It always floored her how much people would give up on their own. She often asked suspects, "Do you know why we've brought you in today?" and they would confess to all kinds of things that OSI had no idea about. Most people knew they had the right to remain silent but lacked the willpower to do so. Pratt was one such case. He had already confessed to being involved with drugs, and he had a positive urinalysis.

"Um, you guys already know everything," Pratt stuttered.

"I know you told the other agents everything you know, but I was hoping you could tell me as well."

Pratt cleared his throat and shifted nervously in his seat. "Well, ma'am, like I told the other fella...we were at a party, and well, there was a beautiful girl there. She was amazing." The young man looked all starry-eyed. "Anyway, my buddies and I were there, and well, this girl had some weed and cocaine." He squirmed in his seat a little more. "Um, well, she offered me some, and I told her no at first, but then we got to drinking, and she said she would let me lick the cocaine off her nipples, and well, ma'am..." His face turned a deep shade of red. "Um, well, she was really hot and all, so I agreed." Pratt exhaled heavily.

"I understand how something like that could go further than you would want it to," Viv sympathized. Pratt exhaled, physically relaxing. "Do you know the name of the investigator who took your statement? Unfortunately, I'm not able to make out the signature here..."

"Um, no, ma'am, there was no investigator. It was my chief and, well, another guy that was there. Not sure about him, but he sure was scary."

"I see," Viv said. Why the hell was the chief questioning witnesses in a drug case that OSI clearly had jurisdiction of? And who the hell was this other guy? At least they had done it properly and filled out all the right forms.

"Was Technical Sergeant Evelyn McGregor there with you?" Viv asked, changing subjects.

"Um, I'm not supposed to talk about that," Pratt said nervously, looking around like the walls might have ears.

"It's okay," Viv said. "You already put in your statement that she was involved in the drug ring. Can you tell me how she was involved? Did she supply you and your friends with the drugs?"

Pratt looked around and squirmed in his seat. She could tell he really wanted to talk, but he was scared. "Um, t-they said I would get in big t-trouble if I told anyone."

"*Who* said you would get in big trouble?"

"My chief," he blurted out, and then dropped his head. "You weren't supposed to know that."

"Know what?" Viv asked in a softer voice.

"You weren't supposed to know that my chief told me to, um...to implicate Mac in the drug ring."

Pratt looked relieved to get the information out. It was one thing to get yourself into trouble—but to negatively and wrongfully affect another person's life? Well, that took a certain kind of ugly person, and Pratt wasn't one of them.

"The worst part was hurting Mac. She was always so nice to me and trying to help me out of this mess, or at least soften the blow. I know I have to face the music, but she was one of the only people who kept being nice to me," he said softly. "They took me off the flight line and made me sit in tools and then be the snack ho on most days."

He dropped his head so that his forehead hit the table in front of him. Then, in a low voice, he said, "Do I have to go to jail now for lying and all?"

Viv gave him a smile that he didn't see. "It doesn't work that way, Pratt. You may have to go to court for the drug charges against you, and you may end up getting some jail time for using. Honestly, your biggest concern will be a federal conviction. It would be a really good idea for you to go see an area defense counsel." She was very big about making sure airmen knew their rights and knew they could seek military counsel.

"Yeah, that's actually how I know Mac. She's my defense person, um...paralegal, I think."

"Thank you for your honesty, Pratt. You've been very helpful today," Viv said. "If this thing gets out of hand and they actually want to prosecute Mac, then will you testify on her behalf?"

"Um, I guess so. Will I be in more trouble for lying?"

"I'll recommend against it since your leadership pressured you to do so," Viv responded. Normally they told suspects that if they talked, they would try to work a deal for them. OSI didn't have that power, but they were authorized to lie about things like that to get a confession. In this case, she thought Pratt could use the truth to his advantage. He was in enough trouble as it was. Unfortunately, the young man was still likely to be court-martialed in a special court.

Viv looked at Pratt and wondered what else he would be willing to tell her. "Pratt, do you know why they told you to lie about Mac's involvement?"

"Um, no, ma'am. They just told me that if I made the statement and said what they wanted me to say, then they would help me out."

"Did they elaborate on what that meant?"

"No, ma'am, but honestly, I was scared half to death. My chief can be intimidating, and they played good cop, bad cop. My chief was the bad cop, and the other guy was the good cop but was still intimidating."

"Tell me about this other guy," Viv asked.

"He was definitely military. Actually, I kinda thought he was with *your* office because he was in civilian clothes but reeked of military."

Viv smiled. "What do you mean, 'he reeked of military?'"

"You know...military bearing, haircut, the works. And he was older. This was definitely not his first time questioning someone. It felt like he had done it before," Pratt said with wide eyes. "Honestly, I needed all the help I could get. I mean, they said they would make sure they threw me in jail and tossed away the key if I didn't do what they told me to."

"Thank you for your honesty," Viv said. "Is there anything else you want to tell me?"

"No, ma'am, just tell Mac I'm really sorry. I never meant to get her into this. It's just that I wasn't sure what to do."

"I know. I'm sorry you found yourself in this situation. I hope it works out for you." Viv stood, indicating that their meeting was over.

CHAPTER
FORTY-ONE

VIV DROVE AWAY from the maintenance squadron. The cold air outside had left her windshield covered in crystals, and she could feel the back end of her car slide a little as she drove. She wasn't sure what to think but knew her next stop had to be Mac. She needed to figure out exactly what was going on and who was trying to set her up. Viv didn't always see eye to eye with Mac, but she liked and respected her. Above all, Viv believed their core values aligned and that everyone should get a fair shake. Her black-and-white mentality didn't allow for any other approach. If someone broke the law, they should be punished. It was that clear and simple. But no one should be punished if they were just doing their job. She got the feeling that there was much more to this than she knew.

She headed to the chapel to find Mac. She walked into the building and ran directly into Chaplain Bastion.

He smiled warmly at her. "Well, hello, Agent Ross. What can I do for you today?"

The chaplain was familiar with her because many of the accused were housed at the chapel while they waited for their investigation to go through. Most of them just helped with services and other activities that the chapel put on. Many of the accused worked in areas of the base that they were not allowed to be in while under investigation.

Often their security clearance was revoked or suspended, and their flight line badge was pulled until the matter was resolved.

When it came to issues of safety and security, the military didn't mess around. They didn't want someone suspected of drug use or anger management problems to be carrying a gun or working on a multimillion-dollar aircraft, so most of them were housed at the chapel. It was a bit of a safe haven for members who had lost their way or made bad decisions.

"Hello Chaplain Bastion, it's good to see you again," Viv responded with a smile. She had always liked the chaplain. He was kind to her and always made time for her when she needed to talk. She wondered if he had ever been angry. She doubted it and couldn't picture it in her head. "I'm here to see Mac. Is she around?"

Deep lines of concern crossed the chaplain's face. "She's at the hospital, I'm afraid."

Viv's eyes widened. "Is she okay? What happened?"

"No, she's fine. It was the security forces shirt. Um, what's his name?" Chaplain Bastion scrunched up his forehead, trying to remember.

"Gavin Hudson?"

"Oh yes, that's him. He's a big man, so I hope that helped."

"Helped with...what?" Viv asked, growing impatient.

"Helped with the impact from the accident."

"Hudson was in a car accident?"

"Well, yes, that is what I've been telling you!"

Viv took in a deep breath and then exhaled, striving for patience. "Thank you, sir," she said, turning on her heels to leave.

The information she had at the moment didn't make much sense. She sat in her warm car and dialed Mac's number. Maybe Mac would have more information so they could figure this thing out. She waited while the phone rang.

Mac finally answered in a low whisper. "Hello."

"Hi Mac, this is Agent Ross. How are you doing?" Viv spoke more formally than she wanted to. She'd hung out with Mac a few times, and there was one time, in particular, she couldn't entirely recall. She knew it had been wild, and she had done a seductive table dance at one point. She owed Mac a solid because a man had gotten aggressive and tried to manhandle her out of the bar. Mac had stepped in and taken the guy down. Viv later heard it had been quite a sight to see; the guy was over twice Mac's size and she'd dropped him like a sack of potatoes.

Unfortunately, Viv didn't remember a thing, but she sure did appreciate Mac taking care of her. She would have paid to see her kick the bastard's ass. To Mac's credit, she'd never said anything about that night. She could have thrown it in Viv's face or used the information as leverage on several occasions, but instead, she'd remained discreet, and Viv felt she owed her for that.

"Hi Viv, how have you been?" Mac responded with a smile in her voice.

Viv sighed in relief. With all that was going on, she really didn't know how Mac would feel about her. "Hey Mac, how are you holding up?"

"Um, okay, I guess. It's been a rough couple of weeks, but I've survived worse."

Viv knew that Mac had had a tough childhood but didn't know any of the details. "I'm sorry to hear that. How is Hudson doing?"

"Hudson is doing okay. He's unconscious at the moment and pretty beaten up, but the doc says he'll live. So, pretty good, I guess."

"That's good to hear. I know you have a lot going on right now, but do you think we could meet up? I have information for you that can't wait and shouldn't be given over the phone," Viv said in a secretive tone.

"Sure, we can meet. When and where?"

Viv liked Mac's no-nonsense way of thinking. She was also one of the more intelligent women she had come across, which was nice. "Up to you, Mac. I'm at your disposal."

"How about my place in an hour?"

"Sure, I'll be there."

CHAPTER
FORTY-TWO

MAC HUNG up and stared at Hudson, still not sure she wanted to leave him. She took a notebook out of her bag, tore off a page, and wrote a note telling him she had been there and that she would be back shortly just in case he woke up. She picked up her phone again and sent Joe a status update on Hudson. She also asked if he had any new updates on the case.

After a few short minutes, he texted back: *Nothing new. Keep me posted.*

Their problems weren't going to solve themselves, no matter how badly she wanted to stay by Hudson's side. As she walked out of the hospital and an ice-cold wind hit her in the face, she realized she had left her car somewhere on Highway 2. She stepped back into the hospital, called an Uber, and waited impatiently for her driver to show up. While she waited, she texted Joe for the exact location of her SUV.

A small sedan finally arrived, and she climbed in the back. The driver was a twig of a man with wire-rim glasses and a potato nose. He turned around and smiled at her with crooked teeth. "Where to?" he asked in a higher-pitched voice than she'd expected.

Joe's texted her back right away and she was able to give him an exact location. Without another word, he took off down the road. Classical music was coming from the car radio, which helped to soothe her nerves. Her little SUV was sitting there where the patrolman had left it. He had locked her keys inside the vehicle, so she was thankful she had a spare with her. She had a terrible habit of losing her keys and always carried an extra one just in case. She thanked the driver and got out into the freezing wind. The door to her SUV creaked as she opened it. She quickly started the engine and sat while the windshield began to defrost.

The winters here were beautiful, but she hated freezing to death all the time. As she sat in the car waiting, she had the weird feeling that someone was watching her. It was that odd little sensation where the hairs on the back of her neck stood up. She had only ignored that feeling one time—and paid a price for doing so. She was thankful it didn't take too long for the vehicle to come to life and get warm inside. She pulled out of the parking lot, looking around but seeing nobody.

As she rounded the corner and her home came into view, her heart skipped a beat as conflicting memories scattered through her brain. She remembered the feeling of fear when she had shown up to her ransacked house. Anger and the feeling of being violated seeped through her. It all came rushing back to her. Just as quickly, her mind shifted to the morning she had shared with Hudson. She felt her cheeks flush as she thought about the heat and passion, his strong, muscular body pressed up against hers. She shook her head to try and clear her thoughts and was relieved to see Viv waiting for her in the driveway. She felt safer with her there and welcomed the distraction.

She got out of her car and the two women embraced. "You look great after the week of hell you've been through," Viv commented.

"Thanks, you look stunning as always," Mac responded kindly.

As they walked into the living room, a listening device placed in the lamp kicked on. He was recording everything they said. He had known it would only be a matter of time before these two met up.

As they walked into her house, Viv stopped in her tracks. "What the hell happened here?"

"Oh, this isn't the half of it. It used to be a lot worse, but we were able to clean things up quite a bit," Mac said as she walked from room to room, checking each corner and opening every closet. She hated feeling this paranoid.

"What happened?" Viv asked again.

"I came home, and my place was trashed. Someone had gone through every room and tossed the place. It doesn't appear that anything was stolen, just that they were trying to send a message."

"I see. Well, that's what I'm actually here to discuss with you. There are some things you should know that isn't sitting right with me. You have to promise that this stays off the record, Mac. I could get into a lot of trouble by talking to you."

"I completely understand, Viv. I appreciate you coming to me with the information. I'll make a deal with you: I'll show you what I have, and you show me your evidence, and between the two of us maybe we can figure this out. I would get in just as much shit for discussing case information as you would..." Mac trailed off. "Oh yeah, I'm already knee-deep in a shit pile." Anger flashed across her eyes. She hated that she was being stalked and that her hard-earned career and integrity were in question. Really, that was all she had—a world where she felt safe and respected. She hated being associated with drugs of all things. It really chapped her ass!

"Sounds fair enough," Viv said. "So, I know you're being targeted. I just spoke with a witness who said he was threatened. They told him that if he didn't implicate you in the same drug ring, he was involved with then they would throw him in jail."

"Okay, that explains why I'm being charged," Mac said.

"His statement said that you were the supplier," Viv went on. "They have pictures of you with Jose Valdez. It shows you accepting a small package of something from him."

"Okay. I can see where this is going. That's circumstantial evidence, but it doesn't paint me in a good light."

"Can you explain what you were doing with the most notorious drug dealer in Spokane?" Viv asked pointedly.

"Yes, two things actually, but it needs to stay between us," Mac said.

"Okay."

"I was seeing Jose about a case concerning one of my clients, who just happened to be Senior Airman Pratt. Jose had been trying to break into dealing on base for a while. He figured the airmen on base had money and would be excellent customers. So, he needed a way in. He hired a pretty young woman who was already hooked on drugs. He sent her to Pratt's party with enough cocaine to show everyone a good time. In exchange, she was taken care of."

"Pratt described this woman," Viv said. "I guess she was very pretty and hard to resist. She convinced the airman to lick cocaine off her nipples. I'm not sure what drunk airman would say no to that but, airman or not, we're talking about young men that are still growing up. Most of them are between the age of eighteen to twenty-three. I know I didn't make the best decisions at that age either. I partied a lot and had a ton of fun. Thankfully, I didn't get caught; otherwise, I wouldn't be OSI today." A little mischievous grin curled the sides of her lips.

The man was listening intently. The ladies hadn't discussed anything that he wasn't already aware of, but he was afraid of what they would figure out when they put their heads together. So, he had been recording everything that went on in both of their homes. He hadn't gotten a whole lot from Viv because he'd been her only visitor recently. Apparently, he needed to figure out a way to track her when she wasn't at home. He had been notified immediately of her little visit with Senior Airman Pratt. He was interested to see what she made of that interview. The reason he survived this long during his hunt for Sahar was by not underestimating people.

"Okay, so you said they bullied Pratt into implicating me. Who exactly are they?" Mac asked.

Viv lowered her head, still struggling to believe what she had heard. "So apparently it was the maintenance chief and another guy. Pratt thought this other guy was from my office, but we don't have anyone that fits his description." Viv paused to let the information sink in.

"You can't be serious," Mac responded. "That can't be right. I've known the maintenance chief for a while… And who the hell is this other player? I can't imagine a chief was involved. Are you sure Pratt isn't just trying to cover up whatever he was involved in?"

"I don't think so. As hard as this is to believe, the young man wasn't lying. I'm a very good lie detector, and he's either extremely good at deception or he wasn't lying. I just don't know the motive behind it all. What would the chief have to gain from this?"

"I'm not sure, but something crazy is going on, and I'm on someone's list. So far, I've been implicated in a drug-trafficking operation, my place was tossed, and Hudson's truck was sabotaged. Actually, we don't have proof of that yet, but I have some pictures you should look at."

Mac went into her office to retrieve printed pictures of everything she had. She showed Viv pictures of the truck at some of the places where the women had disappeared and the grainy pictures that Lola had sent her.

Viv studied each picture carefully. Her eyes widened in recognition when she saw the picture of the man prowling outside of Mac's house. She would know that man's build anywhere. She'd touched that man, made love to that man, and had a relationship with him. She realized Mac was staring at her and quickly recovered.

"You saw something," Mac said, already knowing the answer.

"Um, no. I thought I recognized the man in the photo, but I was mistaken," Viv said a little too quickly. "Look, Mac, I've got to go. They're going to wonder where I've been, and I still have some things to check out. Watch your back, okay?"

"Okay," Mac said, feeling suspicious. "Can we meet up again soon? I could really use your brain on this to help me figure out why I'm being set up."

"Yeah, sure, I'll call as soon as I have something more. Probably in a day or two." Viv stood to leave. "I'll be in touch." She hugged Mac and headed for the door.

"Hey, Viv...if you did know something, would you tell me?" Mac asked.

"Of course, I would. This is as much my butt on the line as it is yours," Viv said over her shoulder as she walked out the door.

CHAPTER
FORTY-THREE

VIV TORE out of Mac's neighborhood. She couldn't breathe. She felt like she was losing her mind. How could her boyfriend be involved? Her mind was racing, and she had to concentrate on slowing down and focusing. There was no denying that the man in the picture was him—she knew that for a fact. He had clearly messed with Hudson's truck, and then only a short time later, Hudson's vehicle crashed with no other explanation. The only thing that made sense was that he'd sabotaged the truck somehow. Then there were those pictures of his truck at several locations where women had gone missing—or worse, later been found murdered. She was determined to get to the bottom of this. She truly hoped he had a good explanation. Deep down, she felt that he wouldn't but didn't want to focus on that yet. She pushed her thoughts aside. Instead of heading back to work, she texted her boss and told him she wasn't feeling well.

Her mind was still bouncing around. There were a few more details she wanted to verify before she confronted him. She got home just before 1600 hours, trying to calm herself to make sure she kept a level head. She didn't believe in coincidences, but she also felt it was essential to have solid evidence against someone before accusing them of anything, and certainly before calling someone a murderer. She kept hoping she was somehow wrong or mistaken. She texted him, *Dinner, my place tonight?*

He was sitting in his office thinking about how to handle the situation. He knew Viv had figured it out, and he really didn't think he would be able to throw her off his scent at this point. He clicked his pen three times, trying to decide. There was only one thing that he could do to rectify the situation. If she had only done as she was told and dropped the cases, then it would have been fine. He did like her and found her useful. He especially liked how she satisfied his sexual needs. The way she smelled, how she felt in his hands, and of course, her submissive side where she unwittingly did things to help cover up his actions. She had been fantastic, but now it was over.

There was an eerie calm that washed over him once he decided what he needed to do. He stopped and picked up some flowers and dinner to put her at ease. He needed to know everything she knew and who she had told. His survival depended on making sure there were no loose ends. It really was a shame. The dinner would be perfect, and the flowers were beautiful.

He pulled into her drive right on time. The night air was brisk, and there was still snow that crunched under his boots. He had changed into civilian clothes and put on her favorite cologne. He knew he was a handsome man and had been able to get what he wanted from women most of his life. This time would be no different than any other. The only one he hadn't been able to control was Sahar, but she had paid for what she had done...or had she? He wasn't sure.

The man knew he was obsessed with Sahar, but he simply couldn't help himself. He felt excited thinking about the night's events. He became aroused with the thought of fear in her eyes. He knew she would beg for her life, cry, scream. He didn't quite understand why that was such a turn-on to him, but he just couldn't get past it. The power he felt when he saw how they looked at him. The feeling of arousal when he plunged the knife into them and how he felt when he slid himself inside and watched them die. He wasn't sure if it was the knife wounds that killed them or the pressure he put on their fragile necks. The explosion he felt each time a life slipped away in his hands was among the most powerful moments he had ever experienced. His goal was to stop Sahar, but he couldn't help enjoying that part.

He was smiling as he approached her door. She had given him a key, but he didn't need it. She had left the door unlocked for him. You would think of all people she would be more cautious since she was a trained OSI agent. She was out on the porch with her hair down, looking relaxed, wrapped in a warm blanket.

He walked up behind her, watching her stare out into the woods. She didn't turn around even though she knew he was there. Trying to keep her voice casual, she asked, "What did you bring for dinner?"

He smiled. Maybe this wouldn't be too bad. He expected her to be livid and accusatory, but to her credit, she wanted to hear what he had to say for himself. "I brought you flowers."

"That was very nice of you," she said in a flat voice.

He set them down next to her on the small wooden table. It was old and tilted slightly to the left. She had thought about replacing it, but she liked the pretty little tiles embedded in the top. It reminded her of her grandma. She took a deep breath. "You didn't answer my question."

"What question is that?"

"What's for dinner?" she repeated, still not looking at him.

He understood; she was avoiding the confrontation. She didn't want to believe that he was capable of any of the awful things he had done. There had to be another explanation, but there simply wasn't. He'd been hunting Sahar, and in doing so, there had been casualties. Thinking back to before the incident, he remembered a time when he wasn't like this. He'd had underlying desires, without a doubt, but he would never act on them. Now, something had changed, and he didn't know how to change it back, or if he even wanted to. He enjoyed the hunt a little too much and couldn't seem to find peace any other way. It was simply the way it was.

She sat there covered in her blanket, gripping the handle of her Glock 19. It was a smaller gun that was easier for her to conceal. Her mom had given her a hard time about getting a concealed carry permit, but it had given her peace of mind. She had hoped she would never have to use it, but she felt more comfortable having it. She just had to stay calm and find out exactly what was the truth and what wasn't.

"Are you hungry?" he finally asked, breaking the silence.

"Not really," she replied. "Do you mind if we sit out here and talk for a bit?"

"Of course not. What's on your mind?"

Viv wondered how he could sound so calm. Maybe she was wrong somehow, and there was an explanation for the evidence. He had been so kind to her, bringing her flowers and dinner. How could he also be the person who had set up Mac, tried to kill Hudson, and possibly killed all those women they knew of? Mac had walked her through the evidence and the women she knew about. The similarities were hard to argue with.

Then there was Ali. She wondered if he had been in contact with her. She decided to start there. "Do you know a woman named Ali? She works at the State Line strip club," she asked in a soft voice.

The simple mention of Ali's name heightened his excitement. He took a silent breath in and then let it out. "What's this all about?" he asked in his deep baritone voice.

"There's reason to believe she may be our killer's next victim."

"Oh? I thought that was Zonira's sister?"

"Yes, she is," Viv responded.

"But I thought Johnson killed Zonira? He's currently in pretrial confinement. He's not able to kill anyone unless he escapes."

"No, I believe there's another person that's been committing these murders."

"What do you know?" he said, dropping the façade.

"I know your truck was seen at many of the locations where the women were taken. I know you had access to Zonira, and I know you messed with Hudson's truck right before it crashed. I also know you were seen on video outside of Mac's house. Did you also trash her house?" Viv finally looked at him with accusation in her eyes.

"Yes, I did," he said, looking right at her. There it was the fear that he craved. "You suspected me of all this, and here you are meeting with me alone. You invited me into your home without any backup." He smiled with an evil glint in his eyes. "Viv, I thought you were so much smarter than that. As a trained agent, I would expect more from you."

She slowly looked down at her lap and clicked the safety off her gun underneath the blanket. The gun gave her courage and made her feel strong and confident. "Why?" she asked calmly. "Why'd you do it?"

"Because I can, and because *she* had to pay for what she did to my team—and what she did to me," he blurted and began pacing.

She wasn't sure what she had expected him to say, but that wasn't it. She was confused and didn't understand what he was talking about. "Who is 'she?'" Viv asked. "You're not making any sense."

"You would never understand anyway," he said, pacing back and forth. The more he paced, the angrier he got. Who was she to get in the way of doing what was right? What needed to be done? He turned and charged her. She was surprised by the cold, dead look in his eyes. The man she had loved wasn't even there. His face was twisted into a wicked grimace that made him look ugly and animal-like.

She pulled the gun out from under the blanket and screamed "*Stop!*" at the top of her lungs. There was already a bullet in the chamber. All she had to do was pull the trigger.

He stopped in his tracks and looked at her like he didn't understand, and then in a split-second, he dove for the gun, and she squeezed the trigger. Even though she was a trained marksman, she had never actually shot at another human before. In her terrified state, she closed her eyes at the last second. Slowly she opened them and looked at the blood running down the front of his shirt. She hadn't hit him in the chest where she had been aiming but had done some damage to his left shoulder.

He looked down in surprise. "You shot me. What the hell!" he screamed.

"Stay where you are, or I'll shoot you again, and this time I'll hit something more important than your shoulder."

"What are you talking about? I never did anything to you," he growled.

"Stay where you are, or I will shoot," Viv growled back.

He took three deep breaths to calm himself. He walked back and forth three times while her gun was trained on him. Viv oversaw him, wondering what to do. She had thought he would be able to explain everything. She wanted him to tell her it was all a big misunderstanding and that he wasn't a killer, but she had seen the look in his eyes. He wasn't going to hesitate to kill her, or anyone else for that matter. She knew that. She could feel it in the way he looked at her.

If she called someone, would they get there in time? Would they believe her? His status as a high-ranking, respected member of the military community would create doubt. She was thankful she had recorded their conversation on her cell phone, but would that be enough? She hoped so.

He watched her fidgeting with the gun. Her hand was shaking as she watched him pace back and forth. If he waited for just the right moment, he would be able to get the gun...probably. He continued to pace, keeping her attention. His shoulder was throbbing. He couldn't believe she had shot him. He didn't think she had it in her. All he could do was pace back and forth like a caged animal and wait for an opening.

She followed him with the barrel of the gun, but he knew the more time passed, the less of a threat he would seem. He tested his theory by moving slightly closer to her. She didn't flinch, just kept watching. He enjoyed the killing part of the war, and this would be no different. He had been so convinced that Zonira was Sahar, but like all the others, she had deceived him.

He knew without a doubt that Viv wasn't Sahar, but she was collateral damage, and he would enjoy torturing her. He had to make sure he got all the information from her that he needed. There was only one way to do that. He was becoming aroused at the thought of her body squirming as he cut her. The look of terror in her eyes. He was enjoying the look of fear in her eyes right now. He gave her credit for keeping it together.

"Stop moving," she demanded.

He stopped in his tracks and stared at her. "What are you going to do, Viv? You know you won't actually kill me. How on earth would you explain shooting me?"

"Don't worry, I'll figure something out," she said. That's when her phone went off, and she looked down for just a fraction of a second.

That was all he needed. He snatched the gun from her hand like it was a toy and trained it on her head. Her breath caught. She sat there not moving a muscle, feeling like a fool for trusting this man and letting him into her home, into her life, into her bed. She dropped her eyes to the floor and stared at her feet. He grinned wickedly. Her defeat was written all over her face as he grabbed her by the back of her head, but she didn't scream or beg or fight. She just allowed him to drag her back into the house like a limp rag doll.

CHAPTER
FORTY-FOUR

MAC WAS FRANTIC. Her heart was racing, and she couldn't shake the bad feeling in her gut. She had been calling Viv for the last hour and getting no answer. After the way Viv had left her place early, she just couldn't shake the feeling that something was very wrong.

She took a deep breath and counted to five inside her head as she held it in and then slowly let it out through her teeth. She was sitting in her little SUV, waiting for the windshield frost to thaw. She had a knot growing deep in her stomach. Her instincts were normally spot-on. There were a few times she had ignored her gut and doing so had not served her well. If she was wrong, then Viv would just have to be pissed at her for coming over unannounced.

Her thoughts were swimming in all different directions, and she almost jumped out of her skin when her phone rang. Her heart nearly stopped when she saw the number of the hospital Hudson was at. She immediately assumed the worst and answered the phone without saying a word.

"Hello, Mac." Her heart melted at the sound of Hudson's deep voice at the other end of the line.

"It's so good to hear your voice. You scared the shit out of me," she said.

He let out a low chuckle. "That's okay, it scared the shit out of me too. The good news is the doc says I'll survive."

"I'm very glad to hear it. How do you feel overall?"

"Like I was hit by a Mack truck, but nothing that time won't mend."

"Do you know how long they'll keep you?" she asked.

"They want me to stay for observation overnight, but they said I might be able to go home if I can get someone to stay with me and help me get around. I was kinda wondering if that someone could be...you?"

"Absolutely, as long as you behave yourself. You can be a real pain sometimes."

"I'll do my best to be a model patient, I promise. How's the case going?"

"Well, I have a feeling our guy is a military member, and that he sabotaged your truck."

"Yeah, Joe told me that someone had been messing with my tires and that the accident was deliberate. Kinda freaked me out that someone wanted me out of the picture. Do you know why I was targeted?"

"No, the only thing that makes sense is that you were getting too close. I met with Viv today and she had some interesting information for me. I get the feeling that she knows much more than she's telling me about. I think she knows who our suspect is but isn't willing to spill," Mac said. "I'm actually headed to her place now."

"I don't know, Mac. If someone came after me and is clearly targeting you, do you think you should go there alone?" Hudson asked. He wasn't used to feeling this protective about someone. He really wasn't sure how to deal with his feelings toward Mac.

"Don't worry, I'm just going to stop by. I have my own protection, so I'll be fine."

Somehow that didn't make Hudson feel any better. He knew Mac could protect herself, but he still got an uneasy feeling and didn't like the thought of her going in alone. "Call Joe and at least let him know what's going on before you head over there just in case," he said. He knew if he pushed the issue too hard that she would just fight him on it. She was one of the most stubborn women he had ever met, and as sick as it sounded, he liked it.

"Fine," she conceded. "I'll call him and let him know where I'm going if it makes you feel better." Mac liked that he was protective of her. It had been a long time since anyone had watched out for her or cared much about what happened to her. A warm feeling spread through her. Maybe after this was all done, they could figure things out between them. Now wasn't the time. "I'm glad you're awake. I'll come to the hospital and bring you some real food as soon as I'm done at Viv's place."

"Sounds amazing. Just watch your back," he said, and she hung up the phone.

Mac drove the short distance to Viv's place. A growing sense of dread was gnawing at her and she wasn't sure why. Viv's car was in the driveway, and it appeared that another vehicle had been there recently. The indents in the snow and dirty slush were hard to miss.

Mac parked her SUV along the side of the road and approached the side of the house. Crouching low, she slowly peeked into the main room. She couldn't see anyone inside. Her body felt tense, and her feet were cold on the slushy ground. She rounded to the backyard where she found a blanket sitting on the porch and a chair knocked over on its side. She slid her winter gloves on before moving anything. If Viv had been assaulted, she wanted the police to be able to find evidence without having to worry about eliminating her prints.

She moved to the sliding glass door and found strands of blond hair attached to the handle like Viv had accidentally caught her hair in it, but that didn't make sense. Viv had short blond hair; she was too tall to snag her hair unless she had bent at the waist while walking through the door. Mac moved the sliding glass door aside, careful not to disturb the hairs.

"Viv," she called softly into the house, but no one answered. She stepped into the house and drew her gun. "*Viv!*" she said, louder this time. She went into the living room, bathroom, and guest bedroom, clearing each room. A lump formed in her throat when she saw a red smear on the white door that led to Viv's bedroom. It was a tiny reddish-brown smudge, but it was enough to make her heart race.

The door was open slightly, and she could smell the unmistakable metallic scent of blood. It was overpowering, which meant there was a lot. She slid the door open with her gloved hand and her breath caught in her throat. All she could do was stare at the carnage in front of her.

There was blood everywhere. It was dripping from the corner of the bed. She could see Viv's blond hair with her face turned away and her back facing the door. Her gut told her that Viv was already gone, but she felt she had to check. She carefully walked over to Viv's body. When she got to the other side of the bed, she saw something she would never be able to get out of her mind. She tasted bile rising in her throat and had to swallow several times not to blow chunks all over the crime scene.

Viv's naked body lay on the bed with multiple stab wounds to the abdomen and genital area. There were ligature marks along her slender neck, and it appeared her neck had been broken. Mac reached forward and gently closed her eyes and moved away from the body. She carefully backed out of the room so as not to disturb anything and dialed Joe. He answered on the first ring.

"Joe, it's Mac. I'm at Viv's place. Someone killed her," Mac said with a shaky voice.

Joe was silent for a long time. "Are you alone?" he finally asked.

"Yes, I checked the house, and no one else is here, though there are tire treads in the driveway indicating someone recently left."

"Don't go anywhere. I'm on my way," he said, hanging up before Mac could say anything more.

CHAPTER
FORTY-FIVE

JOE ARRIVED at the house to find Mac sitting on the front porch, waiting. He walked up with a distant look in his eyes. He liked Mac and thought she was a good person, but he had been deceived before. He had once had a partner he trusted with his life, but his partner became a dirty cop. He'd always felt stupid for not seeing the signs earlier; one day, he was called into interrogation by internal affairs because they thought he might be involved. He couldn't believe they thought he had anything to do with all the shit his partner was into, but it was also hard to believe that he didn't know anything about it.

It turned out his partner had been protecting known members of a sex-trafficking ring in exchange for money and as many young women to spend time with as he wanted. Joe was sickened by the thought of enslaving women and making them perform against their will. He'd never really trusted his partners since then. He always kept a safe distance.

"Are you okay?" was all he could say.

"I'm pretty shaken up. I think I arrived shortly after he..." Her voice trailed off. "It doesn't appear she's been dead for very long. She was at my place earlier today to discuss the case. She knew something but wouldn't tell me what it was. All I found out was that I'm being set up for the drug charges, but I already knew that."

"Who did she say was setting you up?"

"Well, that's the weird part; I guess a chief master sergeant on base and another military guy in civilian clothes coerced a young airman who was one of my clients to implicate me as his dealer."

"Okay, so once Viv left your house, did she say where she was going?" he asked.

Mac was surprised to see a glint of suspicion in Joe's eyes. She knew it looked bad with her being here by herself, but once they processed her, they would be able to tell she had nothing to do with this, she hoped.

"She just said she had some work to finish and took off," Mac said.

Two other patrol cars pulled up. Joe told one of the patrolmen to stay with Mac while he went into the house.

The metallic smell of fresh blood assaulted his nostrils as soon as he walked in. Mac had told him that the body was in the bedroom, and it was really bad, but he wasn't prepared for what he walked in on. There was blood everywhere, dripping from the bed and sheets all over the floor. It was like someone had bathed in her blood. Just the thought of it made him shiver. With all this blood and the amount of contact that had to have been made during the assault, Joe felt reassured they would be able to find the killer's DNA somewhere in the mess. There was no way the person hadn't left covered in blood. He wondered if Mac had seen and passed anyone on her way over. He knew there was no way she could have done this. She wasn't strong enough, and she would have been completely covered.

———

The man had sped down the street away from Viv's house headed for Highway 2. He looked down at his blood-soaked uniform. He had put his Air Force winter jacket over his uniform to cover himself. Before leaving the house, he'd wiped down every surface he could think of. As he drove, his heart pounded against his rib cage as several police cars sped past him, going in the opposite direction. He had been to Viv's house on several occasions, and he might have missed a place where his prints might be.

If they found something, he would simply admit to having an affair with her, which would also explain any DNA they might find in her bed. It would be inconclusive at best with all the blood. He thought about the blood. The warm, sticky feeling of her blood flowing over his hands as he plunged the knife deep into her body. He felt himself becoming aroused again at the thought of entering her during her last breaths. The sound of her neck as it snapped beneath his hands was exhilarating.

Focus, focus! He had to focus. He realized he was speeding and didn't want to get pulled over. He drummed the steering wheel three times with his hand.

How on earth would he explain his state of affairs? *Um, sorry I was speeding, Officer. I was aroused after killing my girlfriend,* he thought and smiled wickedly. No, that wouldn't do at all. He simply wasn't finished yet.

———

Joe came back out of the house. His face was ashen, and he looked as though he was about to be sick. He took several deep breaths, trying to control himself. He'd seen dead bodies before but couldn't recall ever seeing anything quite that brutal. "Um…" He dropped his head and took a few more breaths. "Um, how well did you know the victim?"

"She was an acquaintance. We've gone out a few times together, and we often worked on the same cases. This caused our paths to cross professionally on a regular basis. She's OSI and, as you know, I work in defense. She interrogated my clients fairly regularly, that sort of thing, but I wouldn't say we were close. I liked her, though. She was tough and wouldn't take crap from people. I just don't know how this guy got the drop on her. She was smart and wouldn't have let her guard down that easily."

Joe thought about it for a while. "Do you know if she was seeing anyone?"

"Not that I'm aware of. I know she had a guy a while back, but I think they broke it off. I'm not even sure who he was. You might want to ask Agent Green. He was her partner on base, and they seemed pretty close," Mac said, and Joe wrote it down in his notebook.

He wasn't sure what to think. It seemed like everywhere Mac went; murder victims followed. The connection between her and this killer couldn't be ignored. He just couldn't see that connection yet. Maybe he should dig into her past to see if there was a link that he had missed, but he liked and respected Mac. He would have to approach it delicately. He could start with Hudson but wondered how much Hudson really knew about her.

CHAPTER
FORTY-SIX

MAC WAITED PATIENTLY while they took her statement. She knew Joe meant well, but she just wanted to get out of there and go home. The hesitation and fear she felt about going into her own home didn't help matters much. Fatigue seeped through her body from being so tense. Not to mention the sleep deprivation was starting to catch up with her. All this stress could wear on a woman, and she was starting to feel like the walking dead.

Finally, they released her. Joe insisted on sending a patrol car with her to make sure her place was safe. She didn't object as she crawled into her SUV and turned up the music to keep her focused during the drive. The window was cracked, and cold crisp air curled around her face. It helped a little, but she knew if she didn't get sleep soon, she would stop functioning. After what happened with Hudson, her career, and constantly being on edge, she was beyond tired. It seemed strange to her how so much could change in such a short amount of time. She found herself checking her rearview mirror constantly as she drove home.

She pulled into her driveway and turned off the engine. She locked her doors and just sat there as the young officer walked around her property and checked the inside of her home. She didn't feel like going inside after all that had happened, so she laid her head back on the headrest and closed her eyes for just a moment. She woke hours later surprised and a little disturbed that she had passed out in her drive-way. *Wow, I need to get some solid sleep and find a safe place where I can rest.* She looked behind her and smiled as she saw the young officer sitting in his cruiser, guarding her.

Her body ached as she walked up to his car. "Thank you for watching out for me. I really appreciate it," she said, stifling a yawn.

"No problem, ma'am. Officer Romero asked me to stay here and watch your place."

"Well, thank you, that makes me feel better. Is there anything I can get you?"

"No, I'm fine, thanks."

As she approached the house, she still felt on edge. She drew her gun and clicked the safety off as she entered. Her heart raced involuntarily with the knowledge that she was in someone's crosshairs. Every muscle in her body ached as she went from room to room, clearing the house even though her young protector outside had already done so. Satisfied that no one was there, she checked the locks on all the doors and windows, then went to the shower and stripped off her clothes.

Her heart rate began to slow as hot water ran over her body. Her muscles began to loosen, knowing that the gun was within reach right outside the shower and the police officer was right outside. She could feel the knots melting away. It was hard to focus when she was this tired. Viv's blood-soaked body kept creeping into her mind, followed by Hudson's broken body. She knew Joe suspected she was connected to the murderer somehow, and she was starting to agree with him. There was something about this case. Everyone close to her seemed to be getting hurt or ending up dead. Bodies were all around her.

After washing and conditioning her hair and cleaning every inch of her body, she felt better. Her skin was pink from being scrubbed so hard. She had felt dirty and disoriented leaving Viv's house—guilty like somehow, she should have known. Maybe that wasn't too far from the truth. If she had pushed Viv to tell her what she knew and kept her there at the house, then maybe Viv would still have been alive. She took a deep, cleansing breath. "Should of, could of, would of" was a game she had played often and always lost. She knew better than to live in the past. The only way she could make it right was if she stopped feeling sorry for herself and did something about it.

Easier said than done. Trying to focus on an empty stomach was not a productive way of doing things. Realizing she was starving, she walked into the kitchen to make something to eat. She checked the doors again just to be sure and started rummaging through her kitchen. She concluded there was little to eat in her house. With every-thing that was going on, she hadn't been to the store in a while.

The feel of the gun pressed against the small of her back made her feel better, but something seemed off in the house, and she couldn't quite put her finger on it. The little hairs kept standing up on the back of her neck while she went to the sink to rinse off an apple. *There.* On the side of the sink was a brownish-red smudge. She took a closer look and was fairly certain it was blood. Had he been here again? Her skin began to crawl. She dialed Joe's number and walked outside to let the young officer know. Thankfully, he was still at Viv's house and headed her way.

When Joe walked into the house, she could tell that he was getting suspicious of her. She really couldn't blame him. He had every right with all the evidence that was mounting up around her. If she were in his shoes, she would have thought the same thing.

"Hello again, Joe," Mac said, trying to sound pleasant.

He didn't answer. He simply walked over to the sink with gloves on and took a swab of the brown spot. He put it into a little evidence bag and marked it. "Did you notice anything else out of place?"

"Not that I know of, but I admit I was a little out of it when I came in. I fell asleep in my car in the driveway."

He noticed her wet hair. "Could you take a look around?" he asked impatiently.

"Of course," she said, walking around the house. "You don't think I had anything to do with this, do you?" she asked as she roamed around the house.

"I honestly don't know what to think, Mac. Either this guy has a thing for you, or you're involved. There's no other way to explain all the destruction that keeps following you around."

"I see where you're coming from, Joe, but why would I call you to the house and show you what looks like blood in my sink if I was behind anything?"

"You have a point, but you have to admit something is going on that involves you directly."

Mac agreed to keep Joe informed if anything else happened, and he left. She thought it was interesting that people would automatically think she was involved rather than believe she was set up. *I guess it's easier to believe bad things about people than good.* At this point, she really wasn't sure who she could count on. Most of the people on base thought she was guilty of being a drug dealer, which was absolutely crazy. The one person who knew she was innocent had just been killed.

Maybe she could go back and track down Senior Airman Pratt and see if he would tell her the same things, he told Viv. She wasn't sure if that would stick, considering the evidence would come from her unless Pratt would testify on her behalf, but that was also a gamble. If she ended up in a court-martial, it could go either way, regardless of if she was guilty or not. It all came down to what the members thought. She always found it interesting how perception ended up being nine-tenths of the law. Her gut was always spot on when meeting a new client as to whether she would be able to get an acquittal for them or not. If her client looked like a thug, then their job as defense got a whole lot harder.

It was important to clear her mind so she could think objectively. She made a sandwich with a few leftovers she had in the fridge. It wasn't much of a dinner, but it would have to do. Once she poured herself a glass of wine to try and relax, she went into her office to go over the case. The house was still a mess but not as bad as it had been. She had been going from room to room systematically cleaning things up. Her temper flared whenever she thought about the home invasion.

All her hard work to afford this place, and now she didn't even want to be there. If she left it all and went into her mother's business, she would be able to afford just about anything. It just wasn't the life she wanted. Her mother's empire was wrong on so many levels, and it really didn't matter how much money there was.

Her eyes grew heavy, and she dozed off again in her office chair.

CHAPTER
FORTY-SEVEN

HE WAS TRYING to keep his calm as he drove to the cabin. He couldn't speed but wanted to get away, to hide and make it all go away. His thoughts kept wandering back to the look on Viv's face. He didn't like that he enjoyed what he did so much. He used to be a decent human being, someone that others liked and even cared for. Now he was obsessed and couldn't stop. But then his mind fixated on how it felt, and the self-loathing washed away. Who was he kidding? The only thing that mattered now was stopping Sahar, no matter what the cost. He was powerful and in control. There was nothing to apologize for. Though he knew that wasn't entirely true. His time with Viv had not gone exactly the way he'd wanted it to. She hadn't lasted long enough, and he was left wanting more. She wasn't right, and he felt unsatisfied. He needed more time.

When he pulled up to the cabin, he paused to listen and ensure no one was there. It was secluded, and no one ever came out here unless he brought them...and those people were no longer alive. He took a deep breath and watched the house. No movement aside from a raccoon scavenging for food. The man watched the animal's beady little eyes behind its black mask, and he thought he looked similar. After the incident, he felt he was always keeping a mask in place. His eyes had turned dark and predatory where they used to be a soft, kind brown. When he looked in the mirror now, the man he used to be had disappeared. Maybe when the hunt was over he would go back to normal.

He slowly got out of his truck. The dried blood on his uniform made a strange cracking noise as he walked. He had stopped by Mac's house and washed his hands and face just in case he got pulled over. He knew she wasn't going to be there because he'd watched her pass him, completely oblivious to his presence while on her way to Viv's house to discover his handiwork. It was a good thing he hadn't stayed to enjoy Viv further. He found it strangely erotic that Mac saw his work. There was something about that woman. He knew he would kill her soon, but she was the one he would savor. He would take his time with her and worship her body before he plunged his sleek knife into her taut, flat belly.

He had always liked Mac even before the incident, but now she had become a bit of an obsession. Deep down, he wondered if she might be Sahar with slightly different features. Maybe after she was gone, he could finally stop killing...but then his mind wandered to Ali.

Ali was stunning with her long, strong legs and confident, almost cocky demeanor. She walked around like she was untouchable, just like Sahar had. She thought that little .22 she carried would protect her, but that was nothing. He doubted she even knew how to shoot it, unlike Mac, who he'd have to be careful with. He had gotten to know her well over the years and knew she had been training in martial arts since she was a little girl. Her dad had taken her to classes with her sister before their lives turned to shit and their dad took off. He knew she had continued her training as a way of coping with the loss of her father. Hell, he had actually taught her a few moves during their sparring sessions.

She had shared a lot with him. He smiled at the thought of wiping that smug look off her face, but he had to remember not to underestimate that one.

He didn't think Ali would be a problem. She would be fun and arousing to play with, and then she would be ready to join the others in his garden out back. He liked visiting the garden. It made him feel at peace. But for now, he needed to prepare. Without question, one of them was Sahar, and he was determined to figure out which one.

He felt on high alert and couldn't seem to settle down. He walked the perimeter of the property three times, checking his cameras and motion sensors to make sure no one had been there. Then he went into the house and locked every lock and checked every window three times. His breathing was still erratic, and he knew that things would get out of control if he stayed in this state.

Three breaths in and out, slow and controlled. He needed to regain control, or they would find him. He went into the bathroom and stripped off his uniform that was still covered in Viv's blood. He looked down at his naked body where there were red streaks from where the blood had soaked through. He was lucky that Viv had grazed his shoulder when she shot him, only leaving a small abrasion. He walked naked into the little room at the back of the cabin where his washer and dryer sat. He turned the washer to the hottest setting and let the tub fill up. He put each piece of his uniform in, including his boots, socks, and underwear. He dumped in a little detergent and closed the lid. He took a deep breath and tried to remain focused, but he could feel his mind slipping. He wanted to do it again, and he knew it would be soon.

The shower felt invigorating and helped clear his mind. He stood there watching the reddish-brown blood run off his body. It was mesmerizing the way it swirled down the drain. It felt like he was watching Viv's life wash away. She was gone now. He might miss her a little. She had been good to him, but then she'd become a liability. It was as simple as that. *Everyone is expendable,* he thought. He felt better when he watched the life drain from their bodies. The rush he felt; it made him feel godlike to be able to decide whether someone lived or died. Viv had to die, but for now, Mac could live. He knew many people that stayed in combat too long and felt that way. It became normal—it had to.

Ali crept back into his thoughts. He knew things would be tense for a while, and he knew he should wait. The possibility they would find his DNA or fingerprints at Viv's house was very real, and he would need to answer for that eventually. Then again, if things didn't go well then maybe it was best to experience Ali before he was detained. Then he could think of her—how she smelled, how she tasted, the look in her eyes when he plunged the knife deep into her skin, the warmth of her sweet blood spilling from her body. He found himself becoming aroused just thinking about it.

He rechecked the house. Every lock was secured, and all was quiet. He retrieved his book and looked at Ali. He stared at her for a long time until the decision was made. He would need to have Ali soon. Then he flipped to the pages where he had put Mac's pictures. He had several of her. Just seeing her made his pulse quicken. He took his large cock in his hand and began moving up and down. She would be the ultimate kill. A challenge worthy of him. The ultimate prize for his garden. Or was it Ali he needed first? He hadn't been able to take Zonira with him. Though maybe Mac was Sahar in disguise? She would complete his project. Then maybe he would stop killing. He wasn't sure, but it felt right.

He kept trying to remain focused but could feel an itch he couldn't scratch deep down, almost like an addiction. It was all he could do having Mac this close in proximity not to reach out and touch her. He wanted to touch her in so many awful ways. If she was truly Sahar, then she deserved to die. He started daydreaming about what it would feel like to strangle her. To put his hands around her beautiful neck and squeeze and watch the life drain out of her big brown eyes. He realized his hand was starting to tremble slightly. He was starting to feel like a crack addict needing a fix. He craved the next kill and had a deep need to stop her once and for all. He could feel his skin crawl with anticipation. He couldn't focus.

CHAPTER
FORTY-EIGHT

MAC SLEPT the entire night in the chair in her office. When she woke there was a kink in her neck that she feared might be permanent. She stood up and stretched, trying to get her back to forgive her decision. She moved this way and that, stretching and trying to get her body to respond. After a while, she figured it was as good as it would get under the circumstances.

She went into the bathroom and looked in the mirror. *Ooh man, I look rough!* A good night's sleep was essential at this point. If she kept going this way, it might be the end of her. Good thing Hudson wasn't around to see her. She wasn't exactly sure where that was going, but it would have bothered her for him to see her in this state. She thought about the dinner she had promised to bring him the night before and hoped he would forgive her for not showing.

She went into the kitchen to start a pot of liquid life, AKA coffee. Her coffee addiction worried her sometimes and she knew she shouldn't drink as much as she did, but now wasn't the time to stop. Staring into space, standing in her kitchen deep in thought, she almost jumped out of her skin when her phone rang loudly, breaking the silence. It was her SAT phone. She answered, knowing it would be Lola.

"Hey Sis, how's it going?" Lola asked.

"Not well, but I'll be okay."

"You always are. So, I got another ping off your neighbor's camera. Thought you'd want to know that the same guy was lurking around your place again. I still didn't get a good image, but I think we may be able to get his fingerprints," Lola said excitedly.

"*You* can run prints?" Mac asked.

"Of course, silly! What exactly do you think I do for a living?" Lola giggled.

"Actually, I'm not really clear on what you do. I just know you have some wicked hacking skills."

"Damn right I do. I know more about people than I ever wanted to."

"So…" Mac said, "what's your idea?" Lola's mind was brilliant, but sometimes she had trouble focusing.

"Oh yeah, he touched your front doorframe and didn't appear to be wearing gloves."

"How do I get the prints off?"

"Oh, that's easy. Do you have any powder?"

"What kind of powder? I certainly don't have any fingerprint powder."

"Nah, you don't need that. All you need is baby powder or powdered makeup. It should do the trick. Just shake a little on the surface. If you have a makeup brush to gently apply with, that would be even better."

"Yeah, I think I have something that will work. Hang on." Mac returned a few minutes later. "Okay, I think I have everything."

"Good, now go to your front door and open it, careful not to touch the outside of the door," Lola instructed.

"Got it, the door is open."

"Now dip the brush into the powder and gently brush it onto the doorframe above the doorknob. He also touched the knob, but that probably has your prints on it as well. For some reason, he put his hand on the frame when opening the door."

Mac did as instructed. "There's a print," Mac said excitedly. "It looks like it might be a thumb, but it doesn't have any ridges or swirls."

"That's not good news. He may have worn clear latex gloves. Send it over anyway. Take a piece of clear tape and gently put it on top of the print. Careful not to smudge it any further. Once the print has been transferred onto the tape, carefully place the tape onto the screen of your phone and take a screenshot and then send it my way."

Mac followed her instructions and sent the print. "Thanks, Lola, I really appreciate your help. It would be helpful to know who I'm up against. That has been the worst part of all of this."

"No problem, but I can already tell you by looking at this that I'm not going to get anything. It was worth a try. I'll go through what I have again to see if I can find something else to work with. Take care and watch your back," Lola said.

"Thanks. Will do," Mac said, and hung up the phone.

It unnerved her to get confirmation that he had been in her house. She had suspected he'd violated her home again after finding the smudge of red and brown in her sink. The fact that her sister had video confirmation and it wasn't her imagination was unsettling. Hopefully in the near future she would at least know who she was up against. She was aggravated that she couldn't figure it out.

She wandered into her office and looked over the pictures of the victims and then her possible suspects. She had already eliminated Hudson since his truck was taken out by the person in question. Something was nagging at the back of her brain that she just couldn't quite figure out. Something was familiar about this person, but she just couldn't put her finger on it.

She walked away and started pacing the house when her phone rang again. At first, she thought it might be her sister but realized it was her regular cell phone.

"Mac, it's Chief," came a gruff, deep voice over the line.

"Hi Chief, what can I do for you?"

"I wanted to check in to see if you're doing okay. I heard you were the one who found Agent Ross..." He trailed off, not bothering to finish describing what happened.

"Yes, I did," Mac responded flatly.

"Could you possibly come into my office and give a statement?" Chief asked.

"Of course, sir. When would you like me there?"

"Does fifteen hundred hours this afternoon work for you?"

"Yes sir, I'll be there."

Mac knew better than to meet with Chief without talking with her area defense counsel. Even though they were friends, he still had an obligation to report any suspicions he had about her. It seemed like every time she turned around, there were more suspicions flung her way. She was seriously getting tired of it. She called her boss and was pleased when he answered on the first ring. He was normally in with clients and a lot harder to get ahold of.

"Hi Boss, this is Mac. How are things going?"

"Other than missing having you around and getting my ass handed to me, everything's peachy," he said with a smile in his voice. "Seriously, when do you get to come back?"

"I wish I knew. Now I'm being called into the SFS chief's office. Did you hear about Viv?"

"Agent Ross? What's going on with her?" Stanton asked.

"Oh." She paused. "I'm sorry to be the one to tell you this, but I found her body. She was murdered in her home."

The line went silent for what seemed like a long time. "Are you okay?" her boss finally asked.

She was relieved to hear genuine concern in his voice and not accusations like other people. "Yes sir, I'm okay, though a little shook up. I get the feeling that I'm a suspect, though it was clear I couldn't have done it."

"I'm worried about you, Mac. It seems like some nasty business is following you. I would certainly hate it if they were able to make any of this stick."

"I'm with you on that one."

They chatted about the cases that were going on and how things were progressing. Stanton complained about the new paralegal they had sent him. Apparently, the new person couldn't hold a candle to Mac. It made her feel good to hear she was missed.

"Now, what's this about you meeting with Chief…and which one are we talking about?" Stanton asked.

"The Security Forces one. He says he wants a statement from me about Viv's murder," Mac explained.

"I see. Please call your ADC before meeting with him. If you can't get ahold of him in time and you're read your rights, just remain silent."

Mac called Kibble and let it ring. It finally went to voicemail. She left her name and number again, hoping he would call back before her appointment with the Security Forces chief, plus she wanted to update him on what Viv had told her about Pratt and the maintenance chief.

Her guard was up. Chief had always treated her like a little sister, but with everything going on she just didn't know who to trust. She took a few deep breaths and started putting on her uniform. She realized she hadn't been in uniform in a few days. Most people liked their civvies, but she liked her uniform. It was comfortable and had plenty of pockets to keep all her stuff. Any time she was in her civilian clothes she was always looking for things, like a pen for instance. The uniform had tons of pockets for pens, paper, gum, and any other little thing you wanted to carry with you. It was important to make sure you cleaned out the pockets before washing them. She had made that mistake a few times and ended up with a ruined uniform thanks to pen ink or gum.

After staring at her phone for a while, willing it to ring, she went back to the bathroom to splash water on her face and put her hair up in regulation style. After scrubbing and applying some much-needed makeup to her face, she looked kind of normal. She still had plenty of time before she needed to be at Chief's office, so she decided to check on Hudson.

"Hey, I was just about to call you," Hudson said. "Guess who's getting released from terrible food and uncomfortable beds?"

"I'm so sorry for not bringing you food last night. I'll fill you in when I see you. When can I pick you up?" Mac asked. "Were you still planning on staying at my place or…?" She trailed off.

"If that's okay with you. I promise not to be too much of a pain, but I will need a little help if you're up for it?"

"Um, sure, no problem," she said, but Hudson heard something else in her voice.

"You seem hesitant. Are you sure you're okay with me staying with you? I certainly don't want to be a burden."

"No, you won't be. I was just hesitating because I need to meet with Chief to give my statement about Viv and won't be able to get to you until later tonight."

"What about Viv?" Hudson asked, and Mac inwardly cringed.

"I'm really sorry to tell you this, especially over the phone, but Viv died. She was murdered in her own home. I was the one who found her."

Hudson exhaled. "Wow, Mac, can't get much worse than that. How are you holding up?"

"Overall, I'm okay. I just want this to be over with and for things to go back to normal."

"Sounds like a plan. At the very least, I can provide you with a fun distraction." He chuckled.

"Oh really? What kind of fun did you have in mind?" she teased.

"Well, unfortunately I'm not at peak performance, but I'm sure we can be creative," he said. He smiled, thinking about seeing her again, though he wasn't entirely sure if he was ready to face how he felt about Mac. She was everything he'd ever wanted in a woman and more, but he was hesitant to trust her.

After the hell his ex-wife had put him through, he hadn't let anyone else in. She had left him scarred with walls built around his heart. He'd gone on a few dates and even had a short fling once, but his lack of ability to trust always got in the way. But with Mac, things felt different. Ever since he'd landed in the hospital, all he could do was think about her. Even in his drugged state, he dreamt about her standing there in the kitchen with that towel at her feet. His brain started to short circuit just thinking about her beautiful curves and olive skin. She was beyond stunning. He knew he was a lucky man to be able to get a second chance with a woman like her. She was so much more than beautiful. He loved the way she laughed, her smart-assed comments, and the fact that she didn't take any shit from him or anyone else.

Mac's voice pulled him back to reality. "Hudson, did you hear what I just said?"

"No, not really. I was zoning out, sorry."

"No worries, just sit tight and I'll come get you after I'm done with Chief."

"Sounds good. And Mac? Be careful."

CHAPTER
FORTY-NINE

MAC ARRIVED at the Security Forces Squadron building at precisely 1445 hours. She had always been taught in the military that if you were fifteen minutes early, you were on time, but if you showed up on time, you were late. She signed in at the front desk and told them she was there to see Chief Deleon. Her nerves were frayed, and she felt on edge. She knew she was safe on base and things would be just fine, but for some reason, the little hairs on the back of her neck stood up, and she had that uneasy feeling deep in her gut. She knew to listen to her instincts, but she simply couldn't pinpoint the danger. She was on a secured base in a secure squadron. Even though Viv had told her that the maintenance chief was somehow pressuring an airman to implicate her in a drug ring, that didn't mean her life was in danger. She wanted to know what the SFS chief knew about what the maintenance chief was up to, and why he had told Senior Airman Pratt to write a statement against her.

She walked into his office. He stood there, tall and stoic, with his back to her. She cleared her throat to let him know she was there.

"Hello, Mac," was all he said.

"Hi Chief, how have you been?"

He turned and looked at her with sadness in his eyes, and then he smiled. She wondered if she had imagined it, if only for a second. It was probably just her tired eyes playing tricks on her. She didn't think he had known Viv that well, but she assumed they had worked a few cases together. Mac also wondered what he knew about the allegations against her. The chief's group was a small community, and little happened on base without them knowing about it. It was an odd sensation trying to wrestle with the man she knew him to be and the possibility that he knew something about the false accusations against her.

Her stomach flipped as conflicting information roiled within her brain. Of course, she knew not to believe everything that an accused airman said. She honestly didn't know what to think. She sat down across from Chief and simply looked at him, not sure what to expect.

"Mac, I called you in today to see how you're doing. With everything that's going on, I'm worried about you. First this business with drugs, and then Viv. How are you holding up?"

"I'm okay, just taking it day by day," she said. It felt like he was studying her. "Chief, are you okay?"

He looked at her and quickly adjusted in his seat, trying to find his focus. "Of course, I'm fine," he said while quickly slapping a calm look on his face. He absently clicked the pen in his hand three times. "Enough about me. Is there anything I can do to help you?"

"No," she responded. "I'm sure this whole mess will blow over once they figure out, I'm not involved with drugs or any of the murders."

"What do you mean, 'murders?'" Chief asked.

"Well, my theory is that Viv's and Zonira's murder are connected," she told him. She still wasn't sure how much she should trust Chief, but she figured telling him that much wouldn't hurt. She had no reason to suspect he was involved in the murders in any way. He just might have information about her drug charges, and she intended to find out what he knew.

"So, before Viv died, she told me that the maintenance chief and another person coerced Senior Airman Alex Pratt into implicating me in drug charges." She had never been one to sugarcoat or beat around the bush.

The room went silent; he just sat there looking at her. It had to be only a few seconds, but it felt like a long time. She found herself holding her breath, waiting for his response. She truly hoped it was all a misunderstanding or Pratt was just making it up to get himself out of trouble.

"Did Pratt provide any proof of this meeting?" Chief asked.

"No, I'm not sure what proof he would have other than he said the maintenance chief and this other guy were in on it together. I have a hard time believing that you didn't know about this. You know everything that goes on with the chiefs on base. And I just can't figure out why Pratt would fabricate something like that."

"You know how these young kids can be. They find themselves in trouble and then start pointing fingers at everyone they can. What on earth would the maintenance chief have to gain by implicating you?"

"I have no idea. It really doesn't make any sense, but I'll figure it out. It's what I do best."

She gave him a generic just-the-facts statement about what she had witnessed at Viv's home and then excused herself. Her mind tried to sort through the possibilities. Chief Deleon might have gotten dragged into something that the maintenance chief was trying to cover up. She saw the look in his eyes. He knew something but wasn't willing to tell her. She wasn't sure exactly how she fits into the problem, but she knew she had to get to the bottom of it. She cared for Chief Deleon and couldn't fathom him deliberately hurting her career after all he had done for her.

First things first, after she got Hudson settled at her place, she would find Pratt and interview him. She had to be very careful because she didn't want to be accused of tampering with a witness, especially a witness against her as it currently stood. Maybe she would ask her attorney or one of her paralegal friends to do a thorough interview with him. The only problem was, she needed to read his body language. It might tell her if he was being truthful. It was one of her best tools. When she had asked Chief, he hadn't blatantly denied the allegation; he just said it didn't make sense. At the moment, very little made sense to her, but she would stick to her word and get to the bottom of this. She felt she was close but missing a couple of key puzzle pieces.

CHAPTER
FIFTY

MAC ARRIVED at the hospital to pick Hudson up. He was sitting on the edge of his bed, waiting for her. A huge smile crossed his face at the sight of her. It was a very nice smile. "Hey, thanks for coming and getting me."

She smiled back. "No problem." He had changed into some gray sweatpants and an old-looking black t-shirt. He had some visible scrapes and scratches along his face and arms, but he still looked amazing. The woodsy pine smell that she liked so much hung in the air from his recent shower. His hair had started to grow out and showed a little bit of gray in the stubble on his face and at his temples. For a man in his late thirties, he was looking very good. There was a bit of an age difference between them, but nothing to write home about. Mac realized how much she liked this man. Not quite love, but she certainly had feelings for him. Now she just had to figure out how to break down some of those walls of hers and trust him enough to let him in. She had survived this long by trusting no one. Her father had always said, "Keep your head on a swivel and trust no one, and you'll stay safe." That was just before he disappeared, and she and her sister were put into government protection.

She was still standing in the doorway with a far-off look in her eyes when she heard Hudson say something. "Um, sorry, what was that?"

"You looked like you were off in another dimension. Anything you want to talk about?"

"Nah, just thinking." This was going to be interesting. She wasn't sure what to expect from him staying with her. She knew he couldn't stay alone, but she also wasn't used to sharing her space. "It's nice to see you're feeling better."

"I'll feel great as soon as we get the hell out of this place. If I eat any more nasty hospital food, I think I might go on a hunger strike," Hudson said, smiling.

Mac looked down for a moment with a bit of concern on her face. "Okay, confession time: I have no food at my place. I haven't gone to the store, and I'm not exactly the best cook. I can make a mean mac and cheese and a PB and J, but my culinary skills are limited at best," she said with a shy smile. She had always meant to learn how to cook better but never really taken the time. She kept it simple and ate clean. Mostly grilled chicken, salads, fruits, veggies, and the occasional cheat meal—but she always went out for that sort of thing. She tended to gain weight easily, and with it always being just her, it'd never really made much sense to cook an actual meal.

He smiled at her again. "Not to worry, I happen to be an excellent cook. My mom taught me. You would like her. She's feisty, tough, and doesn't take shit from anyone...like you. The two of you are a lot alike in that department. Especially the part about not taking shit from anyone. Come to think of it, you two would either get along great or go to war. Hard to tell."

She wasn't sure how she felt about meeting his mom at this point and felt she needed to get to know him a lot better before that happened. There was a lot they still hadn't discussed. Sure, there was a lot of chemistry, and he was sexy as hell, but that only got a girl so far. She liked the fact that he had a good relationship with his mom. It said a lot about him.

"So, are you ready, or are we going to hang out here for the night?" Mac said, changing the subject.

"Absolutely," he responded, and moved to get off the bed, then suddenly had to sit back down. The doctor had told them his ribs and shoulder would need time to heal fully, and his equilibrium might be off for a while because of the whiplash and concussion he sustained during the accident. She was just happy he could walk for the most part since he was close to twice her size.

She went out into the hall to get his nurse for a wheelchair. He had been fighting her over leaving the hospital that way. "Seriously, what does it matter how you leave the hospital? If you screw around too much and don't let your body heal, you're going to be in even worse shape, and I'm certainly not carrying your huge ass around."

"My ass is not huge. I've been told it is quite a nice ass," he said with a grin.

"I'm not debating that fact. I'm just saying if you don't get into the wheelchair like a good patient, I'm going to put you back in the hospital myself," she said with a smile, not meaning a word of it. She enjoyed their playful banter.

He finally relented and lowered himself into the oversized wheelchair. She gathered his bags and walked beside him as the nurse pushed them out of the room. They stopped by the nurses' station so he could sign the discharge paperwork and promised to see his regular doctor for a checkup within the week. They headed out to her little SUV. She let out a giggle at the comical sight of him trying to fit his huge frame into her clown car. It was actually referred to as a compact SUV, and with Hudson trying to fit into it, the "compact" part certainly lived up to its name. He moved the seat all the way back, not uttering a word of complaint even though he looked uncomfortable.

Mac was catching him up on all the things that had happened while he was in the hospital.

"Okay," Hudson said when she was done, "so we know you're being set up, and we think my chief might know something. Joe found someone who apparently messed with one of my tires on camera."

Mac had left the part about Lola out of it. She wasn't ready to share Lola's existence with anyone because it could put them both in danger and open the door to her past, and she would have to explain all the horrors that lived there. It was better to let Hudson think she was just another normal person with a normal past, for now at least.

"Then Agent Ross came to visit you, and later you found her murdered. Have you checked on Ali lately?"

"Yeah, but probably not recently enough. I spoke with her a few days ago, and she said she was fine. She's still packin' heat and badass as ever. I like her," Mac said. She could appreciate a woman who was smart enough to go to med school and did whatever it took to get there.

She stopped by the store for some much-needed supplies. She left Hudson in the car so she wouldn't have to worry about both him and the groceries. She was picking up a carton of eggs when she got the weird feeling that someone was watching her again. That feeling had been happening a lot lately. The bright lights in the Safeway suddenly felt blinding, and the little hairs on the back of her neck stood on end. She knew she was safe with all these people around, but she just couldn't shake the feeling of being watched. She took several deep breaths to calm herself. She looked around the store, slowly regarding each person she saw. Some of them stared back at her, and others just looked down and passed her by. None of them seemed like a threat.

They all just seemed like normal people at the grocery store. Something made her gut turn. She quickly gathered the rest of her food and then stopped by the pharmacy to pick up Hudson's prescriptions, gauze, and ointment. The hospital had given them a little care bag to tend to his wounds, but she had nothing extra at her house. She figured it was better to be safe than sorry.

Mac returned to the car to find Hudson fiddling with his phone. She unloaded the groceries and took one more look around, not seeing anything to be alarmed about, but her heart still raced. She took another deep breath. She was probably just being paranoid, but she still didn't like the feeling. Now it seemed she sensed danger around every corner, especially after seeing Viv with her body all mangled and cut.

Hudson looked at her as she slid back into the car. "You, okay?"

"Yeah, I think I'm just tired and a little on edge with everything that's been going on lately."

"That's understandable," he said and covered her hand with his. The electricity that went through her spine made her mind wander back to the morning they had shared before the accident. His strong jaw had stubble running across it, and his hair had grown out since he had been in the hospital. He looked good and clean-shaven, but there was something sexy and rugged about him now. She wondered how that stubble would feel against her hand when he kissed her neck, or between her... *Nope, stay focused.* He needed to heal, and then they could have lots of fun.

She smiled absently as they fell into a comfortable silence the rest of the way home.

CHAPTER
FIFTY-ONE

THE MAN HAD GONE BACK HOME after a meeting. He couldn't get his hand to stop shaking. He went through his normal ritual as the sun started to go down, checking the perimeter of the house, making sure his garden hadn't been disturbed, and confirming each lock in the house was secure. It was getting dark out already, and with the sun going down the temperature would plummet. He started a small fire in the fireplace. His cabin was small, warm, and cozy.

The winter days in Washington were short and cold. The sun normally didn't come up until 0700 hours and went down usually no later than 1600 to 1700 hours. It made the days short and the nights long. Thankfully, they were getting to the part of the year when the days started getting longer. He liked the night. It was a time he could relax and finally be himself. He hated always having to hide who he'd become. He enjoyed what he did. He had never felt so alive. He vaguely remembered his former life before the incident—before she had blown him up and had to be stopped—but in reality, she had unleashed his need to hunt.

It made him feel powerful, in control and better than ever. He knew he had to find ways to maintain normalcy but really, was *normal* what he really wanted? He knew that was what society expected from him, but it no longer felt right. The doctors said that his head injury had caused damage to his cerebral cortex. They said he might experience impulse control and anger outbursts. Some of those things had happened at first, but now he had found out how to control them. He thrived off the high-risk environment he had created by hunting Sahar. He felt he had to do it to feel whole and satisfied, and she needed to be stopped. After the incident, he simply found it impossible to focus on anything but what needed to be done. He had once been good at connecting and keeping normal relationships, but ever since his traumatic brain injury he simply didn't feel bad for what he was doing. It was a necessary evil when at war, and he had to finish what he'd started.

The look of fear on their faces when he toyed with them and eventually killed them was like an itch he couldn't scratch. No matter how many times he did it, he wanted more. It consumed his every waking moment. He dreamed about it in vivid detail when he slept. He thought about it during the day, often having trouble focusing on the most mundane tasks. He often found himself visualizing his next kill while sitting in a meeting as the other military members droned on about the mission and all the other insignificant things that used to seem so important to him. It was interesting to think back to when he spent his days busying himself with mentoring others and furthering the mission; now his days were filled with fantasies. Brutal sexual fantasies were always there. He tried to shut them out of his mind, but he was obsessed, and everything else seemed insignificant in comparison.

Sahar crept into his thoughts. He thought her persona as Ali was stunning, with her long, strong, shapely legs. The way she danced brought most men to their knees, begging for more. He wanted to see her beg for her life. He craved the feeling of power and fear in her eyes. He wanted to watch her when the realization and acceptance of her pending death settled on her face. The twisted expression of terror would make her features more enticing to him. He'd plunge his knife deep into her but not enough to kill her, just to get her warm blood flowing. That was when they normally knew they were going to die. It was his favorite part. She would plead and try to appeal to his human side but fail to realize it was too late. He had become something else entirely, a hunter, and she needed to be stopped.

He would lick the blood from his fingers, enjoying the salty metallic taste it left in his mouth. She would watch him in horror, pleading for him to stop as all the others had. He would wrap his strong hands around her frail little neck, feel her gasp for air, press down until she lost consciousness, feel the life almost leave her body only to let up on his grip and watch her gasp and spit, trying to bring precious air back into her lungs. Just as she regained her ability to focus on him, he would slide the knife back into her warm skin, careful not to kill her. Before she lost full consciousness, he would enter her with the feel of her sticky warm blood against his chest as he squeezed her neck even tighter.

The pain would be intense, and most would pass by then, but he hoped Ali would last longer. She was strong and would fight. He loved it when Sahar fought. It made him feel that much more powerful. When she gave up too easily, it left him feeling unsatisfied and wanting more. No, he knew Ali would fight him. There was absolutely nothing like it in the world. The most earth-shattering orgasms came from watching the life leave a woman's body. Her body was still warm and sticky underneath him even after she was dead. He couldn't get over the feeling, the rush it gave him.

Being normal had become less and less sustainable. He had tried to be normal with Viv, but she'd known there was something off about him. He'd even had a hard time getting an erection if she wanted him. He'd needed her because she was his best source of information, and she was easy to control. After her marriage had fallen apart, she became easy to manipulate. She was so sappy and wanted so badly to please him. It made him physically ill, but she had served her purpose and given him the information he needed. She was also good at misdirecting others for him, even though she didn't realize it. For an OSI agent, she was awfully trusting, but that was to his advantage. Why not trust him? He was a respected member of the United States Air Force. He had earned that trust and certainly enjoyed using it to his own advantage. People never questioned his intentions, even if they should. He loved that feeling of power. One of his therapists had written a note that he feared his patient had become a narcissist, but he had actually become so much more.

He licked his lips, thinking about how enjoyable Ali would be. He felt himself getting aroused just thinking about the life draining from her. The way her beautiful olive skin would start to turn a light tinge of blue. How her sensual lips would gasp for air, praying that someone would come to rescue her before it was too late. He knew no one would ever hear her scream or know where to find her. No one knew about his hiding place, and there was no way to hear her all the way out here. He went to his hiding place, pulled out his book again, and looked at the pictures of Ali and then at Mac. The culmination of his masterpiece would be that beautiful creature that he would truly love devouring.

He had begun to rub himself when an alarm went off, notifying him of an approaching vehicle. He jumped off the couch, frantically putting away his book. How had they found him? He ran to his monitors and saw his worst nightmare: a police SUV making its way up his driveway, shining a huge light on his property. His truck was sitting out front, so they had to know he was home. *Deep breaths, count, one, two, three*—there was a knock at the door.

The man glanced at himself in the mirror and tried to remain calm. Maybe it was nothing, or at least nothing to do with him. He splashed cold water on his face and yelled out, "Just a minute!" He slowly opened his front door, unlatching the three locks that hold it in place.

Outside stood two men in uniform. One was tall and lanky, his partner shorter and stocky. "Good evening, sir," the tall one said.

"What can I do for you this evening, officers?" the man said in his most even, practiced tone.

"We're looking for a missing child that has wandered off from one of the rental cabins by the lake. Have you seen anything?" the shorter officer said.

"No, I'm sorry, but it's been quiet here all night," the man replied, taking a deep breath and feeling relieved that they weren't here for him.

The tall officer handed him a card. "Please give us a call if you see a young boy."

"Thank you, Officer. I will." The man closed and locked the door, feeling the sweat running down his back.

CHAPTER
FIFTY-TWO

HAVING Hudson around ended up being much more pleasant than Mac originally thought it would be. He was helpful—or as much as he could be with his injuries. She'd feared it would take a lot of work to help him, but it didn't. He was getting around fairly well for the most part. He had a hard time opening things with his shoulder still bothering him, and he couldn't do anything terribly physical because his ribs were still healing, but overall, he had proven to be quite self-sufficient. He'd even cleaned up after both of them a little. He would be on convalescent leave for a while longer and had nowhere to be so he kept himself busy around her house, always greeting her with a smile when she returned from work.

It had been a week since he'd been released from the hospital, and so far, it had gone well. Mac was still at the chaplain's office, just helping where she could. She had finally talked with her attorney, Kibble, and he was running down the lead she had given him on Pratt. He agreed that she should not question him because the prosecution could easily twist it into tampering with a witness. She hadn't shared everything else that was going on because she wanted Kibble to focus only on her case and clearing her name.

She had met with Stanton and walked him through the new evidence surrounding Senior Airman Terrell Johnson and her suspicions about a serial killer targeting women in the area. She gave him Joe's contact information and told him to reach out. She also told him about the possible connection to the murders in Coeur d'Alene and gave him Detective Zachariah Ward's contact information as well.

Mac had decided to wait it out. It seemed like every time she got closer to the case, someone else got hurt. That wasn't to say she had given up, but between living with Hudson and having to report to work every day at the chaplain's office, she was staying busy. To her knowledge, no one else had gotten hurt. It was almost like the killer had gone dormant, at least for a bit.

She had just arrived back home from work on a Friday afternoon to find Hudson out on her back porch leaning against the wall while two juicy steaks were grilling. She could see little blooms of cold air coming from his mouth. He had a huge jacket draped over his shoulders and had his jeans and combat boots on. It was freezing out. What on earth was he doing grilling this time of year? She laughed at the sight of him. His arm was still in a sling, so he had to set his beer down each time he tended the steaks.

He looked relaxed and oh so sexy. He had let his beard grow out a little, and his hair was getting longer. She wasn't entirely sure what she liked better. But, damn, he was hot no matter what he did. The way he looked up at her with that sexy grin when she came out to the back porch made her melt. She knew this couldn't last, but boy was it enjoyable.

She walked up to him and stood on her tiptoes to kiss him. "You keep spoiling me this way and I may never let you leave," she said and swatted him on the ass.

"Promise?" He grinned. He had never experienced a connection like this with a woman before. He had always felt alone, even when he was in previous relationships. Mac made him feel grounded and centered, like he was finally home. He felt he had found a piece of himself that he'd always been missing. He couldn't help himself; he knew he was falling for her. As much as he tried to push the thought from his mind, he couldn't deny the fact that he felt at peace with her. He just hoped she felt the same.

Mac disappeared to change out of her uniform before dinner. She had no makeup on when she returned and wore a pair of old sweats and a frayed green t-shirt. Her dark hair was pulled back in a no-nonsense ponytail that made her look younger than he knew she was, and just like that, she took his breath away. He was staring at her long enough for her to become uncomfortable. "What?" she asked.

"Nothing, you're just beautiful, that's all," he replied with a grin.

"I see," she said, cocking her head to the side like a cute puppy would. "Trying to butter me up. What is it that you want exactly?"

"All kinds of naughty things. We could start with a pair of hand-cuffs and a blindfold." He grinned wickedly, then walked over to her and caressed her cheek with his hand. He lowered his head to meet hers. In a low voice, he said, "What do you say, Mac? You up for a little sexy time?"

She laughed. "Only if you feed me first."

So he did just that. He fed her a delicious steak and a perfectly cooked baked potato with just the right amount of sour cream, bacon bits, chives, cheese, and salt. He even served it with her favorite wine. It was the perfect meal.

Being here with him seemed sublime. She wondered to herself if it was a little too perfect. Forever the pessimist, she contemplated their future and if he was truly too good to be true. No man had ever treated her this well. She really hated the thought of it coming to an end; she let herself think what it would be like if it didn't. What if they did stay together? She brushed the thought away. Things just didn't work out that way for her. She had tried a few times, but then she would do something stupid and sabotage the relationship, and the guy would run away with his tail between his legs.

As he reached down and kissed her again, she thought it would sure be fun to enjoy this while it lasted. Even injured, he was the best lover she had experienced. Not that she had many to compare him to, but she wasn't a virgin either. He took his time; he was gentle and always ensured she was fully satisfied before he was done. He was a rare breed.

They made love for hours. She had no idea how he kept up the stamina with broken ribs and a bum shoulder. His movements were limited, without question, but he never disappointed. She sure could get used to this.

She fell asleep snuggled up next to him, careful not to press on his injuries. He made her feel safe and secure. It was the best sleep she ever remembered having. The sound of his breathing, his scent on her sheets, all had the effect of lulling her to sleep every night. Her dreams were filled with a fairytale life that involved her and Hudson getting married and living in a pretty little house out in the country where they would raise their children. She woke the next morning with a smile on her face and a feeling of sadness about what would never be.

CHAPTER
FIFTY-THREE

MAC GOT ready for work and left Hudson sleeping. He had nowhere to be and still had a lot of healing to do. She thought he looked so peaceful lying there in her bed. She only had a queen, which didn't quite fit his mammoth body, but overall, it did the job. He slept on his side since sleeping on his back caused him pain these days, and his feet hung slightly over the end of the bed. One large hand was over her side of the bed like he was searching for her in his sleep.

Her morning was uneventful, and by mid-afternoon, she was ready to head home. She wondered what Hudson was up to when her thoughts were pulled back to reality by her phone buzzing. She didn't recognize the number but answered it anyway. "Hello?"

Granny San's sweet old voice came across the line. "Mac, is that you?"

"Yes, it's me. Is everything okay?"

"Oh no, I'm worried sick. Don't you know? I haven't heard from Ali since last night. It's like she dropped off the face of the earth and is nowhere to be found."

"Okay, take a deep breath and tell me about when you last saw her."

"Okay, okay, so she left for work last night at about six p.m. to go to her job. You know, the one where she dances so she can go to med school? Poor girl."

"Yes, I know. Did you try to call her?"

"Yes, I tried her cell, and I called her work too, but they said she worked her shift and left. She's not due back in until tomorrow night," Granny said. "I just know something has happened to her. I feel it in my bones just like if she was one of my kids. That girl has been through enough. She needs someone to care for her!"

"I'm on my way, Granny. Stay put and wait until I get there."

Mac shot Hudson a quick text: *Headed to CDA to check on Ali. Sorry for the last minute, but something is up. I'll keep you posted.*

She walked into Chaplain Bastion's office to ask if he minded her leaving early. He said he didn't but would need her in the morning for an event at the chapel that he could use her help with. She thanked him and assured him she would be there bright and early.

Cold air bit at her cheeks as she sprinted from the building to her SUV. She made a beeline to I-90 and headed to CDA. Her heart was racing, and she had to remind herself not to speed too much. She had always been a bit of a speed demon with a lead foot, but she couldn't afford another ticket, so she slowly let off the gas. It wouldn't help anything if she never made it.

Her phone rang inside her little vehicle, giving her a much-needed distraction. Hudson's baritone came over the line. "What do you mean 'you're checking on Ali?' What's wrong?"

"Not sure," she responded. "Granny just said she was missing. I'm headed up there to see what I can find out."

"Do you have protection with you?"

"Yes. I promise to be safe. Don't worry so much."

"Easier said than done, and you know it. There's a very real killer out there who might just try to go after you for meddling so much," he huffed. "Come back and pick me up so I can come with you. You need backup."

"I'm already halfway there, and you need your rest. I'll be fine. I'm going straight to Granny's house and then I'll report what I find to Zachariah Ward at the CDA police department. I promise to be careful. I'll check in as soon as I'm done. I might even be home by dinner. What are we having anyway?" she asked as a way to distract him.

"Just get it done and come home. I'll come up with something here in the meantime."

"Sounds like a good deal," she said, and hung up before he could argue more.

Her heart skipped a beat when Hudson referred to her place as "home." She turned up the music on the stereo and sang along. It was something she often did to calm herself. Once she pulled into Granny's driveway, she cut the engine and the music only to find herself sitting in an eerie silence. She had a bad feeling about this and hoped it was nothing more than Ali meeting a guy and staying at his place. She was a grown woman, after all, and had a right to do as she pleased.

Granny came out of the house looking worried and as though she hadn't slept. "Oh, thank you for coming, Mac! Where is that handsome fella you're normally with?"

"He wasn't able to make it. Any news from Ali?"

"Nope, nothing new since we talked."

"Do you mind if I take a look around her place?"

"Not at all, that would be just fine." Granny retrieved the spare key then came back and let Mac into Ali's place.

The two sides of the duplex were like night and day; Granny's side had an elderly lady feel while Ali had furnished her place in bright, vibrant colors and dark woods that brought the small space to life. It reminded Mac of the macaws in Mexico. She loved the birds and found them enchanting.

Mac carefully went through her home with Granny standing watch in the doorway. She asked Granny questions as she went, but nothing seemed out of the ordinary. There were medical books on the counters and takeout-food menus in the kitchen but nothing that would lead her to where Ali had gone. Mac was growing more concerned. Normally if a person went missing, the first twenty-four hours were crucial to finding them. She hoped Ali was safe, but her gut told her otherwise. She thanked Granny for her help and told her that she would notify the police.

"Oh hon, I already tried calling them, and they wouldn't listen to me. They kept saying that she probably ran off with some guy. But that's just not Ali's style. I know what she does for a living, but that's just logistics for her. She only does it to pay for her school."

"I know, Granny." Mac laid a hand on the old woman's shoulder. "I believe you, and I intend to find her. I'll let you know as soon as I know something," she promised and headed back to her car.

Twenty-five minutes later she found herself at the CDA police department. As she got out of her SUV, her stomach growled loudly, and she realized she hadn't eaten for the better part of the day. She took a deep breath and headed into the station.

At the front counter behind a protective wall of plexiglass sat a heavyset redheaded woman with a headset smashed into her wild hair. She was apparently talking with someone who was excited because her side of the conversation kept getting interrupted. She raised her finger, indicating that Mac should wait a moment.

Mac sat down in the small area until the woman was done with her conversation.

"Yes, ma'am, what can I do for you?" the woman finally asked.

"Hello Alice," Mac read from the woman's nametag. "I'm here to see Officer Ward. Is he available?"

"Is he expecting you?" Alice countered.

"No, ma'am, he's not, but I have something urgent to discuss with him. Could you please let him know I'm here?" Mac asked, giving the woman her best smile. Mac had never been very good at kissing ass, but she was willing to try.

Alice disconnected her headset, lifted her substantial frame out of the chair, and walked out of her small reception area through a door into the main bullpen of the police department. Mac had never met Zachariah in person and only talked to him on the phone. She had pictured him as a younger man who smiled a lot, but people never looked the way she thought they would.

Alice came back two minutes later with a tall slim man with gray hair—not at all what Mac was expecting—but then he smiled a smile that reached all the way to his eyes. "Hi, you must be Mac. Joe has told me a lot about you. What brings you in today?"

"I was just wondering if you had a few minutes to talk," she started, not wanting to blurt out that Ali was missing and she thought there was a serial killer on the loose who had abducted her.

"Sure, no problem. Why don't you follow me back to the conference room?"

She followed him through a maze of old gray cubicles and rows of open desks to a back conference room. The floors were a weird blue color that looked like they were ten years past when they'd needed to be replaced. The conference room table was beaten up in multiple spots and was a few sizes too large for the room, pushing the chairs close to the walls. It was about what she had expected. The states rarely received good funding for their furnishing. There had been a lot of budget cuts throughout the years, and it showed.

"So, what can I do for you?" he said as he sat down.

"Has Joe brought you up to speed concerning the multi-jurisdictional case that we've been looking into?" she asked.

"I know some of it." He pulled a small beat-up green notebook from his jacket pocket and looked at his notes. "I'm aware of the missing person's case of Lilianna Broadsmith and, of course, the murder victim, Mrs. Elise Morrison. It's my understanding that Joe might have another case in his jurisdiction, Abigail something or another. Then there's your case on base... Zonira, I think."

"Okay. That basically covers it. I'm here today because Ali Ahmad, the sister of the murder victim on base, has gone missing. We think she might be the next victim of our serial killer," she said, holding her breath for a few seconds.

"I see," he said with a quizzical look on his face. "Do you have any evidence to support your theory?"

She knew this was going to be an uphill battle. As a matter of fact, she didn't have any solid evidence; it was all circumstantial at best. She knew she had multiple women who were either missing or dead, and that they all looked the same, except for Viv. She was an anomaly, but the modus operandi was very similar. Viv's stab wounds appeared to be the same, and the strangulation was very similar to the photos of the other woman. Viv had had ties to the case and had met with Mac shortly before she was killed.

Mac hated to think the killer had been watching her house and gone after Viv because she'd been there. She pushed the thought from her mind. Guilt would get her nowhere. She didn't believe in coincidence, and this case had way too many of them. She took a deep breath.

"Joe seems to believe in your theory," Zachariah said, "but honestly, I don't currently have the resources to go hunting for a stripper that may or may not be kidnapped by a nut job and may or may not be in Idaho, let alone in my jurisdiction. I'll tell you what I'll do: I'll get with Joe and see if we can locate the young woman in question. The problem with a multi-state case is that it requires us to bring in the FBI. Talk about slowing things down and muddying the waters! I'm pretty sure none of us want that."

Mac didn't care what would be a good move from a jurisdictional standpoint. All she wanted was for someone to give a rat's ass about a missing young woman. She also knew she had zero authority to get anyone to do anything. Even if Ali had gone missing on base, there would be jurisdictional issues depending on whether the federal government wanted to investigate themselves or hand the case over to the locals. She felt herself getting frustrated and feared for Ali's safety. She figured he might play with her for a few hours before he killed her. If he felt safe, he might keep her alive even longer, but Mac hadn't nailed down the exact time frame he liked to keep them alive. It seemed like this guy was all over the map.

He had dumped a body, there were two missing women they knew of, and then Viv's and Zonira's bodies were left at the scene. It really didn't make much sense. Most serial killers were ritualistic. They liked to kill a certain way and found comfort in following a specific killing regime, but she also knew that killers were not predictable. Each one she had studied had presented with their own interesting way of doing things. So, his actions only made sense if his time had been cut short with Viv and Zonira. Then there was Elise Morrison from CDA, whose body had been dumped in the woods and found by a hiker. She wasn't entirely sure if that case was related, but the woman had an unsettling resemblance and the same wound pattern.

Mac stood and thanked Officer Ward for his time and assistance. He promised to get with Joe and check things out. He said if they had enough evidence between the two of them to get the FBI to come then he would make the call. She knew his hands were tied but still felt disappointed. Joe would be in the same boat. A multi-state investigation required the FBI's involvement without question, and there was really no way around it.

Shoulders slumped, she left deflated.

CHAPTER
FIFTY-FOUR

MAC SAT in her SUV in the parking lot, unsure of what to do next, so she called her sister. Lola was the only person she knew who could track someone anywhere in the world. Lola answered on the first ring. "Hi Sis, how've you been?"

"I'm good. I miss you," Mac responded.

"Miss you too. I ran those prints through all state databases and didn't get a hit. I'm working on hacking into the military databases to run it as we speak."

"Thanks, I appreciate you looking into that. I have another favor…" Mac trailed off. "I was wondering if you could ping a cell phone for me."

"Well, here I thought you had a challenge for me!" Lola chirped with a follow-up of swift clicking on her keyboard. "What's the number and general area?"

Mac rattled off Ali's number. "I think she's either in Idaho or Washington somewhere," she said, unsure if that would make tracing too difficult.

"So…the phone is no longer on, but it last pinged near Newman Lake right before the Idaho border. If you follow Highway 290 to North Idaho Road then onto East Moffat Road, you should be close."

"Wow, that's amazing! Is there any way to find out what kind of homes or cabins are out there to give me a little more direction?" Mac asked hopefully.

"Let me see what I can do, and I'll call you back. Be safe. Do you have your gun?" Lola asked.

"Of course, never leave home without it."

"Hey, don't go alone, okay?"

"Don't worry, I'm not going to engage. I just want to see if I can find any clues. I'll be fine. I promise."

She hung up and put her SUV into gear. She wasn't exactly sure what she was looking for but figured it wouldn't hurt to go check things out. It was like finding a needle in a haystack. Once she got out by Newman Lake, she would probably lose cell service as well. Parts of the lake were densely wooded, and technology wasn't used in the deep woods.

She headed that way. She certainly didn't hold out any hope of finding any clues, but her concern for Ali's safety drove her to look. The fact that her cell phone had pinged near Newman Lake didn't mean a whole lot. She might have gone out for a little getaway and forgotten to tell Granny. On the other hand, what twenty-two-year-old would turn off their cell phone?

On the way there, she was careful to maintain her speed. Navigating back across the Washington state line, she turned off the highway and made her way into the wooded area where her sister had told her was the phone's last-known location. As she toward the lake, more farms came into view. The road curved like a large snake winding back and forth. She slowed down to a crawl. In parts of the road, the dense woods blocked out most light.

She crept along, not wanting to slide on the ice. The roads were not terribly well maintained back here. If she had to guess, the locals oversaw this part of the lake. She passed a small grouping of houses that jutted out on the lake. They were stacked almost on top of each other, and she wondered why people wanted to live like that.

Her tires slipped a little heading down a steep part of the winding road and again as she tried to stop at a stop sign where the road stopped giving her the option to go right or left. She figured it best to stay near the lake and took a left. A little farther down, where there were fewer houses and home to little more than deer and other wildlife, she saw a lump on the side of the road. It appeared to be a bag of some kind, but with the snow piled up around it, it was hard to tell.

She pulled up and got out to see what it was. She slid on her winter gloves just to be on the safe side. The bag had been tossed at some point, and the contents had spilled out on the road. She crouched down to inspect them, not wanting to disturb anything. There was a red tube of lipstick, a silver compact, and a small black brush. Next to that, sticking halfway out of the bag, was a leather animal-print wallet. She held her breath as she opened the wallet and found the bill holder full of ones. Her pulse increased as she flipped the wallet the rest of the way open to see Ali's beautiful face smiling back at her from her driver's license photo.

She pulled out her cell phone and sent a text to Hudson and Joe. The message lingered for a moment, but then came back with an error message saying it couldn't be delivered. She kicked herself for not giving them her location.

How the hell did Ali's bag end up on the side of the road? Had he ditched it so that no one could track her phone, or had she tossed the bag hoping someone would find it and then find her? Either way, it was a good clue, and Mac was happy that she was in the right place— but where to now? Guilt gripped her for not trying harder to get Ali to leave the area until this guy had been caught. As stubborn as Ali was, it probably wouldn't have made a difference, but if she'd had tried harder then maybe, just maybe, Ali would be safe right now. If she had gone to stay with a friend, this might not have happened.

"Shoulda, coulda, woulda" wasn't getting her anywhere. She cleared her mind and listened. It was a beautiful area, serene and quiet. She could hear nature all around her: birds chirping, small woodland creatures scurrying about. For what seemed like a long time, she heard nothing else, and then there was something. It sounded like someone was chopping wood, maybe a tree—and then she heard the unmistakable high-pitched scream of a woman cutting through the forest. She couldn't tell exactly what direction it had come from.

Mac was starting to shake so badly from the cold that she was having a hard time keeping her teeth from chattering in her head. She quickly collected all of Ali's things, hoping she would be able to return them soon, that Ali would still be alive.

She went back to her SUV and climbed in, grateful for the warmth that lingered there. She started it back up and hesitated. She checked her phone and tried to resend the text message with no luck. Finding her courage, she pulled her gun out of the glove box, made sure it was fully loaded, and put it in the passenger seat. She put the car in gear and began to creep down the road, looking for anything that would give her a clue to Ali's location.

As she rounded the corner, she saw a long dirt road almost resembling a trail jutting off the main road. There was the distinct impression of fresh vehicle tracks leading there. A few signs warned passersby: *NO TRESPASSING* and *PRIVATE DRIVE*.

Welcoming place, she thought. She stayed there idling for what seemed like a long time, not sure if the little road would lead to anything or if she was wasting precious time. She took a chance, angling her SUV down the path. It turned out to be a long driveway. There was a cabin up ahead, but she could only see a corner of it. Darkness was beginning to engulf her surroundings. On the off chance that she was in the right place, she didn't want to alert anyone to her presence. She was fairly certain that the scream had come from this direction.

Mac tucked her little SUV between the trees off the road. She hoped the owner of the place hadn't seen her. If she was in the right place, giving him advance notice wouldn't be in her best interest. If she was in the wrong place, then she could easily get shot for trespassing. She sat there for a moment, debating whether she should turn back to get help. If she drove back to the main road in range of cell service, she could get backup—but would Ali still be alive by then? If that was her screaming, then it could already be too late.

A large crashing sound came from the cabin. Her mind was made up.

She exited her SUV. She owed it to Ali to try and help. Her breath escaped from her mouth, crystallizing in front of her in little puffs of fog. She tried to relax, but her body was so tense that her muscles ached. Partially from the cold, mostly from sheer fear.

CHAPTER
FIFTY-FIVE

THE MAN WATCHED Mac approach the house and felt a large grin spread across his face. *Fortune favors the prepared mind*, he thought as the motion sensors alerted him to her every move. He could just sit back and watch those beautiful huge eyes, terrified in the dark. He absently wondered what she was doing out here with no backup. This day just couldn't get any better. It seemed his prey was just coming to him on their own.

Earlier that morning around 0200 hours he had found Ali getting off work, ripe for easy picking. It was almost like she was waiting for him, gift-wrapped. A toy for him to play with. She went out to her car without her gun or any other protection on her. She'd barely even put up a fight, not that she was any match for him, but he had expected more. It didn't take long. He had simply crouched down in the back seat of her car. It was a little red Nissan Versa that had simple locks to pick. At first, he didn't think he could hide in the back because it was so small, but once he got in, he was pleasantly surprised at how roomy it really was. Then she came out in all her stunning beauty, but with the club's bouncer in tow. He was a gentleman and walked her to her car, probably hoping to get a little action.

Funny. He'd done the same thing with Sahar the first time they met. She was clearly up to her old tricks. He crouched down and flattened himself against the back seat. He figured the bouncer would see him. He waited, holding his breath, not wanting to alert the big goon that there was someone in her car. The bouncer was huge, standing at least six foot four and looked more like a walking building than a man. His proficiency in hand-to-hand combat would help, but it would be difficult to take down a man that size. He himself was not so small, but he wasn't as young as he used to be, and over the years his body had taken a beating.

They approached her car and the man slipped down even lower, hoping to go undetected. He slowed his breathing. Thankfully, the parking lot was very dark, and it was hard to see anything inside the vehicle. He hoped that would work to his advantage. He couldn't believe it. It must have been his lucky night; the overgrown ape was too busy looking at Ali to notice his surroundings. The man could have probably sat straight up in the back seat and the ogre wouldn't have even noticed.

Ali smiled at the big man and thanked him for walking her to her car. She pushed the key fob to unlock the car and let herself in. She sat in the driver's seat, turning over the engine. She had to wait while her windshield cleared so she could drive. The bouncer stood outside her car for a few seconds and then realized he was dismissed and walked back toward the club.

She locked the doors just in case and waited. She was rubbing her hands together, trying to keep warm while the little car slowly began the thawing process. As it did, she relaxed back into her seat. It would still be a few more minutes before she could safely drive home. She was very happy that she had paid the extra money for the model with the heated seats. It made all the difference in the world when waiting for the rest of the car to thaw. She had a remote start, but for some reason, it had stopped working long ago, so she waited.

When he felt certain that no one else would disturb them, he sat up in the back seat. She caught his reflection in her rearview mirror. Her eyes widened with fear, giving him an instant erection. God, she was beautiful. She looked even more stunning when she was terrified. He watched her curiously; she seemed to be frozen in place, unable to move. He wrapped his arm around her chest to keep her immobile.

With one practiced motion, he lifted the syringe to her neck and injected midazolam. He liked the drug because it was fast-acting and didn't have a ton of side effects. He had messed it up a few times trying to figure out the right drug to use and the right dose, but he had finally perfected it. He knew if he used any more than two to three milliliters, things wouldn't go well, especially for a woman as small as Ali.

As the injection went into her neck, she reached up and scratched across his forearm. He muffled a growl and pulled his hand away, but it was too late for her. The drug was already taking effect. Her eyes were drooping, and within a few short seconds she was resting her head against the steering wheel.

The man was very pleased with himself. He loved the thrill of the chase. It reminded him of being in Afghanistan and running down the enemy. He missed the thrill of that life, though he did like the creature comforts this world allowed him. There was simply nothing better than taking the time to slowly kill rather than the rushed jobs they were afforded overseas. He hadn't always enjoyed it this much, but deep down he knew there had always been this part of him lingering. He absently wondered what would happen when Sahar was finally stopped for good.

The doctors and psychiatrists talked about all these crazy acronyms that were supposed to explain why he felt the way he did. "PTSD" and "TBI" were their buzz words. They told him he might have trouble with his altered mental state, but he wasn't having any trouble at all. He was focused and knew what had to be done. He had found his true calling.

It was funny how things worked out. They had done a Medical Evaluation Board on him, and they had all reviewed his records. He thought it was going to be the end of his career. He really hadn't minded that much other than knowing finding a new job would be a hassle. He knew how to be an airman, and he was really good at faking how to be a good military member. He had been relieved as they did their thing.

They returned him to duty and coded him not to deploy again. He knew that meant he was on borrowed time, but he was okay with that.

It just gave him more time to play and perfectly covered up the need to find her. He might have gotten caught if he had been put into an unfamiliar situation where he couldn't easily navigate how to act or speak. He had been raised in the military from the young age of eighteen. It was all he knew, and he certainly knew how to get people to think what he wanted them to.

He gently moved Ali from the driver's seat to the passenger seat. He even buckled her in place before taking her to his home. She was out cold for longer than she was supposed to be. Maybe he had misjudged the dose? After all, she was a small woman. He checked her pulse a few times as they drove. For her to die too soon would just not do. He had plans for this one, questions that needed answered. He wondered what he would do after he was done. Maybe he would retire and go somewhere warmer to kill. There were plenty of bad people out there that needed to be stopped, plus it was hard to dig graves when the ground was always frozen. Florida sounded nice. He had put his time in and deserved a little break, plus all the tourists out there would provide plenty of enticing opportunities to rid the world of nasty people. His mouth watered just thinking of the beautiful women in skimpy clothing waiting for him.

CHAPTER
FIFTY-SIX

HUDSON PACED around Mac's house like a caged animal. She had been gone for too long, and her phone just kept going straight to voicemail. It was now dark outside as he watched little snowflakes fall from the sky. He wasn't sure what to think, but he knew something was wrong. His body ached from the tension and injuries he had recently sustained. In all actuality, he should be dead instead of just banged up a bit. He paced back and forth and then picked up the phone and dialed Joe.

"Any word?" was all he said when Joe picked up.

"No, nothing. Do you have any idea where she might have gone?"

"No, she just said that she was going to check on Ali, but I called Granny Sans, and she said that Ali had been missing and never came home from work last night and that Mac had gone to the CDA police department to file a report."

"Yeah, Nathaniel told me about her visit. He called me earlier and said Mac came by convinced that there was a serial killer on the loose working in both Washington and Idaho. We discussed the case, but there's little to no evidence supporting her theory. We're both looking into the cases, but we certainly don't have enough to get the FBI involved in a multi-state manhunt. We aren't even completely sure that the missing women—including Ali—are related. Obviously, they all look alike, but that's the only connection we see at the moment. Ali could have met a guy and gone off to have a little fun, not realizing she had worried her neighbor."

"So, what you're saying is there's no sign of her since she left the CDA police department over two hours ago?" Hudson asked in desperation.

"Yes, that's what I'm saying. I put out an APB on her SUV with instructions to notify me if anyone sees her, but other than that we have to just wait."

"Okay, thanks for your help, Joe. I'll let you know if I hear from her."

"Don't worry so much. If anyone can take care of herself, it's Mac. She's one of the most badass women I've ever met. Consider yourself lucky. I'm sure she can handle whatever it is she's gotten herself into." Joe hung up.

Mac reminded Joe of his ex-wife, Eli. She had also been a cop. He missed her and was still determined to get her back one day. She was a one-of-a-kind woman. He had tried to date other women, but no one compared to Eli. He kicked himself daily for the stupid decisions he had made back then. He had been working undercover on a trafficking case involving young women who were being plucked off the streets by a sadistic man. They were being shipped in crates and sold overseas to the highest bidder. Some of the young women were not women at all; they were just girls. Most of them were over eighteen, but some of them weren't. It made Joe's stomach turn every time he thought about that case. He had been working with another detective who was also undercover. She was supposed to get picked up for sale as one of the girls. They spent so much time together that his judgment got clouded, and he ended up sleeping with his partner. Eli never forgave him and probably never would. All he could do was hope she came back to him one day. That had been one of the most challenging times of his life. It was the same case where he'd found out his partner was dirty.

Hudson continued to pace. He thought about eating something to distract himself, but he just wasn't hungry. At this rate he would wear a hole in her floor. Joe had been right; he felt like a very lucky man. Mac was a rare breed, and he didn't think he would find another woman like her. Just thinking about her brought him comfort and warmth. She was out there and could be in danger. He was working himself into an unhealthy state. He had to think as she did. What did they know about the case? If he could figure out how to solve the case, then he could possibly find her. He stopped pacing and tried to clear his head. Worrying wasn't going to get him anywhere—he needed to focus.

He went back into her little office and started pulling together everything she had on the case. There were pictures of all the known and suspected victims. She had autopsy reports of each of the dead victims. Hudson wondered how on earth she had gotten ahold of those. It didn't really matter. He started organizing them and poring over every report.

Each one of the victims had the same type of stab wound. It appeared the murderer favored a particular knife. They all showed forced sexual activity prior to death, but no semen or other identifying fluids were left behind. Each victim was first stabbed, then strangled with large hands. In most of the cases, the coroner had said that the stab wounds and the strangling could both be considered the cause of death, but it was inconclusive as to which one caused the victim to pass first.

Hudson felt sick to his stomach as he read. There were no reported fingerprints left behind no hair or skin. Who on earth could do this to another human being? Then he began to wonder how he could do this to someone and not leave any DNA behind. He thought about it for a while. How could someone get away with not leaving DNA behind everywhere he went? The obvious way would be to cover your body and then dispose of everything once the job was complete. That could certainly be it, but how did that lead him anywhere?

Hudson was deep in thought when his phone started to buzz on the kitchen counter. He picked it up without even looking at who was calling. "Hudson," he boomed into the phone.

A sweet voice came over the line. It almost sounded musical. "Hi, Hudson. You don't know me. I'm Mac's sister, Lola."

He didn't say anything for a few moments. He hadn't even known

Mac had a sister and berated himself for not asking her more questions.

"Hudson, are you there? This is important," Lola said.

"Yeah, I'm here. Sorry, I didn't even know Mac had a sister. You just caught me off guard. What can I do for you?" Hudson was intrigued but also distracted and feeling impatient. He wanted to get back to finding Mac, but then he wondered just how much her sister knew about what was happening.

"There's a lot about Mac that you don't know, but that's for later. Right now, I'm worried about Mac."

"Agreed. What do you know?" he said more forcefully than he meant to. "Sorry...I'm also worried. What I meant was, how much do you know about what's going on with your sister?"

"Much more than you might think. I've been tracking this case with her since day one. I'm the one that provided her with all the information that she has on the case like the autopsy reports that you've been looking at all afternoon."

He became very aware of his surroundings. "How on earth could you possibly know what I've been doing all afternoon?"

"That's not important," she snapped. "I need you to focus. I gave Mac coordinates to where Ali's phone last pinged, and I haven't heard from her since, and now Mac's phone is out of range as well. I need you to find her. As beat up as you are, you may want to bring backup. Mac tried to get the local authorities involved, but they blew her off. Do you know anyone that can help?"

"Did her cell ping in Washington State?" he asked, thinking of the jurisdictional issues.

"Yes, out at Newman Lake," she said and rattled off the location she had given Mac.

"Thank you, Lola. I have someone that I think can help. Could you do me one more favor? It could be difficult."

"Anything to find my sister."

"Could you run property records against every active-duty military member that works on Fairchild and tell me who has property out on Newman Lake?" She didn't say anything for a few seconds. "I'm sorry, it just sounded like you had some killer skills," he said.

"And I thought you had a challenge for me," she shot back.

He smiled. He liked her already. "Thanks, Lola. If I find her, can I call you at this number?"

"Yeah, keep me posted. I'll send the data to your phone. Touch base with me before you leave cell coverage. It should be approximately twenty to thirty minutes before you get to the lake."

"Will do."

He thanked her, hung up the phone, and called Joe.

CHAPTER
FIFTY-SEVEN

MAC'S BOOTS crunched in the snow as she made her way up to
the small cabin. It was getting harder to see, so she slowed her pace to
take in her surroundings. The trees towered over her head, covered in
thick snow. It was deeper out here than in town, but someone had
taken the time to clear the driveway. The dirt showed through on the
drive, but thick snow still covered the ground under most of the trees.
It would have been much easier to walk on the dirt driveway and not
sink in, but she wanted to be careful to approach undetected since she
wasn't sure what to expect.

It was quite beautiful. She wished she was here on a different
matter. It would be nice to get away from town and stay in a place like
this from time to time. She got the feeling that much more ominous
things happened in this house that didn't involve the thoughts running
through her head, like long afternoons of sex and relaxation. She
thought about Hudson and regretted not letting him know where she
was going. All she could do was hope that her phone would pick up a
signal at some point and her text would go through. She knew she was
in over her head, but there was no turning back now. If she did, Ali
might die, and Mac just couldn't live with that on her conscience. She
already felt guilty about not insisting on more protection for Ali. She
had seen the danger yet chose not to push.

The man was enjoying the view. Mac was very cautious as she approached. She couldn't see the cameras; they were tucked deep within the trees. He thought about what to do with her. He had never had two people to kill at the same time. He had kept Ali alive so that he could play with her for a while. He wanted answers and was in no hurry with this one, and now he was happy with his decision. Maybe, just maybe, he could figure out which one was Sahar and then maybe have a little fun. He got a little excited thinking about the things he could make them do to each other.

He had always liked girl-on-girl porn, especially the rough stuff where one of the women was slapping or whipping the other. After all, if one of them was really Sahar, then she owed him. He wondered if he should do Mac or Ali first. Not at the same time. That would be too quick. It would have to be Ali first. The more he thought about it, the more he was convinced that Mac was supposed to be his since she was obviously Sahar. He wanted her to watch and see what happened to bad people who blew other people up. He knew she was there to finish him off, but that wasn't going to happen. He imagined the fear in her eyes, knowing she was next. He wouldn't rush it. He needed to take his time with them to make sure they both lasted long enough. If he rushed, it wouldn't be as satisfying, and he needed to be satisfied. He needed to make her pay.

It might help him stop for a little while. That would be good. He could retire. He had thought about selling this place, but then there was the matter of his garden of bodies in the backwoods. Would someone be able to locate them? It would lead back to him if they did. That was a problem for another day. Now he had things to do. He licked his lips and rubbed his hands together, anticipating. He couldn't wait to see the look on Mac's face when she realized who he was. He smiled again to himself.

He thought about Ali, tied up and beautiful. He could hear her whimpering and thought about her dark almond eyes. He had been careful to use a soft cotton rope he'd learned about on a bondage website. It left fewer marks, and it was cheap and very hard to trace because it could be bought almost anywhere or ordered online. Either way, it was very common and easy to replace if he used it all up. He knew now that she wasn't the one, but he had to take her. She had seen too much.

Mac's teeth were chattering. She was dressed in warm clothes, but with the sun down, the temperature was plummeting. She ran her tongue across her lips absently, and the spit instantly froze in place. The cold was even seeping into her boots because she'd spent so much time with them buried in the snow. She mentally kicked herself for not fully preparing for this. She was making her way around a house and not even sure if she was in the right place.

She peered inside a bedroom with nothing in it. She kept a low profile as she came around the corner of the house and found an office lined with monitors, but they were blank, and the window was locked. Her hair was starting to freeze to her head, and her ears were starting to burn from the cold. She moved to the south side of the little cabin and looked into a tiny room. The window was higher than the others, and she had to go up on her tiptoes to see in. She gasped.

There was Ali, tied up to a bed. The door to the room was closed, and it appeared to be otherwise unoccupied.

Mac took a deep breath; thankful she had finally located her and that she was alive. Ali appeared mostly unharmed, aside from her bindings. Mac tried the window and was relieved that it slowly slid open. Not sure what to expect, she reached down and touched her gun that was strapped to her side. Feeling reassured, she tried hoisting herself up to the window. There was no way she was going to pull this off. Her stretched-out body barely brought her high enough to reach the window, and although she had good upper-body strength, she didn't have the right leverage.

She looked around the property behind her and found an old stump. *That will do*, she thought. With some difficulty, she pulled the stump over to the window and climbed up on it. She carefully pulled up on the window, hoping the stump below her feet would stay in place and she wouldn't make too much noise. With some difficulty, she hoisted herself up and launched her body through. She landed on the other side with a soft thump, grateful for the carpet that muffled the sound.

Ali was looking at her with wild, frightened eyes. *Of course, she has to be terrified*, Mac thought. Ali started shaking her head violently.

She walked over to comfort Ali and put a hand on her arm to calm her down when the lights went out in the room. Mac froze for a few seconds and listened. She pulled her gun from its holster, hoping her eyes would adjust to the darkness. It was no use; it was pitch black. She tried to remember her training.

I'm enjoying this just a little too much, he thought to himself, but then again, life was short, and he really needed to stop and smell the roses. He breathed in deeply, enjoying the scent of fear in the air emanating from both Ali and Mac, his pretty little flowers. Then, he silently picked up a book from a side table and threw it on the floor about ten feet to his left.

Her gun immediately trained on the sound. "Stop where you are, or I'll shoot," Mac said, facing to the left of him.

He came a little closer. He could hear her breaths, rapid and short, as he slid on his thermal imaging glasses. They were the coolest things. It amazed him what could be found on the internet. He could see the heat signature of her body as she slowly moved around the room. The anticipation was so inviting. He almost couldn't help but reach out and touch her warm skin. He put his hand forward and stopped within inches. She was so beautiful and made just for him. He had known that for a long time. He had brought her in and made her feel special. He promoted her career and helped her make rank. Because of him, she had been a rising star until he decided to take it all away with the drug charges. It was fun to watch her wither and squirm as all credibility and support left her. She was getting entirely too cocky for her own good. Everyone needed to be humbled from time to time, and now he was certain she was Sahar in disguise.

Her mentor had told her to use all her senses during an attack. *Breathe in and breathe out.* Her heart slowly began to regulate. She took in a deep breath, trying to use her sense of smell and hearing to locate him. She shut her eyes, trying to concentrate when she heard a movement to her left.

He stepped back to make sure she didn't sense his presence. He needed this to last so he could find out why she had blown him up. A shot rang out in the dark and grazed his shoulder, ripping through his flesh. He screamed out in pain, not expecting her to be able to hit him in the dark. He had clearly underestimated her. He quickly spun on his heels and extended one long arm into a fist that connected with her beautiful face. He heard a loud thump as her body hit the floor.

He took off his glasses and turned on the lights. Mac lay on the floor, a large bruise forming across her cheekbone and temple. He had hit her harder than he'd meant to. He looked down at his arm where blood was seeping down his dark shirt. He stuck his finger in the blood and then placed it in his mouth. The metallic taste of warm blood, even his own, sent shivers down his spine. He smiled down at Mac. She was, without question, worthy of being his final masterpiece. Now he could see that she had always been Sahar. He didn't know how, but he knew it made sense.

The man moved around the room while Ali watched silently, feeling hopeless. He lifted Mac onto the queen-sized bed next to her squirming body and methodically tied each limb to the bedframe, making sure not to cut off circulation or let the ropes dig in too tight. He liked them to be unblemished when he played with them. He ran a finger across the bruise on Mac's face. He was sorry she had caused it to be there, but sometimes these things couldn't be helped. He checked each rope three times, making sure they were secure.

He moved to Ali, checked her ropes to ensure she remained secure, and removed the tape from her mouth. It hurt like hell when he pulled it off, but to her credit, she didn't scream. She simply flinched when he ripped it off and then lay in silence looking at him.

He wondered if she had accepted her fate. Some of his victims fought to the end, and others were like Ali. They just waited for things as they came, accepting their inevitable torture and death. He enjoyed the ones who fought more. He thought Mac would fight, which would be a nice contrast to Ali's compliance.

CHAPTER
FIFTY-EIGHT

HUDSON DROVE FASTER than he should have in his new truck. The insurance company worked quickly to replace it. *Thank goodness for USAA and their quick turnaround.* He got the same large four-door Chevy Silverado, but this one was a three-fourth ton in silver with a three-inch lift and larger tires. He liked the badass look of the truck and didn't want to wreck it during his first couple of days of ownership. The road was slick from the cold weather, and the temperature had dropped after the sun went down.

Next to him sat Joe, who reminded him for probably the tenth time to slow down. "We won't be able to save anyone if we're dead! Now slow down. We still have to wait for Lola's call anyway."

Hudson slowed his truck to a less insane speed and took a few deep breaths.

They took the exit off the highway onto the two-lane road that led out to the lake. Little snowflakes fell on the windshield one by one. The sky looked ominous with its pregnant clouds stuffed full of precipitation, ready to unload its winter wonderland. Hudson quietly prayed that the weather would hold out for them. It would make navigating the backroads and seeing fresh tire tracks by the lake much easier. Nothing could be done to help the cold wind biting his cheeks, but he could certainly hope for the rest.

Hudson had brought the case files with him. He'd figured he'd need something to distract his mind while they waited. He had tried to call Lola several times, but the number she'd called from went straight to a voicemail that wasn't set up. He was willing to wait a little longer, but then he was going in to see if he could find them. He was afraid that if he gave that psychopath any more time, it wouldn't end well for either lady. It might already be too late. He couldn't think of that.

They sat on the side of the road, waiting. Hudson checked his gun, and Joe looked at him. "You realize you're a civilian here and have no jurisdiction over this case. If you discharge your weapon, there could be serious consequences."

"I know, but I can't just sit here while Mac and Ali could be in trouble. I know there are no absolutes, but I'll just have to handle that one when it comes my way. I promise to do my best not to shoot the bastard. I'm happy to let you have that honor so long he's stopped, and we get the ladies back alive and safe."

"That sounds fair enough. So, what do we know about this guy?" Joe said as a way of distracting Hudson. He was getting fidgety, and the big guy was making him nervous. He had known Hudson for a long time and had never seen him this way about anyone, not even his ex-wife. Mac must have really gotten under his skin. He thought about Eli and what he would do if she were in danger. *Yup, pretty much the same thing—go in with guns blazing.*

"We know he likes asphyxiation and stabbing while sexually raping his victims. We think he has a certain type, and we think there are at least five victims—three dead and two missing—not to mention Mac and Ali, who we hope are not currently being held by him." Hudson said *him* like it was a dirty word.

"Okay, so other than that?" Joe went on, seeing Hudson getting agitated again. "We know he owns a dark truck. That might help us locate him as we work our way through the lake properties."

"But that could be any number of lake residents. You know how many people drive trucks in this part of the country?" The skin between Hudson's eyes knitted together in frustration.

"True, but you never know what could break this case wide open. Some of my guys were out here looking for a missing child a couple of days back. They found the kid lost in the woods, but they came across a cabin tucked back down a long drive while they were searching the woods. They knocked on the guy's door and the guy that answered looked all disheveled and was breathing hard. The more seasoned of the two cops said that the guy at the cabin made the hair on the back of his neck stand on end. The guy didn't do anything wrong; it was just a gut feeling. The guy was older and had a military haircut. After Lola calls, why don't we check that place out first?"

"What the hell Joe, why didn't you lead with that? That has to be the place. Lord only knows what that creep is doing to them."

"Shouldn't we wait for Lola?"

Hudson answered him by putting the truck in gear and hitting the gas. As they moved toward the lake, Joe saw his cell service disappear. He was worried about bringing a civilian in without backup, but he also understood that their evidence was circumstantial at best, and honestly, he would do anything for Hudson. They had been like brothers for a long time, and more than once, Hudson had had his back in some nasty situations. He'd even stayed with him when his ex-wife had left and he'd drunk himself into a stupor, almost losing his job.

It was pitch black outside now, and there was no light along the road. Hudson put on his brights so they wouldn't get into an accident. He had to bring the truck's speed to a minimum because the road snaked around the lake, switching this way and that. It wasn't just the back and forth but the steep inclines and low dips. There were parts of the road that were particularly treacherous because of large overgrown pine trees that blocked the sun from thawing during the day. With no guardrails, one false move could send his truck tumbling down a steep incline. Hudson's instincts told him to speed because his gut told him time was short, and he feared the worst, but Joe was right. Dead people couldn't save anyone.

CHAPTER
FIFTY-NINE

THE FOG in Mac's head slowly began to fade. It felt like a jackhammer was pounding behind her eyes. She closed and opened them several times with no change. It was so dark in the room that she couldn't even make out shapes. She could feel a softness under her back and legs. Her mind was reeling, trying to remember where she was. She tried to pull one of her arms down, only to have it jerked back into place by the rope attaching her to the headboard. Panic began to grow when she realized she was tied to a bed. Her hands and feet were completely immobile. She closed her eyes again, trying to remember what had happened.

It all came crashing down on her at once. She recalled seeing Ali in the house strapped to the bed and hoisting herself through the window. She thought she'd shot him but wasn't sure if she had imagined that or not. Her mind felt cloudy, but she was pretty sure she had. The side of her face still ached from the shiner across her cheek. Her sense of panic was getting the better of her as she began to hyperventilate. There was movement next to her that helped her calm and listen. He must have tied them both to the bed. Containment made sense. It would be easier to control both women if they were together and restrained. She inwardly cringed as she realized she could no longer feel her gun pressed against the side of her body.

In her head, she slowly counted. She would be no use to either of them in the midst of a panic attack. Carefully, she moved her wrists back and forth to see if there was any way to loosen the ropes. They didn't seem tight or rough, and they weren't cutting off full circulation. She had a little tingling feeling in her fingers from her hands being suspended above her head. The rope must be soft and not tied too tight. *That's a good thing,* she thought. Softer ropes would sometimes loosen easier and wouldn't leave terrible marks.

She tried to think positively as she wiggled her feet back and forth to loosen the ropes. After a few moments, she realized that the more she pulled, the more the ropes tightened against her skin. Unfortunately, he had tied the rope with a slip knot that would just keep getting tighter the more she struggled, so she changed tactics.

"Ali?" she asked softly.

"I'm here," Ali answered in a whisper. "Thank you for coming for me. Sorry he ended up getting you too."

"We aren't done yet. There's still hope."

Ali didn't answer for a long time, and then she asked, "What's the plan?"

"I don't know yet," Mac admitted. "What do you know about him? You've been here longer. Have you seen his face? Can you describe him to me?"

Ali thought for a moment. "He's over six feet tall with dark hair. He looks to be about in his forties, but it's hard to tell. His eyes are a dead blue gray. They looked right through me like I was a piece of furniture rather than a human being. It was super creepy."

Mac encouraged her to continue. "Did he do anything that stands out to you?"

"He checks everything three times. He's methodical about it. When he was tying you up, he checked each of your ropes three times. He always checks the locks three times. Weird, right?"

"Yeah, definitely interesting." *He could be suffering from obsessive-compulsive disorder probably brought on by anxiety or stress,* Mac thought. Many times, obsessive thoughts were hard to control for someone suffering from OCD. It was an interesting disorder and one that she had learned about in her studies. She thought about how she could use it to her advantage. Nothing automatically came to mind. Still, it was good to have as much information as possible to defeat the enemy.

He walked into the room and flicked on the lights, and all of that optimism went out the window. Her mind went blank, and she froze.

He stood there staring down at her. She couldn't speak, couldn't breathe. All the blood drained from her face, and she felt lightheaded. The man who stood before her was all too familiar. He had been her mentor and very much like an older brother. He had helped her when she needed it and helped to promote her career along the way. Her mind argued that this simply couldn't be right. There was no way this could be the killer. It simply didn't make sense. She stared at him, barely breathing, but the longer she looked, the more she could see the cold deadness that lived in his eyes. She remembered his eyes being kind and warm. Now, they looked uncaring. No, that wasn't quite right. They were almost inhuman.

She worked to regulate her breathing. Panicking right now wasn't going to solve anything. The shock began to wear off, replaced by anger. She was furious that he had deceived her this entire time. Her leader, mentor, and friend! She felt stupid for not seeing it, and also betrayed. How could she have been so blind? The Security Forces chief master sergeant stood there looking full of himself. Whether he was somehow pleased with the situation or himself, she wasn't sure. *Sick bastard*, she thought.

"What the hell, Chief Deleon?" was all she could think to say.

Ali whimpered softly next to her. At first, she thought Ali was just afraid of the monster standing before them, but then she realized Chief was holding a rugged-looking hunting knife. "You're a highly decorated chief master sergeant in our United States Air Force with twenty-seven years of service. What the hell happened to you?" Mac demanded.

He smiled at her with an ugly glint in his eyes and a grimace on his face. "You know, Mac," he said calmly in his deep voice that echoed in the small cabin. "I think you know what you did to me. When I was blown up in Afghanistan, everything became clear. I finally know what makes me feel whole...and now it's time for you to pay for what you've done."

Mac stared at him, completely confused.

"Before, I always thought I needed power and prestige, which is why I worked so hard to become a chief master sergeant. Now, I realize that being a chief in the military is insignificant in comparison to hunting you down and making you pay for blowing up me and my team. Now it's my turn to decide who lives or dies; the most intense high I've ever had," he said with an evil grin. "So, Mac, tell me: *Will you live, or will you die?*"

CHAPTER
SIXTY

HE ABSENTLY RAN the knife along the side of Ali's body. With a quick flick of the knife, he slit her silky green top open. Her eyes widened in fear, sucking in her stomach to avoid getting cut by the knife.

Mac watched, feeling helpless, unable to help her. She was getting frustrated not being able to figure out a way out of the situation. She was trying to clear her head and not let the panic rising in her throat take over when a loud shrieking noise came from the other end of the house.

Chief looked up curiously. That could only mean one thing. Someone or something had just broken through the perimeter of his property.

He looked at the ladies tied to the bed. "Now y'all wait here while I'm gone. I'll be right back," he said, chuckling at his own joke. He stood to his full height and squared his shoulders to make himself look even more intimidating. With a quick about-face, he left the room and headed toward the sound.

Mac looked at Ali and whispered, "We have to get out of here, *now*. This may be our last chance."

Ali moved her head up and down in agreement. She was afraid to make any noise and hoped Mac had a good idea.

"So, I think if I can get some slack in the rope around my wrists, I might be able to slide one of my hands out. I need you to slide your foot next to mine so I can use it for leverage."

Ali did as instructed and pushed her foot up against Mac's, giving her as much lift as possible. They could hear the monster moving about in the next room.

Mac stretched, trying to give herself a little slack. If she could maneuver her hand into the right position, she just might be able to create enough slack to slide her hand out of the binding. She pulled and stretched as far as her body would go. She heard him coming back toward the room. She quickly dropped back into place just as he walked back in.

He said nothing, just walked into the room, not looking at the women. There was a frustrated look on his face. He checked the ropes on each of the women three times. They both watched him as he methodically moved from one to the other. He growled and was talking to himself as he did so. After checking the ropes, he left the room again. They could hear him move about the cabin and then head out the front door. The cabin's old floorboards creaked as he walked on them, letting them know exactly where he was in the house.

Mac felt grateful she was able to track his whereabouts. She put her foot back on top of Ali's and began to push and stretch as far as she could. She wiggled her wrist, feeling it loosen slightly. "Ali, I need just a little more," she said, panting lightly.

Ali stretched her strong dancer's leg over as far up as she could, giving Mac just enough leverage to unhook her right hand. She moved it around, trying to restore circulation. As soon as she could feel her fingers again, she released her other hand and got to work on Ali's. It didn't take long for her to release one of her hands. They both began to move quickly, releasing each of their limbs until they were finally free.

"Can you walk?" Mac asked, thinking that Ali had been tied up for a while and had also been sedated.

"Yeah, I think so," she said, getting to her feet cautiously. Her strong legs felt wobbly underneath her, but she regained her strength after a few steps. They moved to the open door and froze to listen. Mac glanced around the room, looking for a weapon, but saw nothing of use. She stuck her head around the doorframe, hoping he wasn't playing with them, but no one was there. She moved forward with Ali just steps behind her.

Mac wasn't sure what her next best move would be. This was the man who had helped her become an expert marksman, and he had even taught her different ways to take down an opponent twice her size. He would be able to anticipate any move she threw at him.

They rounded the corner into a small kitchen. This was more like it. A kitchen always presented several types of weapons. She flipped on the lights, no longer caring if he knew where they were, quickly throwing open cabinet doors trying to find something. Ali came over with a large knife, and Mac had a cast iron skillet in her hand. Not the best, but it would have to do until they found their guns.

It was odd; their boots were neatly lined up at the front door. It almost appeared like they were welcome visitors. She wondered why he would leave them at the front if someone stopped by, but then she thought about their location. No one would just stop by way out here. No one knew where they were, which also meant no one was coming to help. She again kicked herself mentally for not giving someone her location before barging in guns blazing.

They came to the main living area of the house. Ali was in front this time while Mac stayed behind her. The floorboards creaked as they moved. Mac spun around with the frying pan in her hand when the lights went out. She cursed out loud. "Ali," she whispered.

"Right here," Ali responded, and touched her arm.

A motion sensor kicked a light on somewhere in front of the cabin, casting just enough light for Mac to see he was standing right in front of them.

Mac swung the skillet as hard as she could into him. He screamed in pain and dropped to one knee, holding his face. "Run!" Mac yelled.

Ali took off at a full sprint, not looking back. Mac was right behind her until she felt his strong hand grip her ankle. The momentum sent her sprawling face-first into the old wooden floor. She felt a few splinters embed themselves into the soft flesh of her arms. Ali was standing there staring at them, not sure what to do.

"Get help!" Mac screamed at her.

Ali grabbed a pair of boots, flipped on the main room's lights, and ran. She hoped it would afford Mac a slight advantage. She didn't think about a jacket or anything else until she was out in front of the cabin and realized she would freeze to death if she didn't find someone quickly. She ran as fast as her legs would carry her down the long winding driveway. She passed Mac's car, which was pulled off to the side. She stopped for a moment to check the doors, but it was locked. It wouldn't have done her any good anyway since she had no idea how to hotwire a car, and she was certain Mac wouldn't have just left the keys in the ignition. Ali finally found the end of the driveway and came running full tilt out into the road.

At that exact moment, Hudson's truck came around the corner. His headlights lit something in the road, and he slammed on the brakes. His truck slid slightly forward, almost coming in contact with whatever was on the road. They were sitting too high up in the truck to see Ali's small frame.

At first, Hudson thought it'd been a deer and was thankful for not hitting it. He jumped out of the truck and found Ali trembling in front of his headlights, barely clothed and wearing a pair of Mac's boots. He gathered her in his arms. Joe came around the other side with a blanket that Hudson kept in the back of his truck.

"Where is she?" was all Hudson could manage to say.

Ali pointed up the long driveway.

Hudson helped Ali into the truck. "What are we up against?" Hudson asked as they turned into the long driveway.

"He's a large man. Not as big as Hudson, but big. He has dead eyes. Mac keeps calling him 'Chief.' I'm not sure if that means anything to you guys, but I've seen this guy at work before," Ali said, beginning to feel calmer now that she was safe. But she was still terrified for Mac. That man hunting her was no longer human.

CHAPTER
SIXTY-ONE

MAC LAY STILL on the cabin floor, scanning the room for some sort of exit. It was still dark enough in the cabin that he wouldn't be able to make out her face. She could hear him stalking around the room, cursing. She saw drops of blood on the wood next to her face. She shook from the betrayal she felt. She had trusted him.

There was movement behind her, and she felt him climbing on top of her. She would be pinned by his weight within moments; if he sat on her, she would be completely immobilized. She quickly rolled her hips and flipped her body over, bringing a knee up into his groin in one swift move. He grunted in discomfort and let his weight crush her. She couldn't breathe.

"Where did your little friend go? You know she's going to freeze to death out there."

"Why do you care?" Mac spat.

"I've been fantasizing about you for a long time, Mac. You and Ali together," he whispered in a low, manic-sounding voice. His lips were practically touching her ear. She could feel his hot breath on her neck. It made her skin crawl. "You know it was meant to be this way. You created me by blowing me up, and now you belong to me. Now it's time for you to give back." He moved his upper body off her and slid the ugly hunting knife across her throat. She felt the prick of the blade cut her skin, but not deep enough to cause serious damage.

"So, Mac—or should I call you by your real name, *Sahar*? How do you want to die?"

She lay very still, trying frantically to think. She tried to wiggle out from under his grip, but it was no use. "Where do you think you're going, *Maaac*? We're just starting to have fun! You tried to kill me; now it's my turn. I know you came here to finish me off, but this time I was ready for you."

This was not how it was supposed to go. She wasn't supposed to die because this sicko had some twisted fantasy about her. She had survived so much in her life. She had to stay alive for Lola. She couldn't abandon her sister like this. She would be devastated and completely on her own. Then she thought of Hudson and what might be. *The hell with that.* She wasn't ready to die. Maybe if she kept him talking, it would buy Ali enough time to get back.

"Tell me what I did to you," she said.

"You know what you did!" He lifted the knife from her throat and slid it under her shirt, slicing it open, and leaving her exposed.

She moved to the left instinctively, trying to get away from him, and felt something sharp slice through her finger. Realizing it was the knife that Ali had been holding, she felt a renewed sense of hope. *She must have dropped it when she ran.* She silently thanked Ali for the gift.

"I want to hear what you think happened," she said.

His eyes glassed over slightly, and it almost looked like he was going to cry. "Why did you have to give me that bomb? I thought you were giving me a gift, but it wasn't... You hurt me and killed my team."

"Where were you when this happened?" she asked, trying to keep him talking.

"You know where we were. In Afghanistan! We were having such a fantastic time until you had to go and blow me up."

She slid her body slightly to the left so she could get a good grip on the knife. His legs were pinning her arms to her sides, but there was still enough wiggle room to get ahold of the handle. She hoped it would appear to him that she was simply struggling to breathe under his weight. It was strange to think it was this man that had taught her to use leverage with a larger opponent and always keep them distracted.

He began to laugh at her in a crazy, manic hysteria. "You think you fooled me, but I knew it was you. Now I want you to tell me why."

"It wasn't my fault! They made me do it," she yelled, hoping he would buy it.

"That's just not good enough. You were supposed to love me." He lifted the knife over his head, ready to plunge it into her stomach. He stayed there suspended for a moment, looking down at her but he didn't seem to see her anymore. His eyes glazed over, and she thought he could only see Sahar and the love he used to feel for her.

She leveraged the moment, thrusting her hips upward, throwing him slightly back, and freeing her arms. As he came back down on top of her, she plunged her knife deep into his chest, stabbing him repeatedly over and over in a state of sheer panic. She didn't stop until she saw his eyes start to glass over.

He looked confused like he couldn't believe what had happened, as he fell squarely on top of her, smacking his head against hers and soaking her in his sticky warm blood. The knife sticking out of his chest cut into her, but she didn't notice. The blow of his forehead against hers knocked her out cold.

CHAPTER
SIXTY-TWO

HUDSON RAN through the front door of the cabin, ignoring Joe screaming at him to stop and wait for backup. He had his gun drawn as he burst through the front door. In front of him lay a man on top of Mac. He wasn't moving, but neither was she. Her beautiful face looked at peace. Her eyes were closed, almost like she was sleeping.

Joe came up beside him to help roll the man off Mac.

Hudson whispered under his breath, "Holy shit."

"Did you know that guy?" Joe asked.

"Yeah, that's my chief from work," Hudson replied, still stunned to see his leader lying on the floor with a knife sticking out of his chest.

They turned their attention back to Mac. She was covered in blood, but they couldn't tell if it was the chief's or her blood. She had a nasty shiner, but that was the only thing he could see. He felt for a pulse in her neck and was relieved to find it strong and very much alive. Her eyes fluttered open with a pained look in her eyes. "Are you okay?" Hudson whispered.

"I will be once you get your big carcass off of me," she wheezed with a small smile on her lips. He quickly moved away, not realizing that he had been smothering her while checking her pulse. Relief washed over him at the realization that she was okay—and still a smart ass.

The entire cabin was bathed in red and blue lights within the next few minutes as the cavalry arrived. Joe had radioed for backup as soon as they had found Ali on the road, fearing the worst. He was thankful that still worked since their cell phones were out. It was a good thing he'd made the call since they obviously needed forensics and an investigative team, among other things.

The paramedics rushed in and convinced Hudson to step aside. He stood there feeling helpless as they tended to Mac. It appeared she had a minor concussion and bruised, possibly broken ribs from the handle of the knife hitting her, and a cut that would need stitches but aside from that, she was going to be fine.

As the paramedics carried her to the door and out to the waiting ambulance, she looked back at Chief. "Is he dead?" she asked.

Joe had been inspecting the body. With a curt nod of his head, he confirmed he was gone.

She nodded and then let herself be taken to the ambulance. She was pleased to see Ali already in the ambulance waiting for her.

Joe and his team took over the investigation and evidence-gathering while Mac and Ali headed to the hospital with Hudson following close behind.

CHAPTER
SIXTY-THREE

MAC LAY in her hospital bed talking with Ali, who had only suffered some abrasions from the ropes and minor dehydration. The doctor had told her that she might suffer from some psychological issues and gave her the contact information of a good therapist who dealt with PTSD. Mac, on the other hand, was a little more beat up. She had stitches, two broken ribs, and bruised several others. The doc didn't want her moving much until the ribs began to heal. She had mostly recovered from the concussion, but they wanted to monitor her because she still got dizzy spells. She was set to go home the next day.

"Thank you for coming for me," Ali said. "I would have been dead for sure if it wasn't for you."

Mac smiled. "I'm just glad everything worked out. I wasn't sure if either of us was going to be okay for a while there."

"Well, here we are," Ali said, smiling. "Did they tell you what they found at that psychopath's cabin?"

Mac shook her head. They hadn't given her a ton of information so far. She was worried about her career since she had gone off independently and disobeyed a direct order to leave the case alone.

"Joe told me that they found three bodies behind the cabin, buried out back in the woods. They're still investigating and may have to wait until spring before doing much more since the ground out there is still frozen. They also found a book full of women. It was some kind of sick photo album where he documented his kills—and future kills." Ali said this last part and looked away from Mac. "We were in there."

Mac reached out and grabbed her hand. "It's over now. He can no longer hurt us." To change the subject she said, "So, what's next for you?"

"I'm going to quit dancing and focus on med school. Also, Joe asked me out," she said without any prompting.

"He's a really good man. I think you two would make a good pair."

Ali nodded her head in agreement. "Well, we'll see. He said that we would have to keep things a little quiet until I testify about the case, but he said that would be no big deal since the suspect is deceased."

Mac wondered what her own responsibility would be in that respect. She figured it would be a bit more intense than Ali since she had killed the man. "I'm probably going to need you to testify on my behalf as well," she said.

A confused look crossed Ali's face. "What do you mean, 'testify on your behalf?' You're a freakin' hero here! They should be giving you a medal or something. Maybe they should make you a colonel."

"It doesn't work like that, unfortunately," Mac said, smiling. "I broke the rules and went outside my jurisdiction. I also worked a case that I was specifically told not to touch."

"Well, you can count on me to set them straight. Without you, I would no longer be here." Ali smiled, trying to reassure her. "You'll be happy to know that my sister's husband was released. They dropped all charges against him."

"Now *that* is good news," Mac replied. "Have you seen him yet?"

"Yeah, he seems to be doing okay. He's trying to get orders out of here and start fresh. He's staying with some friends. He can't bring himself to go back home...with all her stuff there. It's going to take him a long time to recover."

Mac nodded her head, feeling a little disconnected since she had been in the hospital for almost a week and the police still had her cell phone. Something about it being part of the investigation. Thankfully, she still had the SAT phone to contact her sister with. Lola had been furious with her for disappearing like that and almost getting herself killed. They had talked for almost an hour the day after the incident. Mac had calmed her down and reassured her that she would be fine.

Lola had been able to figure out who Sahar was. According to her research, Chief had been involved with this woman while he was in Afghanistan. She had been the daughter of a leader in the Afghan Army, and she was the liaison between the two. She had planted a bomb that blew him and his team up at some point. Apparently, Chief had suffered damage to his frontal lobe and became obsessed with stopping Sahar. He had gone as far as setting up Johnson to deploy early so that he could get close to Zonira.

She thought about Chief and the man he had been. The man she knew before the incident. Setting aside what he had become, she would miss him. He had been such a positive force in her life and her career. The man she had known was not the monster she had killed, and she would mourn his loss.

CHAPTER
SIXTY-FOUR

HUDSON'S huge frame engulfed the door to the hospital. Ali smiled at him, and they exchanged pleasantries. Ali hugged Mac and said she would check in with her later, then made a quick exit to provide the couple with a little space. He had been there every day to check on her. He'd had to go back to work and answer a ton of questions. She thought he looked extremely sexy in his uniform. Luckily, it appeared leadership wasn't holding him responsible for her good actions.

"Hey beautiful, how are you feeling today?" he asked, coming over to kiss her.

She smiled. She still felt electricity jolt through her body every time his soft, warm lips covered hers. "I think you might be blind is how I'm doing," Mac teased. "I haven't taken a shower in days because they are afraid, I'll move wrong, and I have this beauty mark." She swept her fingers near the side of her face that was all black and blue. There was a deep bruise that had started to turn a little yellow along the edges. It wrapped around her left eye, making it look like she was wearing some deep-purple-and-blue eyeshadow someone might wear for Halloween.

He smiled down at her, knowing not to argue. It was a lot like arguing with an attorney; after a little while, you realized she enjoyed it and was always going to win. He wasn't sure what he had done to get so lucky, but he was certainly going to do whatever he could to keep this beautiful woman in his life.

"So, the doc says you can take a shower today as long as someone goes in there with you and helps support your weight. I obviously offered my generous services," he said with a huge, sexy smile across his face.

"Nah, I think I'll have that good-looking male nurse from the third floor help me," she said with a wink.

He acted offended. "Oh really?" He bent in for a deep kiss that made her toes curl and let her know what he thought of her last statement. He stepped into the bathroom, turned on the shower, and stripped off his uniform.

He walked back out looking like a giant chiseled god. *I'd be happy to look at that view the rest of my life,* she thought. Carefully, he moved the covers off her and picked her up off the bed. Her ribs screamed from the movement, but she didn't say a word. He would have felt awful if he thought he was hurting her. She felt safe and warm in his large arms.

"You know, you don't have to carry me. I can walk," she said with a smile.

He ignored her, carrying her to the shower like she weighed nothing, which felt weird because she wasn't exactly petite—but compared to him she was. She liked the feel of his strong body pressed against her.

She wore nothing but a hospital gown. He gently bent at the waist to set her down on her feet right outside the tiny hospital shower, leaned over to lock the bathroom door just in case, and smiled down at her tenderly. She smiled back. He stepped behind her and she felt his hands working the little ties that kept her gown together.

The gown dropped to the floor, and he let out a deep breath. "I may never get used to you. What on earth did I do to deserve this?"

She liked the way he always made her feel like the sexiest woman on the planet. He gently removed the bandages that were wrapped around her ribs. He did his best not to audibly gasp at the damage underneath as they fell away. She had deep swirls of black and blue mixed in with blotchy red patches that ran from underneath her left breast down to her waist. He gently helped her move into the shower as they both stood beneath the stream of water. He pressed his body against hers to help support her, sending a jolt of electricity through her. The water running over her limbs felt amazing. She hadn't realized how much she needed to be clean...*and* feel his body.

He reached over and grabbed the shampoo. She smiled, realizing that he had brought her toiletries from their house. That caught her off guard. She found it a little scary that she referred to it as *their* house rather than *her* house. She pushed the thought out of her mind as he washed her hair, rinsed it, and then put conditioner in it. For a man who normally had short hair, he was pretty good at this. He filled the little blue loofah with soap and began to run it over her naked body. She stood there with her eyes closed as he gently washed her from head to toe. She was getting aroused and tried pressing against his body but couldn't move quite right and winced.

"Not this time, beautiful. This is just about you feeling better. We can play later," Hudson said with compassion.

She stood there with her eyes closed and her body against his. They stayed like that for a long time, just enjoying the feel of their bodies pressed against each other. She enjoyed the feel of his chest rising and falling behind her and his warm breath on her neck. He rinsed her off, gently helping with her hair and important parts. It hurt every time she raised her arms, so he took care of things for her, mindful not to move her too much.

Once they were ready, he called for the nurse to get clean sheets and new bandages before they put her back in the bed. She couldn't wait to get home and back to normal life. At least, she hoped her life would go back to normal, and they wouldn't prosecute her for her actions.

CHAPTER
SIXTY-FIVE

THE NEXT DAY Hudson picked her up from the hospital with flowers and a smile. Thankfully, it was Friday, and neither of them had anywhere to be over the weekend. She tried not to think about what awaited her the following Monday. She would have to explain her actions to a panel of her leaders, and they would decide what to do about her.

That day came entirely too quickly. Hudson dressed her into her service uniform, helping her pin her long hair up so she was in regulation. It warmed her heart how supportive he had been. He said he would do anything he could to help her, and if the worst happened, he assured her she could stay with him as long as she wanted to. He hoped she would consider staying forever, but he didn't want to rush her given everything was still hanging in the balance.

They drove on base together in Hudson's new truck. He pulled up to the wing headquarters building that housed the legal office. It appeared that everyone had gotten in on this thing: the wing commander, the command chief, the staff judge advocate, Public Affairs, her boss Stanton, and even her AFLOA commander were going to all be there to hear her story. Hudson could see that she was anxious and kept fidgeting with her uniform. To be honest, he was nervous for her. He knew how much her career meant to her.

He parked the truck and helped her out of the passenger side. She was having a hard time getting around and was not supposed to drive with her current injuries. He was still hurting a bit himself from his accident, but he was much further into the healing process than she was. He hoped they would be kind to her and not destroy her. The possibility of a cover-up had certainly crossed his mind. The military didn't want this kind of negative publicity.

He walked in with her, squeezed her hand, and sat down in the waiting area. No matter how things went, he couldn't be prouder of her. She squared her shoulders and walked into the wing conference room, showing no fear.

The doors closed behind her with an audible click. She focused on controlling her breath. No matter what, she wouldn't show fear. Not to them. She had done the right thing and would not apologize for saving Ali's life.

The wing commander stood as she walked in. "Technical Sergeant Evelynn McGregor, thank you for joining us today," he said in an authoritative voice.

Mac just looked at him like he had lost his mind. "Thank you, sir," was all she could think to say.

He smiled at her with kind eyes. "Please have a seat," he said, offering her the seat right next to his. That was not normal. A person usually had to be very high on the food chain to even sit at this table.

She slowly lowered herself into the seat without saying a word. She did her best to sit straight and tried not to wince.

"How are you doing?" he asked kindly.

"I'm healing well," she said. "Thank you for asking."

"We've called you here today to thank you for taking the initiative to follow your instincts and save a woman's life. What you did was reckless and dangerous, but the end result cannot be argued with. At the end of the day, you single-handedly took on a very deranged member of our team and took him down. For that, we all owe you our gratitude," the wing commander said.

Mac looked around the room, trying not to let her mouth fall open. Everyone was nodding in agreement. Her boss smiled at her and gave her a thumbs-up.

The wing commander raised his hand to quiet the room. "Of course, we will need your full cooperation and testimony to close this case out, but after that, we would like you to become part of a task force to help prevent things like this from happening in the future."

She cocked her head to the side in confusion. "It would be my pleasure, sir." She sat for a few moments looking around the room at all the high-ranking people smiling back at her and then remembered. "Sir, what about the drug charges?"

"Yes, I almost forgot about that. The maintenance chief confessed that Chief Deleon had pressured him into it. Chief Deleon was there in civilian clothes with him. Apparently, Chief Deleon threatened his career if he didn't go along with it. Apparently, the chief knew about an affair he was having and threatened to tell his wife. As you know, adultery is against the UCMJ, so the allegation could have hurt his career and ended his marriage. The maintenance chief has been asked to retire. He claims he has no knowledge of the murders committed by Chief Deleon."

Mac smiled, thankful that her good name had been cleared and she once more had the opportunity to do what she loved...*investigate.*

The wing commander stood, and everyone in the room followed suit. "Thank you for your service. We're all happy that you're here today. Now, go home and rest. We have a new case waiting for you when you're healed. Joint Base Lewis-McChord would like your assistance on a case when you're back on your feet. We'll work out all the details and conduct a follow-up meeting when you come back from convalescent leave."

She walked back out of the room and found Hudson pacing back and forth, waiting for her. She smiled nervously. "You won't believe this," she said. "They don't want to court-martial me or even fire me. All charges have been dropped...and I think they just offered me a job."

THANK YOU FOR READING MY BOOK!

I appreciate all your feedback, and I love hearing what you have
to say.
I need your input to make the next book even better.
Please leave me an honest review and let me know what you thought
of the story.

RECEIVE A FREE SHORT STORY

Join Julie Bergman's newsletter and get your free short story, updates about future books and get to know the author only at: https://juliebergman-author.com/my-books.

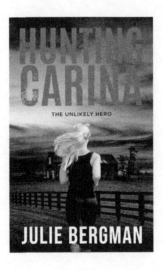

ACKNOWLEDGMENTS

I would like to express my thanks and gratitude to everyone who helped me make this dream a reality. Special thanks to my editor Shavonne Clarke for the amazing guidance on the development, cover design, and production of this book. Last but not least, I would not be here without Self-Publishing School and its amazing program.

ABOUT THE AUTHOR

Julie Bergman is a retired military veteran who served her country for over 20 years. She lives in beautiful Spokane, Washington with her supportive husband, four wonderful children, and a slobbery Olde English Bulldog with attitude. After over 17 years in the JAG Corp and a master's degree in Forensic Psychology, her fascination with crime and the dark side of humanity has spilled into a military-based serial killer novel/series that you won't be able to put down.

Made in the USA
Las Vegas, NV
08 January 2023

65201729R00173